MISSION CLOCKWORK 4

ISLAND OF DOOM

ARTHUR SLADE

DAVA ENTERPRISES

FOR TORI AND TANAYA,
with all my love

PROLOGUE

William "Mad Dog" Middleton faced the gallows rope with a jaundiced eye. He'd lived thirty-six years, the last five in Sumpter, Oregon, during the final dregs of a dying gold rush. In a fit of cold anger he'd murdered three prospectors for their meagre findings and now he was about to hang. It was that simple. He'd never been maudlin and felt only a slight annoyance as he stared back at the gathered crowd: faces he recognized from the saloons, from brawls, all eager to watch him swing. Life had been harsh. He had been harsh. He was happy to go.

His heart didn't skip a beat when the hangman placed the rope around his neck. "Get it done" was all he said, his final words. The trap door opened, and one minute later Middleton was pronounced dead by a doctor. The law had been upheld along with his neck.

Middleton's journey didn't end there. The sheriff, who was also the coroner, barked at the grave diggers, "Take him up to Stony Cemetery and throw him in a hole!" They placed his large body in a wagon and drew it to an unmarked grave in the half-frozen ground outside Sumpter. It was shallow because of the frost and stones. There was no one to mourn him. The men who threw the dirt did their job quickly and left before nightfall. There were other graves. Some miners had died of consumption, others of a gunshot. He lay only yards away from his victims.

A full hunter's moon appeared in the sky, the type William had preferred when he hunted deer. Three men arrived. They were small, wiry and dressed in black, faces covered by balaclavas. They unearthed his body, placed it in a coffin, shrouded William with ice and adjusted several dials on the lid. They were professional resurrection men from the Far East, the finest at their job.

His body was transported by cart to a train and settled beside the first-class baggage, the closest Middleton had ever come to riding first class. At the coast, he was loaded onto a midsized paddle steamer alongside several other coffins from the United States and Canada. There had been three other hangings in the Rockies. One other coffin contained the recipient of a bullet—a natural cause of death on the frontier. There was gold to be found, stakes to be claimed, land to be purchased, all of which often led to arguments and ended in gunfire.

William wouldn't know it, but his coffin was next to one containing the body of a magistrate and sometime novelist named Duncan McTavish. He'd been locally famous for his wit, his loquacious use of words and his love of money. He'd poisoned his wife to inherit her fortune and instead had received a hanging. If he and Middleton were alive, neither would have had much to converse about. Being dead, this presented no problem.

The steamship was named *Triton II* and it plied the

Pacific without the flag of any nation, the caskets rattling in the hold. Most smaller ships would hug the shore for safety as they travelled, but this one had compressed coal and an engine that would be the envy of any navy. It sped directly west, cutting through the waves.

Two evenings later the vessel arrived at an island and was met by armed patrol ships. Messages were relayed by lantern and the ship was guided into a port as large as any in London or France. The eyes of the resurrection men widened, for in the centre of the island was a fortress of glass. The moon painted it a glowing yellow. They knew that inside that palace was the man whom they referred to as the *Dragon Master*. This man was a visionary, renowned for the magnificence of his ideas and philosophies—philosophies that the resurrectionists happened to agree with. And, as it turned out, the dragon master paid rather well.

It was the middle of the night, but gas and electric lamps lit the work of soldiers building barricades to protect the docks. Others hauled wagons of dirt from excavations. Several of the grey-clad soldiers helped them unload the caskets and carry them to a cave a short distance away. The resurrectionists returned to their ship and the search for more flesh.

And there on the cold stones sat two coffins.

Shortly thereafter, four men in white coats came out and, in pairs, lifted the caskets and brought them into the cave. They set both beside a work table littered with flasks, surgery tools and electrical cables. One of the assistants awakened an old man dozing on a cot in the corner.

"Your supplies have been delivered, Dr. Hyde, sir," the assistant said.

The doctor nodded, shook the sleep out of his balding

head, fumbled his glasses on and approached the coffins. The first one he opened was Middleton's. When he saw the size and the condition of the corpse he smiled.

He began his work immediately.

1

A MOST MYSTERIOUS LETTER

A courier in a grey bowler hat and a frock coat approached a tall brick house on the outskirts of Montreal, Canada, unaware of the professionally trained eyes watching him from a bedroom window. He was measured, weighed and classified in the space of a few heartbeats.

"Five feet, six inches," Modo whispered. "One hundred and forty pounds. Twenty-five to twenty-seven years old." He was alone in the room and had reverted to his childhood habit of talking to himself. "Slight limp indicates hip difficulty, perhaps from surviving poliomyelitis." Modo's years of espionage training made the measuring of the man an easy task. It would be even simpler to jump down from his second-storey window and dispatch the courier with a blow or a sleeper hold. Now that'd make the man wet his britches!

Modo carried out this surveillance to break the monotony of his day. He hadn't had an assignment for months now and consequently his skills hadn't been tested by either Tharpa, his weapons trainer, or his master, Mr. Socrates. They continued to train Octavia, his fellow agent and friend; every day she was in the courtyard huffing and puffing and practising her martial arts or shouting her way through her elocution lessons with Mrs. Finchley. But Modo was *persona non grata*—a forgotten and unwanted agent. *I'm going to rot here!*

Three months ago he had twice disobeyed a direct order from his master to send innocent Australian natives into battle. Mr. Socrates had not forgiven him his trespasses.

Modo threw himself back on his bed and opened his copy of *Middlemarch*. The arrival of the courier would likely be the most exciting thing to happen this week. Occasionally, to entertain himself, Modo would go through the painful process of shifting his deformed body and face into one of the many personas he had perfected, such as the Knight, the Doctor and others. He would wander out to the market to practise his French, though the Québécois spoke a different dialect than the Parisians. He did enjoy this little city in the Canadian wilderness with its French residents, Irish merchants and British magistrates. It was like several small countries all rolled into one.

But he always had to return to Montreal House and his life in limbo.

He scratched at the little finger on his left hand. It often itched; the skin was fresh and pink now, but would shed every few weeks. He had lost the finger to an enemy sabre only three months ago and it had, to his great and absolute surprise, regenerated itself: proof that he was the oddest, strangest human being ever to have walked the earth.

He tried not to think of the woman who had wielded that sabre, Miss Hakkandottir, one of the leaders of the Clockwork Guild. The Guild was an organization bent on the destruction of everything British. The Permanent Association, *his* organization, had been formed to preserve

Britannia. Modo had last seen Miss Hakkandottir fleeing into the jungle. He hoped she'd ended up in the gullet of a particularly nasty crocodile. He imagined the beast spitting out her metal hand and couldn't help chuckling.

Alas, even if she were dead, someone else would rise to take her place. The Clockwork Guild was not a small organization and it could strike anywhere in the world with ease. After all, it was most likely the Guild that had burned down Victor House, Mr. Socrates' home in England, forcing them to hide here.

At least the Guild had left them alone for the last few months. He turned a page in his book and tried to disappear back into the town of *Middlemarch.* Would Dorothea ever marry Ladislaw? He was tempted to flip to the end, but stopped himself. He'd done that with *Wuthering Heights* and regretted it still.

There came a hard knock on his door and before Modo could say "enter," or even reach for his netting mask to cover his monstrous face, Mr. Socrates was standing beside Modo's bed. His master had dark circles under his eyes, and his white hair was longer than usual. He looked as though he'd aged ten years in the last few months. The stress of hiding from the Clockwork Guild was obviously keeping the poor man up all hours of the night.

Since toddlerhood, Modo had been raised by Mr. Socrates. *Or rather, trained,* for Mr. Socrates had never been a parent. He'd bought the infant Modo from a travelling curiosity wagon. He'd never changed Modo's diapers or soothed his bruises. He'd given orders for the boy to be shaped, from age one, into a secret agent at Ravenscroft, a secluded country home. Modo didn't leave the house for thirteen years.

"May I help you?" Modo asked.

Mr. Socrates extended his arm. At first Modo thought he wanted to shake hands, then saw what he was carrying.

"This most mysterious letter has arrived for you," Mr. Socrates said.

Modo took the envelope, briefly touching his master's hand. How he wished, just once, that that hand had patted his shoulder or his head in a gesture of kindness.

Modo cast aside these silly feelings and examined the letter. His name was written neatly along the front, and below that was the address of Montreal House.

"But how can this be addressed to me? No one is supposed to know that we're here."

"Not entirely true," Mr. Socrates answered. "Since our *great retreat* from London, I've cut off the majority of communication with the other members of the Permanent Association, but I have left a few trusted channels open."

So, Modo thought, the Permanent Association still operated! The secret organization had employed him for most of his life; its one goal was to keep Britannia ruling forever. Six men, including Mr. Socrates, and one woman had created and now controlled the Association. Even Queen Victoria didn't know of its existence.

His master jabbed a finger towards the letter. "This was delivered to a trusted courier by a French contact."

"But what would the French want with me?"

"Ah, that is the question of the hour. I'm here to discover the answer."

Modo held the envelope up. "It's already open."

"Of course it is!" he replied, lowering himself into the chair across from Modo's bed. "Several eyes have studied it along the way. But the letter is in a code that no one, including me, has been able to decipher. Open it, now."

Modo pulled the single page out of the envelope and unfolded it to see . . .

20-22-11-22:

33-23-28 32-18-21-21 12-15 30-32-29-27-29-20-30-15-11 25-20 16-11-7-24 13-25-22-20 21-13 11-30-29 30-18-15 30-20-31-33-12-31-20-21 30-8-10-23-23-17-22 . . .

"But it's just numbers," Modo said after scanning the first couple of rows. "Without a key it will be impossible to crack. Have you tried the Vigenère Cipher?"

"Do you think I am a fool? That was the first code we applied. The day the French discover that we cracked their cipher will be a bad day for our intelligence gathering. No, whoever sent it has likely used a key that only you would be able to decipher. They would know that you are part of the Permanent Association and that other eyes would attempt to read the missive."

Modo paused. Had he heard that right? *You are part of the Permanent Association.* Perhaps his exile was nearly over.

Another knock at the door. An unusually busy morning! As was his habit, he drew his netting mask from the bedpost and pulled it over his face. He barely had his eyeholes straight before Octavia entered in her exercise outfit—black pantaloons and a black sweater. Her sandy blonde hair was tied back, sweat still on her brow.

"Please, Octavia," Modo exclaimed, "you really must wait for permission to enter!"

"Oh, Modo." She waved away his protestations as if she were shooing flies. "Since when did we have such haristo-cratic stuffery between us . . .?"

He gritted his teeth. Yes, he had shown her his real face once, and he couldn't stand the guarded look she'd given him. Now he thought of the event as the "yours is not the face I've dreamt of all my life" incident. Sometimes she seemed entirely oblivious of his feelings.

". . . I've heard that a letter arrived for you."

"Where did you hear that?" Mr. Socrates said.

"Tharpa told me."

Mr. Socrates raised two doubting eyebrows. "He would not impart that sort of information."

"Well, then, I spied the delivery boy and, then, through the picture window, saw you climbing the stairs. You only go upstairs to lecture one of us, sir."

"Hmm. Perhaps I've trained you too well. Please have a seat."

She chose the end of the bed, nearly plopping herself down on Modo's feet.

Modo was searching for something clever to say when another person came through the door: Mrs. Finchley in a long grey dress.

"Oh, is it an official meeting?" she asked. "Would you like tea?"

"That won't be necessary, Mrs. Finchley," Mr. Socrates said. "Please return to your duties."

"Actually, Mrs. Finchley," Modo said, "would you kindly telegram the gendarmes or whatever it is they call their constables here? My room is becoming rather crowded with vagrants."

She gave him a smile on the way out the door. "I shall send an urgent message."

"Where's the letter from?" Octavia asked.

"France," Modo replied. "But I don't know anyone in France."

"There is that French spy." Octavia brushed a hand through her hair. "What was the little viper's name? Coquette? I mean, Colette Brunet?"

"Impossible," Modo said.

The penmanship had neither a masculine nor feminine appearance and it contained no flourishes, no hint of personality, as though the person had intended to mask any personal style. But the last two sets of numbers contained the same number of characters as the name *Colette Brunet*. He recognized that immediately—her name had come to mind often recently. Perhaps because of the French spoken in Quebec. If this was her name in code it would be relatively easy to decipher the rest of the message: each number likely corresponded to a letter in the alphabet. He just needed to know one of the words. Two would make it easy.

"Octavia is correct," Mr. Socrates said. "Use your faculties, Modo. I did not spend countless hours training you for nothing. Decipher the letter."

"Now?" His heartbeat sped up. Nervousness? No, something else. Colette had written to him. *To him.* Colette who had fought alongside him on the submarine *Ictíneo*. She had been brave and feisty and, he could not lie to himself, bewitchingly beautiful. But when their battles were done, their enemy had vanquished and his defences were down, she had asked to see his face—his real face. They had been adrift at sea; they might never see land again. When he took off his makeshift mask she had paled and turned away from the sight of him in disgust and asked him to cover it. He had relived that moment far too many times. He was stronger now, but it would always hurt.

"Translate," Mr. Socrates commanded.

Modo grabbed a pen and paper from his desk. If C = 10 then O would be—he counted—22. He wrote out the alphabet. A = 8 B = 9, et cetera. It was Colette! But when he went to decipher her last name, it was not *Brunet*, but *Csvofu*. What could that mean? Ah, it came to him. Every word had its own code. Instead of A equalling 8, it was 9 this time. He guessed correctly that the pattern repeated itself and he was able to decipher the first word of the letter, *20-22-11-22*: *Modo*. He began to write it out, his brain calculating rapidly, his mind so focused on the task that he forgot the peering eyes of Mr. Socrates. He didn't even notice Octavia turning up the gas lamp. Soon the words were coming to him almost as quickly as if he were reading regular text. As he deciphered he felt astonished.

Modo:

You will be surprised to hear from me but the situation warrants this communication. I have been well since we met and I often think of you. Perhaps, I could say, it is an obsession. I cannot rid my memory of your face and of my failure to match your inner strength. But my regrets should be of no great matter to you. The important thing is that I have found your parents in France, though I do not know their exact location. You were born in the village of Nanterre, a short distance from Paris. I assume this information will be a revelation to you. I also have dire tidings: your parents are in great danger and I alone cannot protect them. Come to me. The moment you receive this missive you must depart. I shall be in the Le Hotel Grande at noon every day for the next fortnight or longer if necessary. I shall wait for you with eagerness.

Your bonne chance friend,
Colette Brunet

"Well, what does it say?" Mr. Socrates asked. "Tell us, Modo."

Modo looked Mr. Socrates directly in the eyes. There was so much in these few sentences, yet he surprised himself when he said, simply, "If these words are true, then I am French."

"You were born in France, yes," Mr. Socrates agreed gruffly. "I brought you back to England when you were no more than a year old. I rescued you from that cage in a travelling freak show."

Modo sat stunned. He had known about the cage, but had always assumed it was in England. Any time he asked about his parents, Mr. Socrates had one reply: "That is not necessary information." Modo had long ago given up ever knowing.

In one breath he regained control of his emotions. "Then I was born in Nanterre," Modo said.

And if that one fact was correct then the remainder of the letter was most likely also correct. Colette had somehow, for some reason, located his parents and they were being pursued by enemies. There was far too much to consider; he felt as though the constellations in the heavens had suddenly begun spinning in several directions at once. He took another calming breath.

"You're French?" Octavia said, grinning. "That explains so much."

"It's no laughing matter!" Modo retorted.

"You're British now," Mr. Socrates said. "If not by birth, then by education."

"My parents are alive."

"I always assumed so," Mr. Socrates said, defensively. "Remember, Modo, that they abandoned you. Enough of this piecemeal information. Read us the letter."

Modo sat up straighter and put his feet on the floor. He cleared his throat and read, struggling to keep his voice from cracking. When he was done, Octavia was the first to comment.

"I'm most curious about the *bonne chance* friendship. She was a shyster."

"She was not," Modo said.

"The question remains," Mr. Socrates said, "as to whether or not she actually wrote the letter. It may have been forged by another agent or agency."

Modo lowered the paper. "But it sounds like her, the way she speaks."

"Cadence and personality can be mimicked," Mr. Socrates reminded him. "You of all people should know that. You make your living as a mimic."

"I like to consider myself more than just a mimic," he shot back. "Besides, she said *bonne chance* friend."

"It that what she called herself?" Mr. Socrates asked. "*Bonne chance* is a common enough French expression."

"No. It's what she said to me before . . ."

"Before what?" Octavia asked.

He remembered the event clearly. He and Colette had thought they were going to die in a metal pod many fathoms below the surface of the Atlantic.

"Before she kissed me. For good luck," he added quickly.

Mr. Socrates smiled, the wrinkles around his eyes becoming more pronounced. Then he let out a rattling laugh. "You forgot to add that little detail to your report. It seems you have learned more about life than I was aware of."

"It was inconsequential," Modo insisted. He glanced at Octavia. Her face was as serene as a doll's, but he thought he saw a glint of anger in her eyes. She had already known he had kissed Colette. He assumed she had long ago forgiven him. Or maybe he was imagining that glint. Was it wishful thinking on his part? Perhaps it didn't matter to her at all.

"So, we have established a likelihood that it's this Colette Brunet who wrote the letter," Mr. Socrates said. "Why would she look for your parents?"

Modo shrugged. *An obsession*, she had said. About him. Consumed by her guilt, it seemed. Was she seeking his forgiveness for turning away from him?

"The French government obviously knows that you exist, Modo," Mr. Socrates said. "She certainly would have told them. They could be seeking your family, perhaps in the hope that there are brothers or sisters who have your abilities."

"Or, more likely, it's the Clockwork Guild who want my blood," Modo said. He felt a chill. He had meant to say *blood-line*, but somehow *blood* rang more true.

He had rarely ever thought of his mother and father; they were only formless shadows who had abandoned him —uncaring parents like those in so many of the fairy tales he'd read. In any case, he'd had Mr. Socrates and Mrs. Finchley to care for him.

Despite that, now these two people were being pursued by the agents of an evil guild. He had seen what unspeakable things the Clockwork Guild had done to poor street children to create a weapon to destroy England's Parliament Buildings. If they did indeed find his parents, would they be any less cruel?

"Yes," Mr. Socrates said, breaking into Modo's thoughts. "The Guild could very well be in pursuit. I hadn't properly considered the possibility of you having siblings. I'm sure I would have received reports—I paid a great sum of money for the information that brought you to me."

"So you *paid* for me?"

"Uh, no," Mr Socrates said. "I paid for information that led to you." Then he paused. "That isn't quite true. I did indeed purchase you from the owners of that freak show."

Modo spoke slowly, deliberately, so as not to allow his voice to crack. "How much did you pay?"

"That's immaterial, Modo. If I hadn't paid for you, you'd still be in that caravan or in some cabinet of curiosities, or perhaps you'd be dead."

Modo was light-headed. He felt behind him for the headboard, just to touch something solid. It was all too much to take in. A sibling—a brother as ugly as him? Or perhaps not cursed by this affliction at all? A sister?

"I know what you're thinking," Mr. Socrates said.

"You do?" Modo had no idea what he himself was thinking.

"You can't go to France," he said matter-of-factly. "You're too valuable. I'll send orders to my agents there."

Valuable? Modo thought. So the old man didn't hate him. "You have French agents?"

"Of course. It's a smaller organization, but the Association can still infiltrate where it needs to."

"I understand, sir," Modo said, even though he wasn't certain he believed him.

Mr. Socrates took the letter from Modo's hands and, leaning heavily on his walking stick, made to leave the room. He turned in the doorway. "We will discuss this further tomorrow."

Octavia followed him wordlessly and seemed in a huff.

Modo stared at the wall, unable to move.

French. He was French!

2

THE FRENCH CONNECTION

Colette Brunet could not imagine a church more spectacular than the Notre Dame de Paris, but she crept quickly past it without a glance or a moment's pause to admire the way the moonlight reflected off the stained glass windows. She had dressed as a young man, pulling her dark hair back and up into a sweeper's cap, and had created a bruise around her eye with purple makeup to distract any onlookers from noticing her unusual eyes. Few Parisians had Japanese blood.

Her hand was on the pistol inside her dark, long jacket as she followed the limping movements of her target: Father Alphonse Mauger. The priest was striding at a surprisingly fast clip, considering his chubbiness. He looked furtively over his shoulder. Twice she had to throw herself out of his line of sight.

She believed Father Mauger was working with the Clockwork Guild, an organization she had learned about only nine months earlier while hunting for a foreign submarine. That mission on the Atlantic had been amazing and eye-opening, but it had cost her much more than she could have imagined possible. She had stood on the ship *Vendetta* as it was pulled down into the water. Now, she felt the same horrible sensation as her career sank. No longer was she first among *les espions*—the French secret agents at the Deuxième Bureau. The agency had picked her brain about her mission in the Atlantic and become fascinated by Modo, salivating at the thought of an agent who could change his shape. Every bit of information she had given up felt like a betrayal of Modo, but if she hadn't shared it she would have betrayed her country.

Then the bureaucrats—desk sitters!—who'd been jealous of her quick ascent in the ranks pulled out their knives. They cast doubt on her stories of an underwater city. They pointed out her divided loyalties; she was, after all, *ainoko,* half-Japanese and half-French. They whispered lies and scribbled those lies until they acquired the ring of truth.

Then one day, two burly gendarmes came to her desk, grabbed her by the shoulders, escorted her to the front gates of the bureau and tossed her to the curb. She was warned that if she betrayed any secrets of her country she would be imprisoned, tortured and shot.

Now Father Mauger entered the cathedral. If she was correct he was carrying the original documents that revealed the last known location of Modo's parents; the Catholic Church was even more enamoured of paperwork than the Deuxième Bureau itself.

She couldn't think of Modo without a shudder, not of fear or revulsion, though his horrid appearance had haunted her for these many months, but a shudder at her own failure. She had not been strong enough to face his face. Fate had given her a chance to forge a true friendship with a fellow agent, a man more amazing than any other she had met, and she had turned away. How spineless!

Her former employers had sent agents to England to search for Modo and any relatives he may have. She had been on the team up until the moment of her dismissal. She'd decided to take on the task herself, sifting through hospital files and copies of birth records for any mention of a "freak" child, reading nearly every outlandish article of every newspaper published in England: reports about boys in India with three eyes, conjoined Siamese twins, a girl with four arms. Colette found no mention of a shape-changing child.

It wasn't until she'd visited the Imperial Bibliothèque Nationale that she got her first break. There she had struck up a relationship with a librarian who had a particular and somewhat distasteful interest in *les phénomènes de cirque*—circus freaks. He had dropped a massive collection of clippings and diaries onto her desk. She sifted through these to discover an account of a monstrously malformed boy from Nanterre who had been mentioned in *Le Temps* in 1858. It was the right year, assuming Modo was near her age. The article made her reconsider her assumption that Modo had been born in England. After all, the British were known to scour the world for spies. Could Modo have been born in France? Mon Dieu!

She found a transcript of an interview with a midwife who had helped give birth to "a demon straight from hell but born of woman's flesh," so she pursued the midwife to Nanterre. The woman's name was Marie. She had only three teeth and had taken to drink in her later years. Her harrowing account of the birth made Colette cringe; the midwife had actually screamed at the sight of *le petit monstre* as it was pulled into the world. Colette left that meeting with a possible last name for Modo's parents: Hébert.

The next day the midwife died, drowned in the Seine.

Colette would have thought it an accident, except a week later the librarian from Imperial Bibliothèque Nationale fell from the roof of the library to his death. The Deuxième Bureau rarely resorted to such crude methods. She suspected another organization was on the same path, and might even have someone on her trail. It was the British, perhaps. Or the Russians.

She made discreet inquiries and followed the trail of rumours, until she discovered that a family of potters named Hébert had once lived in Nanterre, though no one had seen them for years. She learned that indeed they had had a child whom they were believed to have abandoned, though no one had ever set eyes on the infant. Perhaps it had been left at Notre Dame; this was a common occurrence because many believed their cast-off children would have the greatest chance of a future if left in the greatest church in the land.

And so, a week earlier she had visited the church, but Mauger, the archivist, had not allowed her so much as a peek at his records. This surprised her, since she'd had little trouble getting similar information from other churches. She waited outside the church for him to leave, then followed him through the streets of Paris. After several hours of surveillance she had spotted him meeting with a white-haired man. She'd read their lips from a distance and was only able to decipher the date they planned to meet again: this very day.

The priest appeared anxious as he entered the great doors of Notre Dame, stopping in the doorway to look about like a frightened bird. Colette waited behind a statue until he entered, then snuck in the doors. She crept through the nave of the church, hiding behind columns. The moonlight shone through the massive stained glass windows, splashing colours across the marble floor. She trailed Mauger into the Chapel of the Holy Sacrament and outside again as he crossed the short distance to the stone archives building.

She couldn't follow him directly inside; the building was too small. She hunted around the circumference for another entrance, thankful the priests didn't keep guard dogs. Who would want to steal church records? The only other door she found was secured by a large, ancient lock.

Seeing a darkened window on the second floor, she climbed spider-like up the side of the building, gripping the rough edges of the stone. She was thankful that every morning she completed a vigorous exercise regimen designed by her late father. Her arms and legs were strong. She grabbed the windowsill and it broke off, pieces of stone clattering to the ground. She would've fallen if not for a firm grasp on the protruding and solid nose of a gargoyle. "Merci," she whispered, smiling at him. There was no sign that anyone had heard the noise.

She found a more secure piece of sill on the second attempt. The window opened easily and she slipped in, stepping onto creaking wood. As her eyes adjusted she saw she was on a desk, musty volumes stacked beside her. She lowered herself to the floor, crept across the room and opened the door a crack.

Light. Two figures, one of them Mauger, were visible at the bottom of a set of stairs, their voices distant mumbles. She opened the door enough to slip through and peer over the railing. She was surprised to hear them speaking English.

"Seventy-five hundred." It was Mauger's nasal tone, his French accent quite light.

"Don't be uffish," a reedy voice warned. "I humbly suggest you provide the information free of cost."

Colette thought the second man's voice had an Irish lilt. She'd never seen such white hair; it glowed in the low light. He was thin, his tan suit very stylish.

"I—I will take sixty-five hundred. But no less. This is very important information. You're not the only agency who has requested it."

"But I am here; the other agencies are not. And what if you receive nothing?"

Father Mauger was holding a paper in his right hand, clearly shaking. "That was not the agreement. And why did you bring this . . . this man with you?" He motioned towards a grey pillar. But not a pillar, Colette realized—rather, a brute of a man, standing dead still.

"Is the name on it?" Serpent-like, the thin man snatched the paper from Mauger's hand, then read it. "Names. Addresses. Perhaps this is helpful."

"Fifty-five hundred?" Mauger pleaded. "Mr. Lime, please. I have risked my position."

"It is Lime. Not *Mr.* Lime." He signalled to the larger man, who didn't respond. "Ah, such mush for brains! Can you not obey a simple gesture? Fine . . . I shall use words: Typhon, please separate the dear Father's head from his body."

The monstrous man grunted an answer and batted aside Mauger's feeble attempt to block him. He wrapped one hand around the father's neck.

"No! No—" Mauger choked.

She couldn't let the priest die! Colette cocked her pistol and charged down the stairs, leaping high and landing several feet behind her targets. She pointed the gun at Lime's heart.

"Release him!" she commanded.

Lime smiled as though he'd expected her all along. His teeth glittered in the light of the gas lamp. "Why?" he asked.

"I'll shoot you if you don't."

With his back to her, the beast Typhon continued to choke Auger.

"And what will that accomplish?" Lime asked. "Will it stop the moon shifting in the sky? Will it silence the music of the spheres?"

He wanted to wax philosophical while she pointed a gun at him? He was mad.

"Drop the paper, too," she added. "Now."

Again, that smile. His glinting teeth, if her eyes weren't deceiving her, were made of sharpened metal. "A girl dressed as a boy tells a man what to do." With some drama, he held the paper high and dropped it. On a lucky current of air it floated over and landed between them. She lunged and grabbed it, not allowing the pistol to waver.

"You won't leave this room alive," he said quietly. "Your bones will be broken. Your brains stomped to gruel. Your thoughts will leak onto the earth."

"You must be a failed poet. That's not how this will play out."

"I will it to be so and so it will be. Can the tides of destiny be stopped?"

Madness could only be met by madness, she decided. She fired, intentionally missing Lime by inches and shattering a lantern behind him. Lime didn't budge, though he did open his sneering lips to say, "Release the priest."

Typhon dropped Mauger and the archivist fell to the ground like a sack.

"That's better," Colette said. "Now back away from the priest."

Lime smiled again. "Please, Typhon," he said to his

companion, "kill the whiffling girl in an egregiously painful manner."

The massive man turned, his eyes dead. Colette froze as he lunged; it was as though a mountain were falling towards her. Then she heard her father's voice: *Always be ready to fight!* She lurched backwards, pulling twice on the trigger. The first bullet struck the wall. The second a stack of books. *Steady,* her father's voice whispered. *Aim for the centre of the chest.* The third bullet hit the man in the sternum, but he didn't even stagger. The fourth and fifth bullets punched two holes in his greatcoat, right near his heart. Then she was pulling the trigger madly, the hammer clicking uselessly as the giant thrust out an arm to grab her. His skin was slightly greenish and stitches snaked up the side of his neck. His eyes were cold, unseeing.

She ducked and he snatched her fluttering scarf and pulled, yanking so hard that she was lifted into the air. The scarf unwound from her neck and she rolled across the marble floor, letting the piece of paper go. She'd landed close to the door, so she got up and ran, but something struck her hard in the back of the head. White birds flapped in all directions. No, not birds, she realized as she scrambled to her feet, but pages from a book.

I was almost brained by a book! She nearly chuckled. Then, without a backward glance, she tore open the door and fled into the night.

3

SUCH A PLAYFUL LANGUAGE

Lime chose not to pursue the young woman. She would not dare return. There was no sign of companions. He had known of her existence; both the dead librarian and the dead nursemaid had mentioned being interviewed by her, but neither had any idea who employed her. The woman's East Asian appearance made guessing rather difficult; could it be that even the Chinese were after the same information? It didn't matter. She may alert the gendarmes or her masters, but by then his work would be done and he would be back in his hotel room drinking tea and nibbling chocolates.

Typhon continued to lumber towards the door, following Lime's initial command. *Stupid brainless lump,* Lime thought. "Stop, Typhon," he commanded. The thing turned and his eyes caught the lantern light, giving even Lime a chill. "Come back to me."

The creature slouched back, a slight drag in one leg. He stood right next to Lime, so close that the formaldehyde stink was overwhelming.

"Stand *there*," Lime shouted. "There! There! There!" He

pointed at a spot a few feet away and Typhon eventually stomped into position. Of all the tools his masters had given Lime, this one was a sledgehammer.

It had taken Lime several months of research and inquiries to thoroughly assess the numerous accounts of monster children, first in England, then Germany and later in France. The French, he was beginning to believe, were especially prone to storytelling. Nonetheless, Lime had managed to gather those stories and shape them into the truth. Sometimes it had required a few coins, other times more violent means. He had always been gifted at following leads.

At the behest of the Clockwork Guild, he was pursuing the parentage of a young man named Modo; he didn't know who Modo was, other than understanding that he apparently had wondrous capabilities: uncanny strength, a quick mind and the ability to somehow shift his shape and appear exactly like another. Lime had assumed at first that the shape-shifting was a fabrication, but the more he read and researched the more he began to believe the stories might be true.

He scooped up the paper Father Mauger had provided and read the contents. It was a signed document granting a nameless child to the church. It included the old residence of the parents and their intended new residence. As they had chosen to fill out the papers instead of simply abandoning the child on the church steps, they were probably religious and unlikely to lie to the church, especially in writing.

The priest had crawled into the shadows. He was the last loose end. But what sort of trouble could he cause? Then again, he had too much information. Though the other buyers he'd mentioned were likely made up in an attempt to raise the price, one could never be certain.

"Father Mauger," Lime said, "please show yourself."

The room was silent.

"Father Mauger," he repeated, "I promise not to harm you. You are more valuable to me alive."

"You promise?" The voice came from behind a desk several feet away.

"I do, Father," Lime said. "*I* will not harm you. That is my solemn vow."

The priest crept out from behind a desk and into the light, what little there was of it. He was pale and shaking with fear. He swallowed.

"Typhon, please vigorously break his neck," Lime commanded.

"But you said you wouldn't harm me!" the priest squawked.

"I won't." Lime shrugged. The joke was an old one. He was surprised how many fell for it. "But Typhon will. English is such a playful language."

4

THROUGH THE WINDOW

After his third sleepless night, Modo began to think he was trapped in a re-enactment of *Macbeth,* for he was seeing ghosts and hearing screams. Every time he closed his eyes to sleep, the gaunt faces of his parents rose before him. They were crying out in pain, metallic hounds pursuing them. Or they were tied to torture racks.

The nightmares were particularly vexing. Over his lifetime he'd given little thought to the man and woman who'd abandoned him. Now they were popping up in his head, pleading for his help. How dare they? They'd sold him to a travelling freak show. Sold him!

He owed them nothing.

He also knew Colette would be waiting in Paris, sitting alone at a restaurant table. He had cared deeply for her and had taken a great risk in showing her his face. It had turned out badly.

He owed her nothing either.

He punched his pillow, sending feathers into the darkness. The truth was he had never shirked any duty, large or small. Yes, his appearance was likely the reason his parents had abandoned him. And it was definitely the reason Colette hadn't been able to say goodbye face to face.

If there was one lesson he had learned from the Rain People of Australia, it was that beauty truly was in the eye of the beholder. They had accepted his ugliness, even seeming to worship him as a god. But the gift the tribe had given him was perhaps the greatest gift of his life; they had looked at his face without reservation and with absolute love. They had seen him for who he really was.

His was not a face that the "civilized" could love. But that was their problem.

Modo sat up. For all their faults, his parents didn't deserve to be in such danger. It's my task, Modo thought. My duty! Besides, he wanted to prove his parents wrong; they should never have given him up. He pictured himself breaking them out of a jail cell and how they would beg his forgiveness. Faceless and nameless, they still shared the same flesh, the same blood. And that blood was French!

It had been more than a small betrayal, Mr. Socrates not telling him that the blood in his veins wasn't English. Modo felt weakened by that knowledge, for he had believed that British blood and intellect were what got important things done in this world. He'd been trained to serve England, in fact had served the country well, and yet, he was not English.

He stepped gingerly onto the floor. It creaked as he dressed. It crossed his mind that he should be going directly to Octavia, though it was inappropriate to enter a woman's room at night. He thought of gently poking her shoulder and asking her to make the journey with him. But how could he ask her to both betray Mr. Socrates and risk her life? These were his parents, not hers. And it would be easier without her. He had not shown her his face again since their return from Queensland. He didn't want her to see it. She desired a handsome prince; she'd admitted as much. His friendship, of course, she wanted. But not him.

He must go it alone. He stuffed a wallet in his pocket, knowing it held twenty Canadian dollars and enough British pounds to buy third-class passage on a steamer. He slipped a stiletto into his belt. Into his haversack he tossed a pocket lucifer; the electric device had proven quite handy and cast a surprisingly bright light. He also threw in spare netting masks along with a few trousers and shirts. He would need very little.

He decided to slip out the window. He approached it, wincing at each complaint of the floorboards. He had opened the window several times in the last week, but it wouldn't budge. He applied his strength and the wooden frame squeaked noisily. He was strong enough to tear it open, but that would wake up the entire household.

He tiptoed out into the hallway and paused in front of Octavia's door, lifting his hand to knock gently, then lowered it. She would be angry that he'd left without a word, even more angry when she learned he was going to France to see Colette. Yet . . . *You must be your own man*, he told himself.

He stopped at the hallway window, the crescent moon drawing his gaze. He opened it easily and climbed silently out onto the roof tiles. The pitch was not too steep. Freedom was only a short climb to the ground.

"Are you leaving us, young Sahib?"

Modo nearly fell off the edge of the roof. "Tharpa?"

"Yes, it is I."

The words seemed to float in the air, coming from no particular direction. Then he saw his weapons master leaning against the dormer wall, hidden in shadow. "H-how did you know I'd be out here?"

"I have come to know you well over these last fourteen years. Restless sleeping for three nights in the room next to me means something. And a young man like you can't ignore the news of a threat to your parents so I took the liberty of nailing your window shut."

"Ah, you *do* know me well."

"I know your heart." Sometimes Tharpa seemed more mystical than human. "I repeat my question: Are you leaving us, young Sahib?"

"No," Modo said, "I was only . . . Oh, all right then. Yes, I am."

"Ah, then Mr. Socrates wins."

"Wins?"

"We had a wager between us."

"A wager!" Modo lost his footing momentarily.

"Yes, I said that despite the calling of your heart you would not leave without permission. He believed you would."

The very fact that they'd foreseen his departure as though he were as predictable as a wind-up soldier was most distressing.

"You bet on me?"

"Just a small sum. Do not worry for my financial loss. Now, I suggest you go back through the window. Mr. Socrates awaits you in his office."

Modo shook his head in frustration and stepped back inside the house, followed by Tharpa. It was as though he'd been caught stealing sweet biscuits. To these men I'm still a child, he thought. Trudging down the stairs to the main floor, he saw light under the door of Mr. Socrates' office. Tharpa knocked gently.

"Enter."

Modo blinked in the brightness but strode in, holding his head high. Mr. Socrates gave him a tired smile.

"So, you were slinking out," he said.

"I wasn't slinking."

"You were leaving without permission. When I was a soldier desertion was a capital crime. In India we would tie men to the mouth of a cannon and let the cannonball do the rest."

"That's barbaric."

"It was. I, myself, was not in favour of it. It did inspire discipline though."

"Well, this is not the army."

"No, Modo, what we do takes more finesse than what any company of soldiers does." He lifted his sterling silver letter opener—a miniature sabre—from the desk. "They are a hammer. We are the surgeon's knife."

"I've not been a knife, or should I say an agent, for some months now. It's clear I'm no longer of use."

Mr. Socrates sighed and rubbed at his temples. "What's clear to me is that I have made a mistake."

Modo raised his eyebrows. Had Mr. Socrates ever admitted to a mistake before?

"And what's this mistake?"

"I have let my emotions—my anger at you—get the better of me. You have been trained to a keen edge and you grow bored with inaction. I should have kept you busy with tasks and goals. Instead, a missive from France arrives and its contents stir you up. You become obsessed. I must purge you of your obsession."

"Purge me?"

"Yes. I've decided to send you to France."

Modo blurted, "You'll send *me*?"

"Yes, it's just a small assignment, really. I've booked

steamer passage for both you and Octavia first thing in the morning. I've decided that it's important for us to discover whether or not you have any remaining relatives. I have no idea what the Guild or the French would want with them, if indeed they are seeking them out. It would take years to train another agent as skilled in transformation as yourself. I suppose either organization could be looking at the long game. Or they have some goal that I cannot surmise. You are to be my eyes and ears again. Just don't become overly emotional."

"Emotional?"

"Yes. You shouldn't think of the people in question as your parents."

"And who are my parents, then?"

Mr. Socrates pressed his lips together, a look of confusion crossing his face. "You don't need parents, Modo. You have done very well with the appropriate guidance and training. A trip to France is your chance to free yourself from the past."

Could one ever be free of the past? Modo wondered. It seemed to shadow him wherever he went.

"Does Octavia know that she's been assigned to this mission?"

Mr. Socrates shook his head. "She'll know so in the morning. She'll be pleased to be doing something more exciting than eating croissants in Montreal."

Modo wasn't so sure of that. In fact, when he pictured her and Colette in the same city, a certain queasiness set in.

5

SETTING HIS MIND TO THE TASK

M r. Socrates stood in his office, slowly spinning a small globe, his fingers tracing the Atlantic, France, the Mediterranean and India. He'd visited all these places and would do so again in a heartbeat. But here he was trapped in a house in Montreal, like a fox backed into its hole.

With Modo and Octavia gone, he was left with Tharpa, Mrs. Finchley and the newly arrived Cook and Footman, whom he'd summoned from their hiding places in England. How his great dream of the Permanent Association was shrinking. Yes, he had fellow heads of the Association who had their own agents, but they had sworn to cut off all contact with him and retreat from active duty. It seemed the best course of action until they discovered how the Clockwork Guild had tracked down the location of one of their safe houses.

Despite the retreat, he wished to strike a blow against the Guild. But his special Dragoon project at the Pacific naval base was an egg not quite ready to be hatched. No one —not the Queen, nor the Lord Admiral—knew of it.

He rang the bell on his desk. A moment later Footman opened the door. The Chinese man was perhaps the best hand-to-hand fighter Mr. Socrates had ever employed.

"Please find Cook and accompany him here. I have orders for both of you."

Footman nodded and gently closed the door.

Mr. Socrates was beginning to fear that he had become too emotionally invested in the boy—no, not boy, for Modo was a young man now—sixteen at least—and as such was rebellious. It was to be expected. Were you not rebellious to your own father? he mused. Mr. Socrates had struck out on his own, joining the army at the age of sixteen and attempting to conquer the world. What he wouldn't give to have that vitality in his bones again.

He lifted the grey photo of his wife from his dresser. He had carried it all these years, had even stowed it safely in his kitbag through the Queensland jungle. His memories of her were as faded as the image itself. She had died during child-birth and he had lost his son minutes later, a boy with a weak heart. Mr. Socrates had cradled the dead weight of him in his arms. The world was a hard place but when he looked at the image of his beloved he tried to remember he had once been a softer man. Had once felt the pangs of love.

And so what of Modo? The agent had unequivocally disobeyed him. Twice. And yet, Mr. Socrates found that he didn't have the resolution to punish him properly. The young man was such a spectacular talent, possessed such an impressive intellect. He had devoured every book handed to him, understood concepts far beyond his age. And his shape-changing abilities made him the greatest asset the Association had ever had.

He didn't want to lose Modo to whatever half-wits had abandoned him. Had he attempted to prevent Modo from leaving Montreal, the young man was damnably dutiful enough to try to rescue his parents himself. He had no choice but to give Modo the needed support.

And, if there was a last secret to be gleaned from Modo's parents, if it were true they'd been located, then it was necessary to keep it from the myriad enemies of England. What havoc hostile forces could wreak if they had their very own shape-changing agent.

If it were the Clockwork Guild pursuing Modo's parents, then it was dire news indeed. They had constructed a giant of metal and flesh to attack the Parliament Buildings, had sailed halfway round the world in a warship more powerful than any other on the Seven Seas, and had swooped through the Australian skies in a massive airship. He could not imagine what they'd be capable of with an agent similar to Modo.

No, it was better that Modo nip whatever was developing in the bud. He had sent the girl too because, despite her smart mouth, she did have a vested interest in keeping Modo alive. And there was no one else he could spare.

He had to find out more about this Guild. He had to be proactive and strike at its heart, once and for all. Britain was a big target and the Clockwork Guild must have a large operation to have built such impressive war machines. These things didn't materialize out of thin air. They required metal works, docks and treasuries jammed full of money.

But where had they been hiding all this money, all the armaments? What country would grant them sanctuary?

Cook entered the room, Footman beside him. Cook had been a pleasure to have in the house; while Mrs. Finchley had been adequate in the kitchen, he was excellent.

"I'm sending you on a hunt for documents," Mr. Socrates said.

"Paperwork, sir?" Cook asked. "Would rather you asked me to charge up some enemy hill."

Mr. Socrates gave him a grim smile. "It will have to be a hill of paper. And please, before you go, make me some of your famous asparagus soup and roast pork with dinner rolls. It would be nice to enjoy it at least one more time."

"It'll be an honour, sir," Cook said. "I won't forget the sweet cream butter."

6

YET ANOTHER FRAUDULENT MARRIAGE

Octavia laughed as Modo stumbled under the weight of her luggage, bumping the guardrails of the gang-plank. He regained his balance and they boarded the SS *Ottawa. Serves you right, silly man,* she thought, *not allowing me to carry even one piece.*

She held the second-class tickets in her hand, wondering if such a lowly fare was a sign that Mr. Socrates was becoming a miser. Or perhaps he wanted to teach them some lesson or other. At least it wasn't steerage. Those poor people travelled like cattle.

Octavia and Modo were led by a gruff steward to a cabin near the aft stairwell. Inside was a bed, a minuscule writing table and, Octavia noted with satisfaction, a tiny water closet—they wouldn't have to use the public toilets.

"Well, husband, we've been in worse digs than this," she said as Modo closed the door.

"It'll do," he answered. "It needs airing." He went to the porthole and opened the window.

He was wearing the Doctor's face—that is how she referred to it—one of only a few he had shown her. She found it familiar and distant at the same time. His real face, the disfigured one, still burned in her memory.

"Are you enjoying our second fraudulent marriage?" she asked.

"One marriage to you was enough. A second is a trip into Dante's Inferno."

She didn't like his tone and didn't know what he meant by Dante, though the inferno reference she assumed to be something hellish.

"Oh, you will feel the inferno," she promised. "I was far too kind as a wife last time, hiring a drunk captain and scouring the Atlantic as you drifted to certain death in a diving bell."

"I'm sorry, Tavia," he said, "I was just trying to be clever. It's true. I owe you my life for finding me adrift on the ocean."

"You owe me thrice over by my count. And last night you were going to leave without me."

"How do you know that?"

"I heard your exchange with Tharpa."

"Don't you ever stop spying?"

"My window was open. It's not my fault I have such good ears."

He sighed. "Truth is, I didn't think it likely that you'd go with me. After all, you don't speak French."

"Au contraire, je suis . . . le tout!"

"You just said, 'I am a muddlehead.'"

"I did not! *Tu es le* muddlehead."

She grinned, Modo smiled his handsome Doctor smile, and they both laughed.

"Modo," she said when they had caught their breath again. "Why don't we watch our departure from the deck? The air would be good for us and our humours."

"Then let us go, dear wife."

He offered his arm and she took it, surprised that he held it all the way up the stairs as though they really were married. As second-class passengers they still had access to the promenade and they watched as the *Ottawa* left the dock bound for Liverpool. From there they would board another steamship and land in Le Havre. It was the quickest route from Montreal to Paris, for there were no direct steamships.

Octavia was sad to leave Montreal. For a small backwater city it had heart, the Scots, the Irish . . . even a few English, all working for a new life in a new land. And the Canadian French were so different from the French in France. Rougher around the edges and more likely to swear. Of course, she based her judgments of the French on that tart Colette, whom she'd met in Iceland.

All morning, despite the cold, they read on their deck chairs huddled under blankets, and for lunch they had chicken sandwiches in the second-class saloon. After their meal, Modo withdrew his handkerchief and wiped his forehead, saying, "I must return to the cabin."

Octavia knew what this meant. He could no longer maintain the visage and shape of the Doctor. These transformations could only be held for a few hours at a time.

"I'll wait here," she said. "I'd like to visit the ladies' saloon. Perhaps there'll be some action there. You know, needlework, gossip and penning morose diary entries."

He managed a smile and bowed, grimacing briefly, then turned abruptly. She recognized the sweat on his brow, the look of . . . of pain, that was it. It actually hurt for him to change. And she wondered at his lifetime of changing, of learning to be a chameleon. How much did it hurt him? He had spent so many hours manipulating his bones, his very flesh, all for the service of Mr. Socrates and Britain.

He had once revealed his true appearance to her but had not done so since. She preferred that. It had taken all of her willpower to look him in the eyes in the Australian rain forest. She hoped she would be able to do it again, but didn't want to be tested yet.

She spent a few hours reading *Pride and Prejudice* as other women played the small cottage piano. Later, arriving back at the cabin, she opened the door slowly. Modo was seated by the porthole, wearing his mask. His shoulders and back, so perfectly proportional when he played the Doctor, now looked lumpy and malformed. He was staring out at the ocean.

"I have returned, husband," she said jauntily.

Modo nodded. Without taking his eyes off the water, he said, "If you had the chance to see your parents again, would you?"

"No," she answered without hesitation. She sat on the end of the bed. "I'm not as sentimental as you, Modo. Remember, they left me at the orphanage with a note saying *Burden*."

"Do you think I'm a fool for travelling all this distance to attempt to save my parents from this mysterious threat?"

"I'd expect nothing less of you. You're far more noble than me."

He laughed. "I can't tell if you're serious."

"I am. And there's always the chance that you have brothers or sisters. That's the one thing I wish to know, whether or not I had a sister or a brother. You know, someone as clever and quick and handsome as me."

"If it be, so then watch out world!" He smiled, then

became serious. "It's good to have you along, Tavia. It feels . . . well, there's no one else I'd rather share this journey with."

"You're not going all maudlin on me, are you, husband?"

"Never!"

"Then good. I suggest we dine on the upper deck tonight. As you know I can eat more than ten men. I plan on making those piano-playing ladies roll their eyes."

7

A CLOCKWORK MIND

In the central Pacific, on the island of Atticus, Miss Hakkandottir entered the main doors of the Crystal Palace, walking briskly past the saluting guards. She strode into the copper-plated elevator and barked "Observation deck!" at the soldier operating the controls. The elevator rose in swift silence. Despite her dark mood, the interior of the palace, viewed through the glass doors, was impressive. Her eyes were drawn beyond the twenty-eight-foot fountain to the hundred-foot brass clock that towered over the inner plaza. Its face was a clock within a triangle—the symbol of the Clockwork Guild.

In earlier days it had bothered her that he'd chosen to replicate the British Crystal Palace in Sydenham Hill. The British had built it for the Great Exhibition and had raved about its majesty for over twenty years now. She gladly would have crashed an airship into it, just to see them all moan and gnash their teeth.

But as this palace was brought piece by piece to the island and raised to the heavens, it grew into a building that made the British original look like an oversized greenhouse.

It was beautiful, yes, but more important it was a hundred times more practical than England's flimsy structure. First off, it was nearly impregnable, made not of glass but of a quartz as impenetrable as any stone. Should there be a siege, its own airship dock meant it could be resupplied for months.

The soldier slid open the elevator door and Miss Hakkandottir marched onto the observation deck, a room with translucent white quartz walls that glowed with sunlight. Round observation windows faced all four directions across the Pacific. The roof was retracted and the sea breeze played with her red hair and gently wafted the six-foot feathered wings hanging from the iron rafters. They were symbolic of some Greek story or other but since it was an imaginary tale it wasn't important for her to recall it.

The Guild Master stood in the centre of the room, surrounded by twelve operators sitting at their quadruplex telegraph machines and feeding him strips of paper. He was not a tall man, but he was wiry and strong. He wore a grey military uniform without any insignia and simple gold-rimmed glasses. He could easily have been mistaken for a library custodian. She knew much better. He was the greatest tactician in the world.

He pushed up his glasses and continued to read. This was how he kept his eyes on the world. The world! From here he gave orders to agents in all four corners of the earth, purchased metals or armaments, bought and sold stocks, all without a moment's hesitation. He'd formed a perfect plan in his head and each command spoken, each message sent, brought the plan that much closer to fruition.

Miss Hakkandottir didn't know exactly what the plan was, but she suspected it was larger than bringing the pompous British Empire to its knees. She sometimes wondered if it was his intent to control every single government in the world. A foolish thought, for who could exert such power? Even Alexander the Great failed to accomplish it.

Though he was small and lean, she feared him. For his mind could outpace hers a hundred times over. And though his face was pleasant, behind those glasses his eyes were ice. Rarely did he express anything resembling an emotion. Many years before, when she'd been a captain of a Chinese pirate ship, she'd first been summoned to his Hong Kong lair. It had stunned her to discover that this nondescript, white man was at the heart of a massive criminal organization that ran half of China and nearly all of the opium trade. Even then he had an aura of power.

She knew nothing of his earlier life. He could be Danish or French or Russian. Even British. He had no accent and she'd lost count of how many languages he spoke.

She waited. It was best not to interrupt him during his work. He wrote a final missive and spoke to a telegrapher in German. Then the Guild Master turned to her.

"Ah, Ingrid." His tone was flat. His eyes, such a consistent dark brown that they seemed almost black, examined her. "You've been so helpful over the years."

She tensed up. "Am I about to be retired?"

He let out a dry chuckle. "No. I only experienced a moment of sentimentality. I apologize. I have also been disappointed by your mistakes: the sinking of the *Wyvern* under your command is a fine example."

The loss of that ship had nearly broken her heart. The Guild Master had even allowed her to name it so that it truly belonged to her, though he'd expressed some regret that she'd chosen a name that wasn't from the Greek pantheon. How she'd loved those iron decks and perfect guns. But now it languished at the bottom of the Atlantic. All due to Modo.

"I should have done better."

"Ah, that is true. Though, my design for the *Wyvern* was tempered by my hubris. I should have closed the interior compartments so that a blow to the hull would not have allowed all the lower chambers to fill." Had he just admitted a mistake? She almost fell over. "But don't forget, Ingrid, you lost our henchman Fuhr in the Thames and allowed our mechanical giant to be captured by the British, and you failed to retrieve the God Face in the jungle. A disturbing pattern of losses."

She squeezed her metal hand into a fist. "Am I here to be chastised?"

"No. I seek only to remind you that you are not perfect."

"I am aware of that."

He nodded. "Do you have any thoughts about the disappearance of Mr. Socrates?"

"He is hiding in one of his pampering homes. Do you want me to hunt him down?" The mere thought of it made her heartbeat quicken, her blood lust rise. How she would love to corner Alan—or Mr. Socrates, as he fancied himself—and skewer him right through the heart with her sabre. After all, he was the one who'd cut off her hand. She should perhaps thank him for that, since the metal hand was her greatest gift. But she still remembered the pain of the blow during the sword fight. He would pay for that.

"You're dreaming of revenge, aren't you," the Guild Master said. His eyes were measuring her again. "Don't deny it. You get a crinkle between your eyebrows when you dream of such things. I've toyed with the idea of flushing him out, along with the rest of the Association. We shall remove the members of the Association from the board one by one. But at this point, I don't want to take any resources away from Project Hades and the myrmidons."

She'd heard him mention this project several times and she knew the bodies that were arriving daily at the island were part of it. She also now knew that *myrmidon* meant warrior; she'd asked Dr. Hyde for the definition. She was growing tired of having to know every single Greek myth. If only she understood the grand plan behind it all.

"What is it you want me to do?" she asked.

"There've been interesting developments in France. Our search for more—how shall I put it—flesh is progressing at a satisfactory rate."

"And why do you mention this?"

He paused, deep in thought. She knew better than to ask another question at this point.

"I was considering sending you there," he said a second later, "but I have reconsidered. Lime is progressing nicely and you and your airship skills are needed here. Our assembly of the myrmidons is of the utmost importance."

"You want me to transport bodies?"

"Yes. An airship is faster than waiting for boats. I have ordered you a larger airship, though construction will not be finished for three months. We'll make do with our older airships. Soon we'll have more than enough material."

"Is this a demotion?" she asked, then quickly added, "sir."

He smiled. "No. You enjoy being in the air and your efforts will help the Hades project come to . . . well . . . to life." Another dry chuckle.

"If these are your orders, then I will follow them. But there is little challenge to transporting the dead. Would you prefer I bring them back alive? That would be simple enough. I would only need a dozen or so Guild soldiers. And irons."

"Ah, Ingrid, that is an intriguing idea, but far too time-consuming. And I need the extra soldiers here. You may depart southwest now—there are materials in New Zealand. I shall contact you along the route if your orders change."

"Yes, sir."

She left him and made her way to the airship tower near the dock. The *Gorgon* could make the journey to New Zealand in four days. She commanded her pilot to fire up the engines and her crew to load supplies. The sooner she was in the air, the better she would feel.

8

OPERATING ON INSTINCT

Modo sat at a table in the open-air section of Le Hotel Grande's café, wondering if his shivering was from the breeze or nervousness. Octavia seemed aloof this morning, though they had shared the occasional word about the weather or how different Paris was from London. She'd said she didn't like the smell of the city and he'd said it was no worse than the Thames. They'd spoken little since.

Their fellow diners were all engaged in animated conversations. Modo was pleased to find that he understood most of the French he overheard. He noticed, too, everyone was very fashionable; he'd never seen such an array of ladies' hats in England. Everything in Paris was remarkably stylish, from the people to *les fiacres*, the little horse-drawn carriages; even the tables of the café were a fancy wrought iron topped with glass.

He searched the crowd for Colette, expecting her to appear at any moment. He'd decided to shift into what he called the Knight face, the one that she'd seen before, so she'd be able to recognize him.

"I like the Doctor face better," Octavia suddenly said.

"Better than what?"

"Than this one," she said. "It was more sophisticated."

"Well, I'm sorry that I don't look sophisticated enough for your taste."

"No, it's me who is sorry, husband."

She didn't seem to be sorry. He could only presume it was the impending arrival of Colette that was responsible for her change in mood. It had been a good journey here. She'd even exclaimed how beautiful Paris was when they first stepped off the train from the port of Le Havre. But since they'd woken this morning she'd been nitpicking. In all his years of education, why hadn't he thought to ask Mrs. Finchley to explain the female mind?

They continued to wait in silence. At a quarter to one Octavia began tapping her teaspoon on the table.

"Must you do that?" Modo asked.

"Ah, sorry, husband. I forgot how jangled your nerves are."

"I am not jangled!"

But he was and he knew it. Had Colette given up on waiting here for him? He'd travelled as quickly as possible after receiving the letter. Of course, she had probably assumed he'd be travelling from England, not Canada.

"Your French mistress is late," Octavia noted.

"She's not my mistress, Tavia."

"Well, you certainly were in a hurry to cross the Atlantic to see her."

"You know why I—"

"Modo, I thought you would be alone." A young woman's voice interrupted them.

Modo and Octavia turned to see Colette standing behind them. She was thinner than before, and wearing a black hat and dress as if she were on her way to a funeral.

She held a tan briefcase. Her hair was tied with a purple ribbon, her eyes had dark circles under them and her cheeks seemed sunken.

"A pleasure to see you again, Miss Milkweed," she said, her accent clipping the consonants coldly.

"Yes," Octavia agreed with mock geniality, "a most welcome pleasure."

"And it is wonderful to see you, Modo." She held Modo's shoulder with a firm grip, and her voice softened. "It has been far too long since I last set eyes on you."

"It has?" Modo said. "I mean, it's wonderful to see you."

"Are the two of you married, again?" she asked.

"Yes," Octavia answered.

"Only for show," Modo added. "Please join us."

Octavia gave him a sharp elbow in the ribs; he wasn't certain why.

Colette walked around them and sat down, waving over a waiter to order coffee. "I've not had fish for eleven months now," she said, laughing. It was, of course, a reference to what she and Modo had been eating on the *Ictíneo* when last they'd been together. "Strictly beef and chicken."

"You could do with adding a few pounds," Octavia said, feigning kindness.

"I appreciate your concern," Colette replied, dusting a few crumbs off the table.

She was still as beautiful as Modo remembered and yet she'd lost more than weight—a certain vibrancy, perhaps? Her air of invincibility?

"I avoid fish," Modo admitted, giving her his full attention.

Colette leaned towards him. "Let us get to the matter at hand, shall we? The French secret service is looking for others who are like you, Modo. It is a top priority."

Octavia set her cup of coffee down right between them with a clatter and said, "Who would be leading that search? You?"

"I—uh—am a member of the team."

"So, this could just be an elaborate trap to capture Modo."

"It's exactly that," Colette said, narrowing her eyes to slits. "With a snap of my fingers armed agents will sweep down and surround us. They'll haul you, Miss Milkweed, off to jail, cotton stuffed in your snide mouth, and drag Modo to our interrogation rooms on rue de la Merci." She lifted her hand and snapped her fingers, drawing the attention of a nearby waiter, then waved him away, laughing bitterly at his confusion. "I do not expect to gain your trust, Miss *Weed de la Milk*. But I do hope that Modo will remember our previous, shall we say, adventures and the pact we made with each other."

"And what sort of pact was that?" Octavia glared at Modo.

"Um . . ." He looked to the sky and cleared his throat. He scoured his brain for the answer. Octavia was often vexing, but Colette's presence made him doubly vexed. He could barely think straight. "Did we swear to help each other survive?"

"Yes, you remember!" Colette said. "Good. Good. It was not an oath I took lightly. I come not as an agent for my country, Modo, but as a friend to you. I owe you."

Owe me? For what? Modo was confused. Couldn't she meet his eyes for longer than a few seconds at a time?

"Your parents are living in the country. I've been able to ascertain that much."

Modo's heart sped up and this disturbed him. It was

important to keep his emotions in check. "Please tell me what you know."

"I've done a great amount of research, Modo. I discovered accounts of your birth. I even interviewed a witness."

"A witness to my birth?" Modo said, flabbergasted. "A relative?" Maybe he had an aunt. Or even a grandmother.

"No, not a relative. A midwife. Her name was Marie."

"What did she say?"

"She ... uh ... verified that you were born. And that you were ... well ... she was affected by your appearance."

Just as you were, Modo thought.

"How can you be certain she was describing Modo's birth?" Octavia asked.

"I am certain—unless there is more than one child with Modo's unusual abilities. How old are you, Modo?"

"My age? I can't be certain. I'm sixteen, at least."

"No, Modo. You're fifteen. Your birthday is November first, 1858."

"You're only fifteen!" Octavia exclaimed. "I thought you were older than me."

"I'm wiser," Modo snapped. Then he couldn't help himself. He smiled broadly. He had an actual birthdate! He'd never once celebrated his birthday.

"May I interview this midwife? Was she a friend of my parents? What other information does she have?"

Colette sucked in her lips for a moment and stared into her coffee cup. "I'm afraid interviewing her will be impossible: she's dead. Drowned in the Seine." Modo sat back, dazed, but Colette went on. "And a librarian, who was a great aid to me in my research, also died after falling off the roof of the library. One wonders if he was pushed. And finally, a Father Mauger, who was the records master for Notre Dame de Paris, is also dead."

"Death certainly likes to follow you around," Octavia said.

"Who committed these murders?" Modo asked.

"Two foreign agents, Lime and Typhon. I know for certain they killed the priest. I can only assume they murdered the others. The leader, Lime, spoke English."

"They were British?" Modo asked.

"Well, he spoke with an Irish lilt. He seemed quite mad —spouting mad poetry and such, even as I pointed my pistol at him."

"That sounds Irish to me," Octavia said.

Colette set down her cup and tapped a finger several times on the table. "I am certain that they were members of the Clockwork Guild."

"How did you come to that conclusion?" Octavia asked.

"Instinct."

"Instinct? Are we to trust your instincts?"

Colette wagged her finger. "Only one of you was invited, my dear. And I have learned to trust my instincts. Further, the methods of these killers were more than brutal—one of the hallmarks of the Clockwork Guild."

"What exactly were they searching for?" Modo asked.

"Information about you, my friend. They've retrieved your submission forms from Father Mauger."

"The what?" Modo said.

"The Notre Dame submission forms from 1858," Colette replied.

"Which are?" Octavia said.

"These are forms that parents sign when giving their children up to Notre Dame. Most just abandon their offspring on the steps, but a few want to officially hand the child over to the church. These papers may also have contained valuable information. Shortly after your birth,

Modo, your parents changed their names and moved out of Nanterre. The question is to where. And what are their new names?"

"What was my—their last name?"

"It was Hébert. They were potters."

Modo paused. Potters! His parents made cookware? How . . . how normal. He had pictured his father as a doctor or a military officer, something impressive. But a simple potter?

"Well," Octavia said, "since these enemy agents have all the information, are we stuck just twiddling our thumbs?"

"No. There are other French agents besides me who are working on this same case. They have put together an index of names and occupations in the villages surrounding Paris. There's a high probability that Modo's parents' new names are on that list."

"Why don't you just go take a look at their list, then?" Octavia asked.

Colette let out a long sigh and, for a moment, Modo thought he saw her eyes become moist. She straightened her shoulders and set her jaw. "I have been discharged from the agency."

He caught Octavia shooting him a glance.

"But why?" Modo asked, averting his eyes from his colleague. She was too quick to jump to conclusions.

"They considered the *Ictíneo* assignment a failure," Colette admitted, "and no one would believe me about the underwater city of New Barcelona. We don't have submarines capable of diving to that depth. They even insinuated that I was just imagining the Clockwork Guild. And they . . . well . . . let us just say I was not always the best agent after that. They no longer trusted me."

"They are wise men," Octavia said.

Colette stood up as if to leave. Modo stood up, too,

putting his hand on her shoulder. "Please sit. Octavia, despite her demeanour, wants to get to the bottom of this as much as I. Don't you, Tavia." He gave her a look and she returned it with a grim nod.

"How do we get this information from your former comrades?" Modo asked as they sat down again.

"That's where your spectacular talents come in." Her voice was suddenly energized again, the vitality he remembered returning to her face. She placed her briefcase on the table. "I would like you to assume another persona, break into a building and steal the information."

"Whose persona?" Modo asked.

"And which building?" Octavia added.

"The Deuxième Bureau, our spy agency. And the person I want you to impersonate is Directeur Belanger, the agency's head."

Modo met Colette's eyes. She was clearly enjoying the shock on their faces.

9

A SLIGHT SKIP OF THE HEART

Colette gave the instructions to the driver of the *fiacre*, then allowed Modo to hold open the door to the carriage for both her and Octavia. The folding roof was open, letting in the warm September sun. As they rode the cushioned bench, a luxury she was extremely thankful for, she pointed out a few of the sights, hoping that her descriptions weren't too forced. *He is here! He is right here across from me!*

The moment she'd seen Modo there had been a slight skip to her heartbeat. He was wearing the face she'd known on the *Ictíneo,* but something about it had changed, or her memory of it was different. She was also surprised that she had difficulty meeting his eyes. She remembered them with utmost clarity. Once, in jest, she had called them soulful, and it was the perfect word. In Paris. She'd been waiting for him for so long, checking at Le Hotel Grande every day. As the weeks passed she'd begun to believe her letter had not been delivered.

She had often imagined his arrival with anticipation, and a little fear. What if she were to break down again?

But, mercifully, that hadn't happened. And now it was as though no time had passed even though it had been almost a year since their last meeting.

"Enough of this tourist talk," Octavia said. "We need to get to the meat of our visit to your fair country."

"What a . . . pleasant way of putting it," Colette whispered. "Then let us get to the meat." Colette remembered well Octavia's protectiveness of Modo, or rather, her possessiveness—that was a better word. "We are nearly at the Bureau."

The carriage turned down the rue de la Merci and she thumped briskly on the side of the car. The driver stopped in front of a tall iron fence. Beyond it was a structure Colette knew all too well. From the outside it seemed to be an ordinary seven-storey rectangular building. The architects had taken pains to make it look exactly like a textile factory. In reality it was the very heart of French espionage; from here their tentacles ran throughout Europe, and across the oceans.

Inside those walls Colette had spent far too many hours sifting through paper, searching for clues, taking orders from oafs whose minds worked at half the speed of her own.

"This is the building you will enter, Modo." She spoke quietly so the driver wouldn't overhear. "It is the *Deuxième Bureau de l'état-major général*, or in English, since I know Octavia doesn't understand our beautiful language, it means 'the Second Bureau of the General Staff.' It is the centre of our military intelligence."

"Humph." Octavia gave a dramatic sniff. "It's rather plain."

"That is the *point*." Colette spoke slowly as though explaining something to a child. "Did you expect a big sign saying French Spies Inside?"

Colette was pleased to hear Modo chuckle. Octavia looked out the window.

Colette opened her briefcase and pulled out her dossier. "I have a photograph of Directeur Belanger, though it is ten years old, so you'll have to age yourself appropriately."

Modo examined the photo. "I assume you also have his height, a description of the type of clothing he typically wears, jewellery, his manner of carrying himself and his personal habits."

"It is all listed in great detail."

"And, while I am Mr. Belanger, would you like me to reinstate you to your position?" Modo asked cheekily.

Though Colette enjoyed the fact that he was relaxed enough to joke at such a time, she could not imagine working for the agency again. "I am done with them. By the way, I do hope your French has improved."

"It is adequate. But there are many other more worrisome and unpredictable matters. For example, he'd know most everyone in that building. Who do I acknowledge? Which individuals are his close colleagues? There are too many relationships to understand, faces to know on sight. Normally I spend weeks memorizing the interactions of my targets."

"Monsieur Belanger is—how do you English say?— gruff. He ignores everyone—his wife, his agents. He once kept even *le président* waiting for several hours."

"He sounds typically French to me," Octavia said.

Colette carried on. "Your mission will be less complicated if you enter the building at night. Most of the staff are finished in the early evening. You'll stride right in and take the papers and return to us with a canary-eating grin on your face. Did I say that right?"

Modo smiled. "Yes, you did!"

That face, Colette thought, that face was so handsome and yet she knew what lay beneath it. No, she reminded herself, the beautiful face was the mask.

She managed to return the smile as she handed him the dossier. "First we'll go to a tailor," she said.

"Well," Modo said, "with the two of you picking my clothes I should be the sharpest dresser in all of Paris."

10

THE ROOT OF ALL EVIL

I t was perhaps the most boring week Mr. Socrates ever had endured. He'd spent nearly every waking moment in his office sifting through information brought to him by Cook and Footman in the hope of gleaning some telling detail about the Clockwork Guild's location. Mrs. Finchley would bring him tea and meals, clearing the plates without his even noticing. Tharpa would cajole him into a short constitutional to clear his mind. Data gathering was something Mr. Socrates had abhorred during his life in the military, but it was a necessary evil of his job. From data came conclusions and from conclusions came action.

A few months earlier he'd have had his team of trusted "ferrets," as he called the clerks who worked for him, sift through the newspapers and documents. Instead, he himself was reading shipping records, passenger lists, documents indicating market trends, even patent applications. He wanted to know the prices of metal and the places where it was being bought. Fools often said that money was the root of all evil, but Mr. Socrates knew better. It was metals. If there was anything that had driven the vital mechanization

of war it was metal. First for swords. Then cannons. And
finally, iron-hulled ships.

He did stop to read the papers: The *Montreal Gazette, The
London Times* and *The New York Post.* There were the usual
stories of terrible railway collisions, of political campaigns,
political addresses to Republicans, even an article that
graded butter. He paused over a story about bodies disap-
pearing along the Pacific coast. If he'd had more agents, he
might have pursued it. Most likely it was resurrection men
selling the cadavers to medical establishments. There was so
much to learn about the human body and not enough dead
bodies to go around. In time a pattern began to emerge and
his boredom was replaced with excitement. A large
purchase of metal from Ontario had been bought by several
companies with Greek names. Did the Clockwork Guild not
have a penchant for using Greek names? It was perhaps a
reference to the past glory of that civilization. The metal had
been shipped to an unknown destination in the Pacific.

He worked even longer hours. He read accounts of metal
leaving from Vancouver, from Seattle—and spotted
evidence of a large shipment three years ago to a Chinese
buyer in the Yellow Seas. That piqued his curiosity for he
knew that Hakkandottir had once been employed by the
Chinese triads, the pirates and brigands who fought both
the Emperor and the British Empire. He'd dealt with many
of them, Hakkandottir included. He knew she'd not easily
give up those ties.

Sixteen years ago he had met her in a sword fight on the
deck of a two-masted junk and severed her hand. At the
time he'd been pursuing the leader of a triad, someone
known only as 489. It was a number from Chinese
numerology that referred to the dragon master, the leader.
Mr. Socrates had been reassigned to India, but his fellow

servicemen had never discovered that triad leader. Why hadn't it occurred to him before? This 489 could have formed this Guild. The organization did not have the pattern of a triad, it was something much larger, but would take the same skill set to control. It was entirely possible.

He remembered the junk, Hakkandottir's ship that he had captured. It had been steam powered, with an engine the likes of which he'd never seen before.

Was it all connected? Oh, Alan, you fool. Of course! Their nest is in the Pacific, as far away from British as possible. Now the only difficulty is to pinpoint exactly where they are.

It became clear what he must do. It was a big world, but made smaller by train and steamship. He summoned Cook and Footman. By the time the two were standing before him he was practically vibrating with anticipation.

"I'm about to ask the two of you to charge full-steam up a hill," Mr. Socrates said.

"I was hoping so, sir," Cook said. "I'm ready, willing and able. Just point me in the right direction."

Footman only nodded in agreement, but Mr. Socrates was certain he saw excitement in the Chinese man's eyes.

11

THE HEART OF THE AGENCY

I t had been relatively simple for Modo to take Directeur Belanger's form. He had paid for a room in a nearby hotel and rested for several hours. He then removed his mask and stared at the photograph while composing the face. Colette had fetched the clothing from a haberdashery while Octavia quizzed him about the upcoming mission.

When he emerged, dressed in a dark suit and a long jacket, his belt cinched tight, he was amused by Colette's shocked expression.

"*Sacre bleu!*" she said. "You have captured the image of Directeur Belanger."

"It's a stunning gift, this shape-shifting," Modo had only meant this to be lighthearted, but he was suddenly aware that it sounded like bragging.

"*Très excellent* is what it is!" Colette said.

"I prefer when he looks younger," Octavia said.

"Young or old, the disguise only lasts for a few hours, so let us hasten away," he said. Within minutes they were in another *fiacre* and, shortly after that, had returned to the Bureau.

Despite the plain facade of the stone building, Modo felt as if he were looking at a fortress. The fence was taller than any of the nearby ones and there were several guard stations. There were also plenty of gas lamps, making the courtyard relatively bright. He wiped the glass window of the fiacre, for their breath had fogged it.

Smoke rose from three smokestacks protruding from the roof of the building. In the short time he'd been watching he'd seen three tarp-covered wagons stop at the gates, present papers, and continue up to a large delivery door that led into the lower level of the building. Were the tarps hiding arms, or stacks of files?

"Are you certain you want to do this?" Octavia asked. "I don't know that we can trust her."

"I do have ears," Colette said.

"I want you to hear," Octavia answered. "This could very well be a trap."

"Why this whole complicated ruse, then?" Colette asked. "If it was a trap I could have agents swoop down on us at this very moment."

"Modo is the strongest man I've ever met. To even stand a chance of capturing him you would first need to draw him into your lair."

For a moment Modo thought Octavia was having him on, but her face said otherwise. She really was bragging on his behalf. Well, it was the truth. Even Tharpa couldn't beat him at arm wrestling.

"I know you find this hard to believe, but I trust her, Tavia," Modo said as he patted Octavia's hand. "She may have been a French agent, but her word is good as gold, that is one thing I learned on the *Ictíneo*. And I need this information. *We* need it. I believe Mr. Socrates would agree with me."

"There is no time like the present," Colette said.

A light flashed to life inside the carriage and Modo was momentarily blinded by it. She'd shone what looked like a pocket lucifer directly at him.

"You have a battery-powered lamp?" Modo asked. "I didn't think the French were so advanced."

"Oh, *la petite lumière*? It is an old technology. The English are not the only ones with batteries." She peered at his face. "It continues to amaze me how much you look like Belanger . . . Now, you remember the map I drew for you?"

"I've memorized it."

"Then you will recall that the office you want is in the centre of the fifth floor? And that it belongs to Lucien Quint?"

"Yes, of course I do. You need not repeat the instructions," he snapped. Perhaps he *was* getting nervous. "I have the plan in here," he said softly as he tapped his skull. "You have prepared me well." He paused. "Both of you."

"Then we shall begin," Colette said. She knocked three times on the ceiling of the *fiacre* and the driver drove up to the front gates and stopped. Modo opened the door and stepped down to the street.

"Sois agressif!" Colette whispered. "Remember to be gruff. Not your usual polite self."

"Indeed I shall," he replied gruffly, then smiled.

"Take great care," Octavia said. "Don't go running around like a bull in a china shop."

"The two of you are acting like mothers," he hissed, then turned away before either could get another word in. Truth was, he was happy to be out of the wagon and away from the two of them.

He strode to the front gate. Behind him, he heard the *fiacre* pull away.

"Arrêtez-vous!" the guard commanded.

"Arrêtez-vous, Monsieur," Modo said, correcting him.

"Mot de passe," the guard said.

"Ashenden," Modo barked, for Colette had given him the password. The name had no meaning that he could discern, though he found it odd that they used a British surname.

The man nodded and said in French, "Welcome back, sir."

Modo, pleased his appearance had fooled a guard, didn't give him another glance. He carried on to the main entrance, passing a second guard station. Two hounds growled and their master pulled back on the leashes. "Shut those hogs up," Modo spat in French, then opened the door to the Deuxième Bureau.

He marched smartly down a brightly lit hallway. Of course the French would have electric lights; they liked showing off the latest advances. Modo found this new type of lighting to be garish, not nearly as warm and natural as gaslight. He tried to set aside his worries that the brightness would make it easier to spot any mistakes he'd made in his transformation.

How many papers about England, about Queen Victoria, about Mr. Socrates, about Modo himself would be filed here in this building? If he had hours to spend he could uncover a lifetime of secrets. But there was only one secret that Modo wanted to uncover tonight.

He encountered another agent, who saluted, but Modo just stomped by. A guard at the door to the stairwell also saluted but Modo didn't even look at him, giving the air of a man in a hurry. He burst into his office and closed the door, then immediately exited through the office's back door and climbed the stairs to the fifth floor.

Room 5498 was exactly where Colette's map had indicated. He opened the door and charged in, just as he imagined Belanger would do. This was a mistake, as he banged his knee on a desk. He cursed and turned the key for the light. It flickered to life. These rooms were much smaller than Belanger's and bursting at the seams with perfectly piled papers, folders and files.

He went to the desk Colette had told him about and discovered that the file drawer had been locked. Using two small pins he had in his vest pocket, he took over a minute to pick it. He chastised himself for not practising enough recently. The lock eventually gave a *click* and he pulled open the drawer; all the papers inside had been neatly placed in labelled folders. Ah, the bureaucrats were good at this sort of thing.

He found a thick file marked *Subject Modo: 24601* and began to read. At first there was very little of interest or import, only conjecture on his whereabouts. India! Someone had seen him in India. He laughed. He'd never been to Tharpa's homeland. Then he went back to the drawer and thumbed through several more files, stopping on one marked *Ictíneo/Brunet/Modo*. He opened it and skimmed the French pages until his eyes found this: "Agent Brunet insisted that an agent with the code name 'Modo' was able to change his shape and his facial features. Her description lead investigator Quint (47b321) to doubt her sanity, but after several tests with doctors she was certified as sane. Quint searched records in England . . ."

He folded up the page and stuffed it into his pocket. Perhaps there was something else in the file but it would take days to read through it all. He was here for one file only.

As he replaced the file in the drawer he noticed an envelope had been clipped to the back. Curious, he opened it.

Inside were several pages including a handwritten note in French:

Copy of these pages 1 thru 8 appear under *Brunet, Colette 15901*. It is important detail for file *Modo 24601*. Agent Brunet complains of nightmares and is easily excited. Her discovery of the *Ictíneo* is exemplar, but the loss of the *Vendetta* leads us to conclude that ultimately she failed in her mission. She complains of dizziness and lack of sleep, and when interviewed by the physician she blames this on seeing the face of the English agent Modo, a face she describes as being "gargoyle ugly." She has mental fatigue compounded by physical exhaustion and an extended stay in a sick room is recommended. When Brunet is released again, she should be put on light duty only.

Mental fatigue? Blames this on the face of the English agent Modo? Gargoyle ugly? So, seeing his face *had* marked her. The deaths of hundreds of her comrades, the weeks spent as a prisoner on the *Ictíneo,* the fight for their lives—these were all hardships, but none were listed as contributing to her illness. It was seeing *his* face. His true and ugly self. *That's* what had broken her.

He skipped ahead where three sentences had been underlined:

Brunet has become extremely delusional and is no longer in full control of her faculties. She was sent to Laroque Sanatorium for three months but it did not improve her condition. She was declared unfit for duty and released from employment on July 7th.

She'd spent time in a sanatorium! He'd seen the inside of Bedlam, London's most famous home for the deranged. The people there had been totally cracked. This threw everything into question. Had anything she'd said so far been the truth? Were his parents actually alive? Was he even French?

Yes, that part had been true. Mr. Socrates had confirmed it. And the French agents were looking for his family, so there had to be something to it.

Why was she helping him? Out of pity? Did she feel she owed him?

He put the documents in his jacket pocket along with several other papers that might contain something about his parents. He began to comb through the paperwork, madly hoping to find his parents' current address.

The door swung open and a man walked in. "Directeur Belanger!" the agent exclaimed in French. "I didn't expect to see you in the office this evening."

Modo closed the file drawer with a bang, keeping his voice gruff. "Since when do I report to you?"

Colette had described Quint as a thin, pale man and this person fit that, the electric lighting made everyone look pale.

"Is there something I can help you with, sir?"

"No, Quint. Nothing." Modo kept his sentences short. The more French he spoke the greater the chance of a gaffe. The man would know Belanger's voice well, but Modo had discovered that people often heard what they saw as though it was their brain's job to fill in the gaps.

"I understand, sir. May I have a few seconds of your time?"

"I'm extremely busy."

"I just need to ask you about the Modo case. I've made great headway on the location of his family. And I have an important request."

"What's that?"

"I would like Colette Brunet to be arrested."

"Brunet? Why?"

"Because, sir, she has betrayed her former position. I

have proof she has continued to research Modo even after her removal from the Bureau. She has recently been associating with foreign spies."

Modo stood up. "How do you know this?"

"For the past few weeks I've had her followed."

"Under whose orders?"

"You gave me full rights, sir. Remember? *Do what is necessary* were your exact words."

"Quint! Don't be impertinent!"

"I apologize. But I must tell you that these spies she has been dealing with are British."

"British? Have you proof?"

"Yes, sir." He paused, a glimmer of a smile crossing his face. "You are the proof."

Modo stiffened. How could he have guessed? "I don't follow."

The man reached into his coat and removed a pistol from his pocket in a swift, well-rehearsed motion. "Because, I am not Quint. My dear Directeur may have hundreds under his command, but he would recognize me. I can't believe you are here, that *you* have come to *us*."

"Put away that gun! What madness is this?"

"I've been doing much of the field work on your case for eight months now. I've interviewed Brunet. I've read the reports of your ingenious robbery of the French Embassy in London. Do you think I'd miss the connections? But never did I imagine that you'd walk right into my office."

"Put down that gun at once. You are mistaken!"

"Am I? Then tell me my name." Colette hadn't mentioned any other agents.

"Put away the gun, you fool!"

"Modo, enough of this," he said calmly, this time in English. "I am impressed. You do look very much like

Belanger, except shorter. I was handpicked and trained by him. He comes from southern France and has a meridional accent. Oh, and Quint retired three weeks ago; I inherited his office."

Modo sat down and shrugged in a friendly manner. "You've caught me. Congratulations. What is your name?"

"Philip Laroche. It is a pleasure to meet you. I am—how do you English say—an admirer of your work."

So, what do you intend to do with me?"

"Ah, you'll know soon enough. For now, we have a room where I would like to take you for questioning. It's a quiet place on the lower floor of the building. I'd like to inquire about so many things. This Clockwork Guild, were they just a figment of Brunet's imagination? And the *Association de la Permanence* that controls you. And this Mr. Socrates. So much to review. You'll be detained for some time, but your favourite meals will be served. We aren't barbarians. It will be a pleasant and polite series of conversations, I promise." He waved his pistol. "Now, please, stand up or I'll shoot you."

12

TRANSPORTING THE DEAD

I n her thirty-seven years Miss Hakkandottir had seen hundreds, if not thousands, of bodies, and now she was carrying load after load of cadavers to the island. She had been at it for weeks, and there were three more sitting here now in the car of the airship *Hera* as she floated across the Pacific.

This last batch had been from New Zealand, brought to her by desperate prospectors who had yet to find a vein of gold. Another hanged man, his neck too long. Someone who'd died in a mine by suffocation, the body in pristine condition—a particularly valuable find. And a man who'd ingested poison after losing all his money in a card game. He was an odd shade of yellow.

The ice coffins had been designed by Dr. Hyde, showcasing his trademark ingenuity. Despite the humidity and warmth of the Pacific, the ice melted slowly so the bodies stayed cold, in the same state they had been in not hours before their deaths.

Her orders had been to keep the coffins closed, but her curiosity got the better of her and she opened them one by one to gaze down on the faces of the dead. Hardened, muscular men who had lived tough lives. The combination of gases and cold kept them looking as though they could snap their eyes open at any moment. She mused about how she would look after death and shrugged it off. Death was not something worth dwelling on. *Fearlessness is better than a faint heart,* her father had told her many times. The timing of her death had been written long ago and she could not prevent it.

It was an important but tedious task to transport the dead back to Atticus. In total she had brought one hundred and seven bodies to the catacombs of the Clockwork Guild's lair. There was something sacred about it. She laughed. Sacred? When had she ever been concerned with spiritual matters?

The trip took three days. She did love being airborne. From here she could look to the northwest, where the giant shipyards on the coast of China were building three new steam-powered Guild battleships: the *Hydra,* the *Gorgon,* and the *Medusa.* They would be larger and more powerful than the *Griffon,* her last battleship. No navy would be able to stand in their way. Each ship would be accompanied by a fleet of steam-powered *Triton* vessels. All nations would tremble at the sight of this armada.

She had no desire to be the captain of any seafaring vessel—if she was to be captain of anything it would be in the air. No nation—not England, nor Germany, nor France —had an airship with as much weaponry and speed as the *Hera.* With enough coal and food she could strike London and vanish into the night before they even knew who had dealt the blow. She imagined having a hundred airships at her command. No. A thousand! The stunned world would be in awe of her.

"I want a perfect landing this time," she said to the pilot. The wind was blowing out of the northwest and the cross-wind would make it difficult.

"Yes, Captain," the pilot replied.

She noted that his hand was steady on the wheel. Good. Only the best of the Guild soldiers could work with her.

Below them three small *Triton* boats were cutting through the water at a speed she estimated to be over twenty-four knots. In a short time there would be a hundred of them. The Guild Master had some plan or other at play, but he was always so secretive about his grand intentions. Even Dr. Hyde, whom she could twist into whatever shape she desired, had been equally secretive.

The pilot lowered the flaps and a gust of wind banged the *Hera* against the dock, making the ship rattle and shudder. It was enough to set Miss Hakkandottir's nerves on edge. She grabbed the pilot with her metal hand, ignoring his pleading, and lifted him over the side of the open car. "You'll land perfectly next time." Then she dropped him.

He fell several feet before grabbing on to the landing rope and slipping down to the ground. She was disappointed. Not even a broken leg.

As the soldiers began unloading the cargo, she climbed down the net ladder and strode up the hill towards Dr. Hyde's cave. The Crystal Palace glowed with the red light of the setting sun, the dull Pacific evening still warm and humid. She felt as though she were being spied on from the palace's observation deck. That was how the Guild Master wanted her to feel: watched. He had numerous telescopes and would often look down on his creations; perhaps he was peering at her right now, as she marched up the hill and into the cave. She straightened her shoulders.

Dr. Cornelius Hyde looked just as he had the last time

she'd seen him, nearly a week ago, standing under the gaslight holding two test tubes. The man, old as he was, rarely stopped working. If she were to make a sudden noise, he would startle and drop the tube, smashing it and destroying the contents. She had done that only once before and set his work back by days. So she cleared her throat lightly, until he looked up.

"Ingrid. It is such a pleasure to see you."

"And you, as well, Cornelius. I have brought you more fine specimens. How does your work go?"

"It is frustrating, Ingrid. Typhon was such a success. He made me feel I was born to design human beings." He paused. "That does sound somewhat mad, does it not? But I see so much potential!" He lifted his hands to emphasize his point. "Every molecule. Every cell is connected. Run through with veins and nerves. And with Typhon I was able to animate it all using that metamorph's finger."

"Metamorph?"

"Agent Modo. He's a metamorph—like a tadpole that can turn into a frog and back again—except he likely can change into any human form he imagines. There is something about his cells, his blood, that combined with the right electrical impulses brought Typhon to life."

"You do remember who brought you his finger, don't you?" she said slyly.

"Of course, Ingrid. I praise you every day for that. But I need more of his tissues." He pointed at the empty cages where several chimpanzees had once been. There was also an aquarium on four wrought-iron legs, inside which was a large octopus. It had seven arms. "All other attempts have failed. The secret is in *his* flesh."

"Would you like me to bring him here, piece by piece?" she asked.

"Ah, if only you could. But the Guild Master has promised me more material very soon. Typhon was only the beginning, Ingrid." He grabbed her by the hand. "Imagine, if you could live forever in a larger and more powerful body. Imagine that? Never breaking down."

"It would be glorious," she admitted.

"Well, it is within my grasp. We are marching towards a beautiful and brave new world."

Perhaps he was mad, but he hadn't been wrong yet.

13

A STRONGER WOMAN

Inside the *fiacre*, Octavia's eyes moved from the window to her pocket watch and back. They had asked the driver to stop at an alley where they had a good view of the whole Bureau. The building and grounds looked to be quiet, guards standing upright at their posts. No alarms had sounded since Modo had disappeared into the building. They spoke in hushed tones.

"Remind me how long you expected this little adventure to last?"

"According to my calculations," said Colette, "it would take Modo three minutes to enter the building, four minutes to reach Quint's office, less than a minute to pick the lock. He'll need at least ten minutes to find the proper files. Then he has to retrace his path back to the gate. Therefore, I estimate twenty-five minutes. Though, we should allow him at least ten minutes' leeway."

"Thirty minutes have passed," Octavia said. "Any moment now he should be walking out that door."

"You care about him deeply, don't you," Colette said.

Octavia was about to say something glib, but when she

saw the look on the young woman's face she fell silent. Colette seemed sad, even forlorn.

As much as Colette's question made her bristle, she couldn't help admitting, "I do. There are few like him."

"There are none like him," Colette replied. "I've never met anyone I was so willing to trust. Not since . . . well, my father was the only other man I trusted so completely."

"Your father?"

"He died in Japan. Many years ago."

"I'm sorry to hear that."

"It is in the past. And we cannot change the past." Colette rubbed her fingers together nervously. "Though, perhaps we can atone for mistakes we have made. Perhaps."

Octavia was surprised at the candour in her voice. And the bitterness. "I have no country to serve now. Modo is my country. I must prove that I am worthy."

What kind of statement was that? Was she professing her love for Modo? Or her allegiance? "What do you have to prove to him?"

"Everything," Colette said. "I asked you once, in Reykjavik, if you had seen his face. His real face. You answered no. Has that changed?"

"It's none of your business," Octavia said. Colette's dark exotic eyes, her prying words, her grip on Modo, these things were becoming such an aggravation.

"Well, I will make it your business. I was coy with you then. I said it was a matter of confidentiality. But the truth is I have seen his face. I could not look at him for more than a moment without feeling an absolutely uncontrollable revulsion. He is such a brave man. He is, despite his occupation, guileless. And I rejected him. And it . . . it marked me."

Octavia found herself holding her breath. She'd had a similar feeling when she first saw Modo's real face. It was so different from what she had expected. So twisted. So raw. And not what he deserved. He was such a grand young man that he deserved to be beautiful.

"I too have seen it," Octavia admitted.

"And did you look away?"

"I did not." She remembered that night in a Queensland rain forest, that moment, clearly. Every cell, every nerve, every instinct had been telling her to look away. Such ugliness. She'd wanted to touch his face, knowing the pain he'd felt his whole life, but could only put her hand on his shoulder.

Colette grabbed Octavia's hand and squeezed it. "You are a much stronger woman than me," she whispered. "You are so very brave. I could not look. I failed him. It is as simple as that. I am not accustomed to failure. I do not accept it."

"So how do you reverse this failure?"

"I must admit, I do not know. Will he ever accept me as, well, as a friend? Will he accept my allegiance? He is my country. My country. Just being around him. You know what it is like. I envy you." She paused. "He must love you, you are so beautiful."

"I—I don't know."

They fell silent. The horses snorted outside; the *fiacre* creaked as the driver stirred in his seat, perhaps shivering in the cold. He would wonder what they were doing, but they'd been careful enough to cover their faces when they hired the carriage so that he wouldn't be able to identify them. Only Modo had been visible and he, of course, would soon look completely different.

Did Colette really see him as her country? Did that mean she would fight for him? Octavia didn't understand her own feelings. In her way she, too, had turned away from Modo's face.

"It has been forty minutes," Colette said, her voice steady now. "I fear that something has gone awry."

"What do we do? We don't even have an alternative plan."

"We cannot charge in there. He is a brave and clever man —he'll have to find his own way out. And once he does, we will be here to rescue him."

14

THE STRENGTH OF SEVEN MEN

"You'll open the door to the office and proceed down the hall," Laroche instructed.

Modo nodded and gave the French agent a friendly smile, one that he hoped was disarming. He nearly chuckled to himself—"disarming" was exactly what he had in mind. Laroche was holding the gun in an easy manner that indicated he was completely comfortable with the weapon. That was dire news. Modo stood slowly, opened the door to the office and began to walk down the empty hallway.

"Good, good work," Laroche said, as though encouraging a child. "Now please stay five paces in front of me. We will go to the end of the hall and turn left."

Modo did as he was told, judging the distance of the man behind him by the sound of his footsteps, picturing the gun at his back. Laroche was no fool and had been well trained; he would not come within striking distance. The chances of taking him by surprise by turning and knocking the gun from his hand were slim, and a move like that would most likely result in bullet holes in all the wrong places. Modo glanced around for something he could throw.

"Please look straight ahead," Laroche said calmly. He spoke without a French accent, indicating that he had worked in the field for a number of years. "I assume you are searching for an object to use as a projectile. I should inform you that I won the Bureau marksmanship competition seven years running."

"Recently?" Modo asked. "Or was that in your younger years?"

The man laughed again, a pleasant sound. "Well, it was some time ago, I admit that."

He was grey haired, yet young enough that he may only recently have been assigned to a desk. And perhaps that was why Colette hadn't mentioned him. Or was it the fact that she didn't have full control of her mental faculties? What other major details had she missed?

"Is it true that you're as strong as ten men?" Laroche asked.

"Only seven men," Modo answered. "Ten French men, perhaps."

Laroche laughed. "You mock me, but I know that you are French, too."

"But British by education." Modo was surprised to hear Mr. Socrates' pronouncement come out of his mouth. Maybe there was some truth to the old man's words. Oh, how Tharpa would be shaking his head at him now. Allowing himself to fall into the hands of the enemy. Or at the very least, suspicious allies.

"Please open the stairwell door and proceed down the stairs."

The offices they had walked through were deserted and so was the stairwell. That, at least, was playing in Modo's favour. He could jump down the stairs and flee. Laroche might get off two shots. Of course, at such close range he wouldn't miss. Modo decided to walk slowly down the stairs.

"A bit faster, please," Laroche said. "I'm so looking forward to our conversation. Your disguise is almost impeccable. I am extremely impressed."

"I'll make a note of that in my diary."

They crossed a landing, then continued down more stairs. Light appeared beneath each door they passed; the agency was busy this evening. Soon they were on the main floor. The steps and the walls leading down into the basement were made of stone, like those in a real fortress.

A lone light cast fractured beams across the stairs. In the shadows it might be possible to attack and give himself the extra seconds he needed. He listened, not daring to turn. Before he could decide on the best course, the metal door at the bottom of the stairs scraped opened and two burly men stepped through it. They looked up and were just beginning to salute Modo when instead they reached for the pistols at their hips.

"Halt," Laroche said in French, "this is not as it seems. This man is an imposter. A prisoner."

"Listen carefully," Modo said calmly, also in French, "draw your weapons and shoot Laroche. He has captured me and turned against France. He is a traitor."

The guards' hands were frozen on their guns. One moved slightly, making the keys on his belt jangle.

"Shoot him! That is an order," Modo barked.

They drew their guns. Laroche fired, his bullet sparking off the stone wall, making the men duck. Modo smashed his way between them and through the doorway. There were more rows of desks and several hallways. A collection of French spies looked up from their paperwork, mouths gaping, clearly alarmed by the pistol fire. He dashed past them shouting, "Intruder, intruder behind me! Bar the door!"

He chose a hallway, sped to the end of it and turned awkwardly down another. A shot rang out, knocking a painting off the wall. Even in his mad running he was impressed that artwork hung in the Bureau. There was a large uproar behind him, but he couldn't make out a word of it, except that Laroche was swearing at such volume that his words cut through it all. Modo flew by a row of occupied cells; some prisoners were in rags, looking as if they hadn't seen the sun for years, others were in dapper grey jackets as if they'd been arrested while dining.

A way out! There had to be a way out! He was beginning to feel like a trapped rat. *Get me out of here now!*

He took a deep breath. *Calm yourself.* It was Tharpa's voice—he was always there in the background. Modo pictured the front of the building. There had been large loading doors leading to the lower level. They were on the west side. He veered to his left down a narrow hall and plowed through the door at the end, knocking it off its hinges.

He found himself in a giant storage room. Crates stood along several walls; one lid had been pried off revealing a collection of guns. He recognized them as Chassepot rifles, the main armament of the French forces. He could use one to fight his way out, but he'd be surrounded and shot in the space of a few minutes. Stealth was still the best option. He passed another crate jammed with ceramic dolls, of all things. What purpose they served he couldn't imagine.

At the end of the large room was a ramp leading to the loading door, which was locked and barred. He put his back to it and strained, swearing and pushing until the bars snapped and the doors flew open. He charged out into the dark shouting, *"Intrus! Intrus!"* He couldn't think of anything else to say. His French was failing him and he could only hope the guards would recognize him as Belanger.

A siren sounded, screaming from the top of the building, followed by the barking of dogs; the guards had let loose the hounds. He ran past the nearest guard station and the dogs turned their snouts towards him and leapt into action.

Someone behind him on an upper floor of the Bureau used a voice trumpet to shout, *"Fermez les portes! Fermez les portes!"*

They were going to close the gates! He was still fifty yards away from the exit. He could see the guards swinging the gates closed. He was sweating madly now, his hair dishevelled. They'd shoot him before they even realized he might be Belanger.

"Arretêz-vous!" a guard shouted.

"Je suis Belanger! Je suis Belanger!" Modo repeated as he ran full speed down the lane.

But the guard at the front gate raised his rifle and pointed it directly at him, forcing Modo to stop—and wait for the hounds that any second now would tear into his flesh.

15

MAD HORSES AND AN
ENGLISHWOMAN

The siren sent a shiver down Octavia's spine; the barking of dogs doubled her fear. She stared out the *fiacre* window and could only see that the guards were running back and forth across the courtyard.

"Something has gone dreadfully wrong!" she said.

Colette shoved open the door and shouted, *"Allez vers la porte!"* The *fiacre* began to roll down the street towards the gates, but by its slowness it was clear the driver was apprehensive. Colette banged her fist on the ceiling. *"Dépêchez-vous!"*

The *fiacre* picked up speed briefly, but slowed again as they neared the gates. Octavia spotted a man running across the courtyard, dogs pursuing him. It was too dark to tell if it was Modo, but who else could it be?

"The driver's a white-livered muffin face," she muttered. "I'll jaw with him." She pushed open the door and, without so much as a glance at the cobblestone streets below, in fact with a joyous beating of her heart, she grabbed onto the top rail, climbed the side of the carriage and plopped down next to the driver. *"Sacre bleu!"* he said. She would have laughed at the look of shock on his face if she wasn't in such a desperate hurry.

"Through the gates!" she shouted, pointing madly ahead. *"Donnez la porte!"* She didn't know if those were the right words. "Through the gates right now!"

"Non! Non!" he shouted back.

"Well, off with you then!" She gave him a shove. He tumbled from the driver's seat and bounced along the street. Octavia grabbed the reins and shook them, shouting, "Go! Go!" She had only a thimbleful of experience with horses, but she knew they answered to the whip, so she grabbed it from the holder and snapped it above their backs.

The man who'd been fleeing was standing about twenty yards from the gates, two soldiers pointing rifles at him. Another soldier was holding a pair of hounds by their leashes as he approached from behind.

Octavia turned the *fiacre* towards the gates. The horses let out worried whinnies and fought against the reins. She began yelling, "Mad horses! Mad horses!"

Then Colette shouted out, *"Ces chevaux sont fous!"*

The horses smashed through the gate, knocking two of the guards out of the way. "Sorry, sorry!" she shouted.

Colette kept yelling, *"Ces chevaux sont fous!"*

The guards were so taken aback that they didn't think to raise their guns.

Octavia turned the horses and, as the guards scattered, pulled up right in front of Modo. She would have paid a thousand quid for a painting of that moment: his wide eyes, his mouth hanging open in shock. She pulled back on the reins and let out a laugh, slowing the horses and turning so that Modo had time to leap into the open door of the *fiacre*. She yanked hard on the reins to head back towards the gate.

The hounds had been released and were nipping at the

horses' hooves, causing them to kick and buck. One gave a hound a good kick and he rolled away, and a second hound was soon outdistanced as the horses began to gallop again. Octavia urged them to gallop at such speed that she worried the carriage would shake apart.

Behind them orders were shouted. A bullet hit the back of her seat and split the wood. She laughed. *As mad as the horses,* she thought. Now the *fiacre* was through the gates and bouncing down the cobblestone. She laughed again when she thought about Modo and Colette rolling around in the cabin. She urged the horses down the empty streets, turned sharply left then right then left, having no idea where she was going but only wanting to get as far away from the Bureau as possible.

"You can stop now!" Colette shouted through the window after several more minutes.

Octavia pulled on the reins, but the horses didn't obey. In desperation, she yanked so hard that one rein snapped. "They've gone wild!" Octavia shouted back. The horses' earlier frenzy was turning to fear. Now they couldn't stop whinnying as they galloped even faster through the night.

"I said stop!" Colette yelled. "Stop!"

"Easier said than done," Octavia shouted back. She yanked on the remaining reins, digging her feet into the driver's box. Another rein snapped and the horses veered to the right. She had lost all control. The carriage was already off the road and bumping along the sidewalk, missing lamp-posts by inches. It brushed against a wall and a wheel was knocked off.

"Jump!" she shouted. "Jump for your lives!" And she leapt, aiming for the straw piled at the edge of the street, landing hard and rolling along. She was on her feet again immediately, pleased she hadn't brained herself.

The carriage had already careened down the street and was breaking into pieces as the horses dragged it out of sight. Momentarily she thought her companions were still inside, then she saw something move in the gutter. It was Modo! He was helping Colette to her feet.

"This way," Colette said, gesturing.

Curious men and women, alarmed by the noise, were opening windows and stumbling out of doors, rubbing the sleep or the effects of drink from their eyes. Colette grabbed Modo and pulled him down an alley, Octavia a few steps behind. They ran, twisting and turning up ever-narrowing streets, until Octavia felt her heart would burst. Finally Colette led them into an abandoned building and they stopped to rest next to a stinking cistern.

"Remind me never to let you drive again," Modo said, doubled over and gasping.

Octavia laughed as she tried to catch her breath. "You should be thanking me. Not that I'm keeping count but that would be the fourth time I've saved your life."

"I had the situation under control."

She rolled her eyes.

"Well, perhaps I am thankful," he admitted. "However you did come within inches of running me down."

"Did you get the documents?" Colette asked. She seemed the least winded of the three of them, Octavia noted.

"I managed to take several, but was then interrupted by a man named Laroche."

"Laroche? Has he been assigned to your case now?"

"Yes."

"He's a good man. Very thorough," Colette said.

"Far too thorough; he saw through my disguise. We had a pleasant conversation, a struggle, and I escaped." He patted his bulging pocket. "I do hope the answers we seek will be found on one of these pages."

Colette smiled with anticipation. "We'll go through them as soon as we reach my apartment."

Modo shook his head. "No. Laroche said they've been watching you for several weeks. We can't go there. We'll need to find some other shelter. Any suggestions?"

"Obviously we can't go to a hotel. Nor would my mother's home be safe. No, they'll have eyes on all those places within the hour."

"We need somewhere safe for just a night," Octavia said. "Somewhere we can read the documents, and sleep."

Colette snapped her fingers. "I know the perfect place to hide."

16

SANCTUARY

Modo ducked behind a partially collapsed wall, out of sight of Colette and Octavia, and struggled to change his shape back to the Knight. He was exhausted, and switching to another form was only going to make it worse. But if he walked around Paris with a mask on he'd be noticed and easily remembered by any passersby or gendarme.

When he was done he rejoined his companions. They both gave him a long look, as though searching for imperfections.

"Good, good," Colette said, but he sensed disappointment in her voice.

What face had she expected to see?

She turned on her heel, leading them out of the ruined building and down an alley that opened onto a wide street. Several feet away was a *fiacre* stand, not much more than three walls painted black—a cubbyhole for a driver to warm himself. Colette grabbed Modo by the elbow and marched him up to the stand. She knocked on the side to wake the driver, a white-haired man who sat with a blanket of open newspapers over his legs. He shook them off and stood up. Without a word, he climbed into his *fiacre*.

Colette elbowed Modo and whispered, "Tell him to take us to Notre Dame Cathedral."

"Really?" he asked. "Why?"

"Give the instructions. He will expect them to come from the man."

Modo gruffly told the driver their destination and they climbed inside. As the *fiacre* headed towards the cathedral, it began to rain softly. It was hard to see the outside world, as though they were travelling under water.

"Shouldn't we worry about the driver identifying us?" Octavia asked.

"The gendarmes won't post our descriptions until tomorrow. The afternoon paper may publish them, so we'll have to be gone by then."

"Why are we going to the cathedral?" Modo asked.

"It is a sanctuary," Colette said.

"We won't find sanctuary from the Bureau there," Octavia said.

"I do not expect true sanctuary, but I know the building. There are places to hide if only for a night, and if we need to escape quickly we can dive into the river. Let us hope it does not come to that."

"Once we're there, what next?" Octavia asked.

"We will make our decision at the cathedral," hissed Colette. "You seem to think this is all my fault."

"It was your plan to enter the Bureau," snapped Octavia.

"Modo, how do you work with such a viper?" Colette asked.

"Very carefully," Modo said.

The two glared at him and he imagined them both slapping his face at the same time. He grinned. A moment later they were all laughing.

"The church will be as safe as anywhere," Modo said finally. "No one would expect us to be there."

The *fiacre* continued to jostle down the street. When the rain let up, Modo could see that the city planners hadn't been stingy with the gas lamps; Paris really was a "City of Light." The buildings were just as close together as those in London, but they were more colourful and better kept. The nights certainly weren't as foggy.

After forty minutes they crossed a stone bridge onto an island on the Seine. The *fiacre* passed a large building lined with pillars and countless windows.

"Is that Notre Dame?" Modo asked.

"*Non*, that is Hôtel-Dieu de Paris, a hospital."

The *fiacre* stopped and Modo got out, then took Octavia's hand and helped her down before doing the same for Colette. One had to keep up the pretense that they needed help. He gave the shivering driver five francs and bid him good night.

When the *fiacre* moved out of the way, Modo found himself standing on a small cobblestone courtyard, and right in front of him, blocking a good number of the evening stars with its massive size, was the Notre Dame de Paris. The red quarter-moon lit the stained glass windows and stone goblins that crouched along the side of the building.

He had an overwhelming sense that he had stood on this very spot before, but it was impossible for him to have any memory of this place; he had been an infant when he was brought here by his parents. Perhaps it was the French blood in his veins that made him feel this way. Then he recalled how often he had read *The Hunchback of Notre-Dame*—far too many times. Could merely reading a book make a place seem so familiar? He shook his head and laughed.

"Why do you laugh?" Colette asked.

"No reason," he said, feeling his love of the novel was a private matter. "Where exactly shall we hide? I do need to rest. Any moment now I'll collapse from exhaustion."

"Follow me." Colette led them to a side door on the east wall of the church and they quietly crept inside.

Colette grabbed his hand and guided him into the pitch black. He in turn held his hand out and took Octavia's. Hers was warm.

Colette's eyes seemed to adjust much faster than his, for she was leading them past pews, around pillars and up a set of winding stone stairs that to him were only dim shapes. Their footsteps seemed impossibly loud, as did their breathing. His heart pounded in his ears, as if the church were amplifying his heartbeat. But the higher they climbed, strangely, the more comfortable he felt.

Colette opened an iron grate door and they were hit by the cold. They crossed an open-air walkway lined with gargoyles who vigilantly watched over Paris. The lights of the city were far below them, looking as though they were reflecting the stars.

Colette pushed open another iron door into a dark room. Inside it was warmer at least, but he shivered when he heard the fluttering of bat wings above him. They were in a bell tower, he was sure of it!

"We're safe here," Colette said, patting Modo's hand before she let it go. "Emmanuel will watch over us."

"Where is *here*?" Octavia asked. "And who is Emmanuel?"

Modo had not yet let go of her hand.

"We are in the southern bell tower," Colette explained, "and Emmanuel is the bell above us."

"How do you know the way so well?" Modo asked.

"As a youth I explored," she explained. "It was a game I would play to hide from the priests and my father. He would bring us here every Sunday. I would do my—what do you call it?—*sneaking* during the services."

"So began a lifetime of sneaking," Octavia noted.

Colette clicked on her *petite lumière* and Octavia let go of Modo's hand as though she'd been caught with hers in a sweet biscuit jar.

"Now, let us have a look at those documents."

Modo pulled the crumpled mess from his jacket and smoothed the papers out on the floor. She bent over to examine them, but Modo covered them with his hand and looked perplexed.

"There were documents about you, Colette," he explained.

"Oh," she said. "And what did my kind bureaucratic friends have to say?"

Modo cleared his throat. "There was a report on your mental faculties, including a description of your stay in an asylum."

"Oh that," Colette said. "Yes, I *rested*, as they like to say." But she wasn't quite able to make it sound inconsequential.

"She was in a madhouse?" Octavia said. "We've been following a mad woman around on a merry chase?"

"The proper term is *sanatorium*," Colette said indignantly. "I was put there against my will. I—I really didn't need it. They wanted my job. My desk. My soul."

"Soul?" Octavia echoed.

"Everything," Colette whispered. "Everything I've fought for! They've taken it all away."

She was shaking and Modo placed his hand on her

cheek. "I've been inside those so-called madhouses," he said. "Not everyone there was mad."

"No. Not everyone," Colette agreed, "though the man who believed he was Jesus Christ and Napoleon was certainly unhinged."

"Our debt is paid," Modo said. "Not that I ever thought you owed me."

She shook her head. "It is kind of you to say so, but it is far from paid."

"Well," Octavia huffed. "If you two lovebirds are done, we had better read these files or nothing will be solved *or* paid."

Colette flipped through the pages. "Conjecture upon conjecture. Useless agents! And, wait—" She picked up a page, her eyes flitting back and forth as she read. "No, my apologies, there is nothing."

"But there must be *something*," Octavia said.

Colette gathered up the documents and held them out to Octavia, her eyebrows knitted in despair. "I can't read French, you know that."

Modo took them and leafed through, trying to hide his desperation. He used his pocket lucifer to study every page carefully.

"I was interrupted," he said finally. "If I'd had more time, I might've found something of use."

"Then we've come all this distance for nothing," Octavia said.

Colette sniffed. "We cannot stay in Paris, that much we know. Perhaps we should visit Nanterre again. We may find others who remember your parents, Modo."

"But that will take days," Modo said. "And the Deuxième Bureau will *expect* us to go there. They will have eyes everywhere."

"I am aware of that. I suggest we sleep now. Perhaps in

the morning an answer will come. We will want to leave before sunrise."

Modo sighed and nodded. They gathered what soft things they could find—feeling lucky to discover a few cloth sacks—and made their beds on cold stone.

17

MORE MEAT, PLEASE

L ime, his pistol and knives hidden by a greatcoat, strode past the medieval ramparts that surrounded the outskirts of Montreuil-sur-Mer. The hut they were searching for was along the road to étaples, if the drunks in the pub could be believed.

The town lay on the banks of the Canche River and Lime hated the place. He had grown up in the squalor of Kuala Lumpur, the son of an Irish merchant. It was a small settlement and made ugly by the tin mines that scarred the muddy rivers and lush countryside. He had embraced that ugliness; things were meant to be scarred. As a consequence he hated anything picturesque and perfect. Montreuil-sur-Mer brought out that loathing. Another perfect French town.

His mute companion slouched a step behind him, eyes dead as ever. *Typhon.* Lime disliked the beast's name. It should have been Grunt or Lump or Dunghead. But he had been named Typhon and that was the only name the sack of flesh and muscle responded to. Oh, how the Guild Master loved his word games and his Greek mythology. Lime loathed the Greeks.

He had spent the first three days in the town looking for Monsieur and Madame Hébert. All these French towns-people had begun to look the same. And no one had any memory of potters with the last name Hébert. But there were many potters in Montreuil—half the population. He'd bought their wares, spoken with them, and uncovered nothing.

The first potter he visited was the right age to have been Modo's father, but he'd never been married. The second potter and his wife had ten squalid brats running around half naked; the mother was too young to have given birth to Modo.

Lime took pleasure in smashing the bowls and plates in the fireplace of his room in the Hôtel de France.

Every street he explored, Typhon slouched alongside him. Why the Guild Master had sent the beast with him was obvious. Its brute strength was beyond any Lime had previously witnessed. And, so far as he could tell, the thing was indestructible, but mute and dumb as a stone with only the occasional glimmer of intelligent light in its eyes.

They approached the hut and he commanded Typhon to stand a few feet back. The size and extreme ugliness of the monster was helpful for intimidation, but not so helpful when one needed to appear friendly.

In response to his knock the door creaked open and a grey-haired woman poked her head out. "May I help you?" she asked in French.

He guessed her to be about fifty-five, a little too old to have had a child fifteen years ago.

"Are you Madame Hébert?" he asked.

She shook her head. "*Non*, my name is Lambert. I do not

know an Hébert."

"So you have never met a potter named Hébert?"

"I have not."

Typhon let out a rumbling grunt and the woman looked behind Lime and went pale. Leave it to the monstrous lump of flesh to make a noise now!

"My brother has a simple mind," Lime said, "and he was disfigured at birth."

She continued to stare in fright. "Disfigured at birth? Is he an abomination?" She crossed herself. "Cursed by the devil?"

Lime laughed. "No, only cursed with an abundance of ugliness."

The woman did not smile back. Instead she crossed herself again. Lime glimpsed a man at the table behind her, his back to them. He had reddish grey hair. Then the door closed.

"Thank you," Lime said to the door. Another dead end.

He turned and walked down the edge of the road. The leaves in a tree rustled, a bird chirped. The frost would take care of them soon enough. A moment later he realized that Typhon was missing. The beast's brain was grey useless sludge. He turned to see Typhon waiting in the same spot.

"Follow me, you beef-headed buffalo," he shouted. It had been one of his father's favourite curses. The beast didn't move. "Follow me, Typhon." The monster began to trudge towards him. Such a literal creature.

They returned to the inn and he asked for three roast hens to be delivered to his room. Once inside, he laid his greatcoat on the wooden chair and sat on the bed to gather his thoughts.

"Sit beside the hearth, Typhon," he said, and the man sat on the floor and stared straight ahead, shoulders up against the wall, his legs stretching halfway across the room, bumping and spilling a bowl that Lime had been using to water the beast. Lime couldn't help but be impressed by his size. Even his hands were thrice the length and width of a normal man's, except for the tiny pink finger on his right hand. It was so different from the rest of his greyish green flesh.

He did not understand the science that had brought the creature to life, that made it walk and grunt. Dr. Hyde did, of course, and perhaps the Guild Master himself. Lime didn't care how it had been created so long as it obeyed orders.

He was becoming convinced that Modo's parents were not in this town. It had been fifteen years; they could have moved anywhere. How many potters could there be in France? He was at a loss as to where to look next. Perhaps he shouldn't have killed that priest. After all, Mauger might have had other documents. Or the midwife. She might have been able to recognize his parents. He'd been too quick to kill. Again.

But what was done was done.

There was a tentative knock on the door. Lime unlocked it, letting in a pale, dark-haired chamber boy who carried a brass platter with three cooked hens surrounded by roasted vegetables.

"Set them there." He pointed to the table. The boy did so and left without a word.

Lime began eating, meticulously cutting the flesh from the birds with one of his own knives. They were still pleasantly steaming. The carrots and potatoes were delicious. At least the French knew how to cook.

He heard a *thump* behind him. He glanced over his shoulder. Had Typhon moved? No. The monster was in the same place.

Lime finished the first bird, then set the plate of scraps next to the creature. It stared at the food. "Eat, Typhon," he commanded, and Typhon leaned over, grabbed the remains of the hen with both hands and began to devour them, bones cracking and crunching between his large teeth. He left the vegetables.

Lime returned to the table and the other hens. So where were the Héberts? Had they died? Emigrated? That wasn't beyond possibility. The French were as adventurous as the English. Perhaps they'd moved to India, to Africa, even America. He banished the thought; he didn't want to spend months sorting through passenger lists.

"More meat," a voice rumbled.

Lime shuddered and looked up from his meal. The monster had spoken and was looking directly at him with those horrible eyes.

"Did you say something?" Lime tried to keep his voice steady.

The monster lifted a foot and stamped once, shaking the floorboards. "More meat," he growled.

So it could speak! And therefore it must also think. If so, he couldn't just let it order him around. It needed to know who was in charge.

"Ask nicely," he said.

"More meat . . ." The thing paused, struggling to find the right word. "Please."

Lime carried the last hen over and it disappeared into the maw of the creature. Then it downed the bowl of water, splashing half across its chest, and closed its eyes.

"Yes, you sleep, my pretty one," Lime said, staring at the creature from several feet away.

In time, too much time, he too fell asleep, clutching his gun under his pillow.

18

EYES THAT ARE BLIND

Modo turned his back to Octavia and Colette and let his natural form return. At this stage of his transformation there was little pain; this was where his body was meant to be.

One day when Modo was a child, Mr. Socrates had given him a hand mirror and let him take his first real look at his own face. He had stared in horror. Mr. Socrates then said, "You are deformed. You are ugly. But remember this day, Modo. It's the day you learned that you've been given an incredible gift. Your unsightly countenance may seem unbearable now, but because of it, the world will always underestimate you."

Modo was five years old at the time.

He was no longer troubled by people underestimating him, nor did he fear the horrified glances of strangers. Who cared about them! No. But the fact that Octavia and Colette couldn't stand to look at him. Ah, that seared him.

He had grown more comfortable in his hunchbacked shape. Anytime he changed into one of his many personas, his skin became itchy. During his training, Mrs. Finchley used to slap him lightly with a wooden ruler if he scratched. Habits such as scratching drew attention; spies should not have noticeable habits.

He slipped on his mask so he wouldn't frighten the two women in case he rolled over in his sleep. Not that there would be much slumber. They were certainly in a tricky situation. No matter how hard he focused his mind, he couldn't imagine how they would find his parents. By now Lime and his companion would be well ahead of them.

Finally, he stood and began wandering around.

"Are you leaving us?" Octavia whispered.

"No," Modo said, "I need to walk out my aches. If I'm not back in half an hour, look for me."

"I'll send the hound," Octavia said, gesturing towards Colette who seemed to be asleep.

Modo found he could see quite clearly in the dim light. He passed through an open door and into what seemed to be a storage room. There were old pews up here. Imagine hauling them up all those stairs! He sat on one of them for a few minutes, rubbing his head, then spied an open doorway on the other side of the room.

He was surprised to find the next chamber warm. As he stood in the centre of the small room and it dawned on him just what he was seeing, he grew numb with shock. He had assumed the shadows along the walls were rectangular crates, but now he could see they were cradles. Wooden rattles were set along the ledge beside each one. He stepped over to the nearest cradle and looked inside, gasping when he saw eyes peering back.

In a moment he realized that they were the glass eyes of a ceramic doll. Good Lord, it was a nursery! Way up here? A hearth had been bricked into the exterior wall. This must have been a place where abandoned infants were raised.

He touched the blanket, so carefully tucked around the baby. Each of the other cradles held a ceramic child, also neatly tucked in.

Was I once here? thought Modo. Here, up high, away from the eyes of the parishioners?

"Who walks my halls?" a male voice whispered in French. "A ghost?"

Modo stood perfectly still. Someone else was in the room, but he couldn't tell where the voice had come from.

"Speak," the man said softly. "Please speak."

His pleading loosened Modo's tongue. "It is no one," he replied in French.

"There are no no-ones," the man said.

"A traveller, that is all. I do not want to bother you."

"No bother. No sight. Father is here."

Modo pinpointed the sound. The man was seated in a large chair that faced the hearth. His shadowy figure stood and slowly came around the chair.

"This is my home. My hearth. You are welcome."

"Thank you," Modo said.

"I know your voice," the man said.

Was he mad? "You do?"

"Yes. I don't forget a voice. A tone." He began to hum softly, a pleasant sound.

"One does not hear the bells every day without learning the tones. Please come closer."

Modo could see no harm in doing so. As he did, he could see that the man's eyes glowed eerily white. Cataracts caught the moonlight.

"I heard you draw in your breath," the man said. "Yes, I am blind. For decades now. I have forgotten what it is to see. Tones! Tones are my eyes, the identity of a person, the expression on a face. Do you hear the children crying?"

Modo had no idea what he meant. "No."

"Come closer, young man. Please."

Modo did so, but before he could react the old priest had reached out his hands and touched Modo's face—his fingers were knobbed with rheumatism, but they were quick.

"You wear a mask?"

"Yes. To hide a disfigurement."

"Many are afflicted. Some deaf. Some poor. Some rich. God is mysterious."

"Most certainly so."

"May I?" the man asked, and before Modo understood his intention the man had peeled back Modo's mask. He let out a sigh as he traced Modo's cheek.

"What is your accent?" the father asked.

"Canadian," Modo lied.

"I know your face." He ran his fingers across Modo's ragged cheeks. "You were the sweetest child."

"You know me? That's impossible."

"All is possible."

"Who are you?"

"I am Father Cambolieu."

His fingers continued to trace the lines of Modo's face. They touched his ragged cheeks, caressed his forehead. It felt so gentle and so . . . natural.

"You have always had such a strong face. Even stronger now."

"Thank you," Modo said. "Was this the nursery once?"

"Yes, until Father Mauger closed it down. It was too expensive."

"And when was it closed?"

"1860."

"Where did all the children go?"

"I was told they went to proper homes and to other churches."

"Wh-who am I?" The father's hands were still on his face.

"You are the boy with the blessed face."

What could that mean? "Did you meet my parents? What were their names?"

"Ah, I am good with names. Monsieur and Madame Hébert."

He did know! So Modo was indeed an Hébert!

The man placed his hands on either side of Modo's head, as if measuring the size of it. "How old are you now?"

"Fifteen," Modo replied. "So, you really and truly knew me as a child?"

"You were here only a short time. Four months. As I recall you rarely fussed. Then Father Mauger came and took you, said he had found you a home."

"A home?" He had been sold to a travelling freak show. Did that constitute a home?

"What do you know of my parents?"

"I wasn't allowed to meet them. In any case, the parents —or should I say the mothers, for it was often the mothers —rarely showed us their faces. Most of the children were abandoned on our doorstep. But your parents had marked you for the church. They were very close to God. Sometimes one can get too close to God."

What did that mean? "I—I am trying to find them. They did not return to Nanterre after leaving me here. Do you know where they were going next?" Modo asked.

"I wanted to know everything about my children," Father Cambolieu said. "I would pester Father Mauger incessantly. Sometimes the abandoned babies had names pinned to their shirts. Others had a doll or a soft blanket. I wanted to understand where they had come from . . . why God had sent them to me."

"Yes, yes, but did you know where my parents went?"

"I did. I did. Father Mauger did tell me what he knew of your parents. He said they intended to travel to Montreuil-sur-Mer. I remember it clearly. It is the town I was born in."

The floor creaked behind him and the father seemed to look over Modo's shoulder. "Ah, we have more visitors. It is a glorious night."

Modo knew Colette and Octavia were in the shadows. He adjusted his mask over his face again and motioned for them to stay back. This was his room, his past.

"They are my friends. It is time for me to depart. But there is so much I must ask you," Modo said, grasping Father Cambolieu's hands.

"I have told you everything I knew, except I will tell you my nickname for you. It was Bright Eyes." With that he chuckled. "Bright Eyes. Back then I still had enough vision in my left eye to see that much, at least."

"We must go," Colette said quietly. "The sun is rising."

Modo was reluctant to release the priest's soft hands. He took one and kissed it. "I will return one day and thank you properly."

"I look forward to that day, my son. Go with God. Bless you."

19

A SUDDEN REVELATION

An agitated sleep had put Lime on edge. He awoke to find Typhon sitting where he'd left him, like a child who had been scolded by a teacher. He didn't even know if the monster ever really slept or even breathed like a human, and he never let himself get close enough to check for a heartbeat. He did know that the creature didn't bleed. After that woman had shot Typhon there were holes in his clothes but no blood. For all Lime knew, the bullets were sitting in the creature's chest, rusting to bits.

Lime ordered breakfast. He had already been to the Saint-Saulve church for the third time that week to look at their records, leaving Typhon on a bench near the town wall. There were no Héberts who had arrived in 1858. He was at a dead end. He would telegraph his master and receive his orders. Perhaps the great mind that was the Guild Master would have an answer.

After breakfast Lime took one last walk around town with Typhon a footstep behind. They certainly attracted attention, but the townspeople only watched them timidly. He wondered what their reaction would be if he commanded Typhon to start tearing them to pieces. Now *that* would be a show! Alas, he was not here for such frolicking.

They walked along the ramparts of the citadel; the stone had fallen in several places. Walls that had been built to keep out the enemy, that had lasted nearly a thousand years, were crumbling to pieces. He mulled over what he knew of the parents. They had plied their trade at markets in Paris. The father had been relatively unknown in Nanterre. They had abandoned their child at Notre Dame and had disappeared. Why?

The church documents clearly said that the Héberts had intended to move from Nanterre to Montreuil-sur-Mer, but not a single person in their new home remembered the Héberts arriving sixteen years ago. It was a puzzle. They'd given birth to an abomination and then had given that child to Notre Dame de Paris—the most revered of all churches in France. Why not their local parish? Instead they had travelled a small distance to the cathedral, and had left from there to Montreuil.

Were they driven out of Nanterre? Superstitious, fearful people often saw the devil in anyone malformed. More to the point, did the Héberts themselves experience some sort of religious shame? Did they believe they had given birth to a demon? That his disfigurement was a sign of their own great sin? It was possible.

Religious belief had always been a curiosity to Lime. He worshipped his knife, nothing else. But his mother had been God-fearing and had often talked of spirits and ghosts and demons . . . the demons inhabiting her only son. It wasn't hard to imagine a mother who believed the devil had played a role in creating Modo, a monster-baby. Short of suffocating it, which would have been a sin, why not give it to the church? The priests were the experts in exorcism. Then the Héberts would come to Montreuil and change their names to escape the past.

But he had visited all the potters listed in the Montreuil church records and none could have been Modo's parents. Only those who lived outside the walls weren't in those records.

That gave him pause.

What had the woman he'd seen yesterday said when she saw Typhon? "Is he an abomination? Cursed by the devil?"

Would a woman who believed such ugliness was a curse of the devil abandon a child? Would she and her husband move to the outskirts of a fortified town to hide from their shame?

"Typhon, you blighted old troll, you've given me the answer," Lime said.

The monster said nothing.

"Typhon, return to the inn with me. We have a telegram to send. Then we'll get out of this ugly town."

20

IN THE VILLAGE

Modo watched the passing French countryside from the window of their private booth on the train to Calais. After leaving the city in his Doctor form, he had slipped on his netting mask and allowed his shape to return to its natural state. Lately he dreamed of going out with no mask, no shape-shifting to disguise his faults. The Rain People in Australia hadn't seen his disfigurements as faults. And the blind Father Cambolieu had touched his face and pronounced it strong and blessed.

But Modo did not want to upset Octavia and Colette, so he had put on the mask. They would be at least four hours on the train, so he couldn't yet alter his face. He must save his strength for changing into the Knight face just before they arrived.

He was born in this land, he now knew, and might have travelled a good part of it in the back of a carriage with the freak show, so he couldn't stop himself from searching for something recognizable. How foolish! He'd been so young when Mr. Socrates rescued him. He had no memory of the months travelling on the carriage, but still, maybe he'd been on these very roads before. Then again, maybe he'd never been allowed off the wagon of curiosities. Despite his doubts the scenery all felt familiar. The green land, the thick woods. Perhaps some part of his soul did remember, if there were such a thing inside him.

Octavia had fallen asleep beside him, her head occasionally resting on his shoulder. Colette sat across from him, staring out the same window. The dark circles under her eyes made him wonder about her time in the sanatorium.

"Please don't judge me," she whispered, so low Modo almost didn't hear her. "Don't. Judge. Me."

Modo didn't move, didn't even blink. What to say? He considered closing his eyes and pretending he hadn't heard, but she wouldn't fall for that.

"I don't," he whispered back.

Perhaps she nodded, but if so it was almost imperceptible.

When the conductor shouted the name of their stop, Modo went to the washroom, glad not to encounter any other passengers on the way. He sweated and struggled to change into the Knight. It was the most familiar of his regular personas, and he could maintain the form for at least an hour longer than the others. Perhaps with practice he would be able to wear it for a whole day.

They arrived at Verton and paid passage on a two-horse carriage to Montreuil-sur-Mer. It took about an hour.

The name of the town was familiar to Modo, but it wasn't until they saw the ramparts in the distance that it came back to him. "This is Jean Valjean's town!" he exclaimed. "He was mayor!"

"Who was the blinking mayor?" Octavia asked.

"Jean Valjean," Modo said, "from *Les Misérables*. He was mayor of this town."

Both women stared at him blankly.

"It's a novel," he said.

"Oh. Well, I don't have time to read novels," Colette said.

"He does this every once in a while," Octavia said, "has little outbursts of literary fancy. I've learned to put up with them."

They shared a small laugh and Modo snorted and stared out the window.

Soon they were passing through the medieval walls that surrounded Montreuil-sur-Mer. He wouldn't have been surprised to see knights and siege engines lining the road. Perhaps there had been battles, but it looked peaceful now. Modo couldn't help gawking at each resident they passed. Could one be his mother? His father?

The carriage drew to a stop in front of a brick coaching inn at the centre of town. It was called Hôtel de France and was three storeys tall, with a long slanted roof and three dormer windows on the top floor. It looked to Modo like an oversized country house.

A few people stared at the new arrivals, and Modo wondered if visitors were few and far between.

"Come," Colette urged, "we shall rent our room, eat and begin our search."

"I ain't much for little towns," Octavia said in a falsetto.

Modo wasn't certain whom she was imitating.

"Do not speak," Colette chided, "unless you can speak in French. We agreed to this."

Octavia saluted. "I shall remain silent, Captain Brunet."

"Stop drawing attention to yourself," Colette said, trying not to smile. "Now follow me. That's an order."

She led them into the Hôtel de France and went straight to the innkeeper at a mahogany desk.

"How may I be of service?" he asked.

While Colette organized their lodging, Modo looked around the room, noting several people waiting on a bench with their luggage. There was a small pub area near the desk. He looked for exits, a habit Tharpa had hammered home.

Before long Colette was handing Modo the key to room 12B. "It's at the top of the stairs," she said as they climbed the spiral staircase. "You'll have a nice view of the courtyard. Very romantic. Which is good since you and Octavia will have to continue your ruse of being married."

"I'll be his simple British wife," Octavia said.

After freshening up in their rooms they met in the pub. It was as dank and smelly as any English pub, but the beguiling smell of cooking made Modo's stomach grumble. He ordered roast hens for himself and Octavia; Colette chose lamb stew. He sipped a pale apple cider and their food arrived within minutes.

Modo was hungry but found it hard to eat. Everywhere he looked he saw potential mothers, fathers. The woman who had served their meal was older, slightly hunched over. He couldn't stop staring at her.

"I did ask the innkeeper about the Héberts but he wasn't familiar with them," Colette said. "That may indicate they don't frequent establishments such as this."

"Of course they don't. They're probably upper class," Modo joked, but his own vehemence surprised him. For all he knew they were drunks, sitting in the gutter clutching their bottles.

Colette gave him a peculiar look. "*Oui,* I see. Anyway, it is a small village, we will just have to visit a few of the potters —" She sucked in a breath. "*Mon Dieu!* Don't turn around. Don't even move."

Modo froze. He had never seen such fear on her face.

Colette was staring over his shoulder, slouching down in an attempt to hide.

Modo couldn't resist turning his head ever so slightly. A thin, white-haired man was paying at the desk of the inn.

"The Clockwork Guild," Colette said, very low. "The agents I met at Notre Dame are here."

"That shouldn't be surprising," Octavia said. "They did get a head start."

"The smaller one looks relatively harmless," Modo said.

"That's Lime," Colette said, "the mad poet I told you about. They have their backs to us now. You can look. See the man just behind him?"

Modo turned again and saw a giant whose head was nearly in the rafters. "Zounds!" he whispered.

"A monster with the name Typhon," Colette said. "I shot the brute three times in the chest and he didn't so much as stagger."

Really? Modo wondered. Or was this her madness revealing itself? But the man was so immense he hardly seemed human. Just then Lime turned and glanced at Modo. Modo looked down into his cider.

"What are they doing?" Modo asked. "Coming over here?"

"They have left. Let us hope it is for good."

"You shot that hulk?" Modo asked.

"Three weeks ago. It was a small-calibre gun, but still, no ordinary man would have been left standing."

"You must have missed," Octavia said.

"I did not miss! Three shots found their mark. One bullet directly through his heart."

"You must have been seeing things—after all, you did spend time in an asylum."

Colette reached for the gun that Modo guessed was

hidden in her dress. "Would you like me to use you as target practice?"

Modo thought it best to change the subject. "Well, if they are here, then that's actually good news."

"How so?" Octavia asked.

"They can't have found my parents or they would have already left. So we're not too late. And maybe, if they've located them, and if we're clever enough, they'll lead us where we want to go."

"We will keep our eyes open. Meanwhile, I will poke my nose in a few places." Colette stood up and smoothed her skirt. "You two finish. I have eaten enough."

"You're going to waste away to nothing," Octavia said.

"You sound like my mother," Colette said and walked out the front door.

Modo continued eating silently.

"You seem nervous," Octavia said.

"I'm not."

"But you keep tapping your fingers on the table. It's a nervous habit of yours."

Modo looked down to see his rebellious left hand was doing just that. Octavia knew him too well.

"I am nervous," he admitted. "Now that we're here, so close to where my parents may be living. If they're alive, if they're here, I can't help but wonder what they'll be like. Will they be amazed by what I've become? Or will they turn away . . . again? I don't know what I'll say to them."

"Perhaps you can ask them why they abandoned you." She sounded sad.

"Of course, I won't forget that," Modo said.

"As you know, I wouldn't throw my parents a lifesaver from a sinking ship. I've become my own woman. You'd do well to remember that you have already cut your own path."

Did I? he wondered. Mr. Socrates had forged his mental faculties, Tharpa had trained his body, Mrs. Finchley had shaped his mannerisms and perfected his acting ability. What exactly had he done on his own?

But why was he worrying about the opinions of the people who gave birth to him and then tossed him aside? He was here on an assignment. If they found the Héberts he would warn them of the danger, take them back to Montreal and hand them over to Mr. Socrates, who would send them someplace safe and be done with them.

After dinner Modo and Octavia went out onto the street, keeping an eye out for the Guild agents. Minutes later they heard someone behind them screaming, *"Incendie! Incendie!"* A man came running down the street, his desperate voice echoing in the alleys. Church bells began ringing madly.

"Fire," Modo said. Outside the city walls, he spotted a thin plume of smoke, so he ran a few hundred feet to the ramparts and easily leapt onto them, grabbed the scaffolding and vaulted to the top to scan the area. "A cottage on fire," he yelled down to Octavia. "Not far out of town."

By the time he'd climbed down again, Colette had returned. "Commotions certainly seem to follow us," she said.

"I have a feeling we should have trailed Lime immediately," Modo said.

Colette's eyes grew wide. *"Mon Dieu!"*

They ran through gathering crowds to the city gates. They must have some kind of fire brigade, Modo thought. But it was so slow. Most people seemed confused, as if they'd never seen a fire before.

The three of them dashed through the open gate and down the road towards the smoke. Modo quickly outdistanced Octavia and Colette and soon reached a small cottage engulfed in flames; smoke belched out the windows. Two tethered goats strained at their leashes, madly trying to escape the heat. Modo leapt over a dead hound on the path. The front door of the cottage had been torn off and cast aside. Three farmers stood at the entrance, afraid to go in. "Modo, stop!" Colette shouted.

"Modo!" Octavia yelled.

Ignoring them, Modo took a deep breath and charged through the doorway.

"Je suis là pour vous aider!" he shouted, smoke making his eyes water. The conflagration was heaviest near the fireplace where logs had spilled out onto the floor. A rug and thick curtains danced with flames. Crouching low to avoid the smoke, he pushed through to the next room. He saw a body, rushed over and heaved it up, only to feel it tear in half. Horrified, he blinked his watering eyes until he could see again. He was holding a sack of grain. When he dropped it and stumbled back, he spotted the body of a man a few feet away, splayed across the remains of an urn, smashed pottery and pieces of a chair all around him. A long-barrelled shotgun, bent in half, lay on the floor.

"Modo!" someone shouted.

He began to cough so hard he thought his lungs would rupture. He felt on the verge of passing out, so he bent down and sucked in some of the cleaner air from near the floor. Glancing around, he saw no more victims, so he scooped the man up like a child and careened out of the cottage, amid the flames and smoke, stumbling for several yards, then laying the man on the ground and practically falling on top of him.

As his coughing subsided and his eyes cleared he saw that the man's face was severely bruised and bleeding, a long cut oozing on his scalp.

"*Mon Dieu!*" the man rasped.

Modo held his hand. In French he said, "You are safe now. I am here to help you."

"We're all here to help you," Colette added, placing her handkerchief against the wound on the man's forehead. "What is your name?"

"Jean Hébert," the man answered in a daze. Then he blinked. "*Non, non*, Lambert. I was Hébert . . . long ago."

Modo's heart nearly stopped.

He sat up and shuffled closer to the old man. His father? He looked for something in the man's face that would prove it, but who on earth would have features like his own? He noticed that the man's greyish hair was shot through with red, the same colour as Modo's. And there was something familiar about his jawline.

"Were you from Nanterre?" Modo asked him, glancing up at Octavia and Colette and then back down again.

The man nodded. "W-water," he whispered, rubbing at his dry lips.

"I'll get it," Colette said, getting up and dashing through the crowd to the well.

Octavia leaned in to hold the handkerchief against the man's forehead.

"You're kind," he said to Modo, "for pulling me out of the fire. You risked . . ." He coughed. "I thank you."

"It was my duty," Modo said. What a stupid thing to say! But he was lost for words and his French was failing him. Hébert was clearly dying.

"They . . . a thief and a monster . . . they took my wife. I fought. I fought them . . . I am broken," he said. "That beast."

"You fought well, sir. We will find her," Modo said. "I promise you."

Hébert stared at the sky. Had he died? But then he grabbed Modo by the shoulder.

"I wasn't strong enough," the man said. "You're a good Samaritan. Your kindness will be rewarded." He pulled Modo closer. "There's something familiar in your face. Are you my nephew? Luc, I have not seen you for so long. Years. You've grown." He was coughing more softly now, his breath unsteady.

"I am not your nephew," Modo whispered.

The man convulsed and coughed up blood. Colette was quick with the handkerchief. Octavia had taken a blanket from an onlooker and now covered his legs.

"Do you have any children?" Modo asked. He wished he could just let the man rest, but time was so short.

The man shook his head. "I, no, well, once we had a child but he was . . . We gave the boy to God." He paused. "To God."

"I . . . I am your son. The one you gave to God." He grasped his father's cold hand, cradled his head. "I came to find you. I am your boy. I will take you to a doctor. I am Modo. I am your son."

Colette's hand touched Modo's and he looked up at her.

"He is gone," she said in English.

Modo looked down into his father's dull eyes. Then, seeing the truth, he gently closed his papery lids and stroked his face.

Modo let out a whimper, then caught himself. Octavia touched his shoulder, but he stood quickly. Something cold and painful was growing in his chest.

"Where is his wife?" he hissed. "Where is she!"

"We'll find her," Octavia said. "Please, calm down."

"And what do we do now? Just leave him behind?"

"We cannot wait," Colette said. "They have a good half-hour lead on us and will be travelling with utmost speed."

She was right. Already there was a collection of townspeople and farmers; soon gendarmes would arrive and there would be far too much to explain.

He approached the crowd. "Which of you is the mayor? A priest? Which of you is a leader of any kind?" he asked in French.

Several people gestured towards a man who stepped forward. Modo gave him three gold coins. "Bury my father well. I shall return to ensure it was done properly."

And then, with Octavia and Colette by his side, he ran back towards the gates of Montreuil, rage beating in his heart and coursing through his blood.

FOUR-WHEELED PURSUIT

Modo ran to the centre of the town, not caring if Octavia or Colette could keep up with him, and skidded to a stop in front of the inn. A carriage had just pulled up and a gentleman was stepping out. Modo pulled the passenger aside, grabbed his luggage from the cab and tossed it to the ground. He threw a handful of francs at the driver, shouting, "Drive west!" in English, then in French, *"Conduisez à l'ouest!"*

"Non! Non!" The driver reached for something on his belt.

Modo vaulted up to the driver's seat and shoved him over the edge, a small club clattering on the cobblestones beside him. Modo snapped the whip and the horses surged ahead, the carriage lurching behind them. His mother! They had her and they would dissect her—would do whatever it was the Clockwork Guild was doing to create their monsters and nightmare machines. He would not allow it!

"You are not behaving appropriately," a woman's voice said from behind him. He saw a pair of hands grab the lip of the driver's seat. Colette climbed up the side and, rather gracefully—considering the circumstances—sat beside him.

"This *is* appropriate behaviour," he shouted. He snapped the reins again. "Faster! Faster!"

It was only after he caught his breath and some of his wits that he asked, "Is Octavia aboard?"

"She is. Though whether she will survive your driving is another question. You cannot even keep the horses on the road. Here!" She grabbed the reins. "You hold them like this."

"I was doing well enough," Modo said. "Where does this road take us?"

"Back to étaples. This is the only road to the coast and they will not be racing like we are."

The small window from the cab to the driver's seat slid to one side. A pair of eyes looked out.

"Oh, the French girl is steering," Octavia said. "No wonder we're in such a hullabaloo."

"This carriage is not designed for such speeds," Colette yelled back.

"Well, you two seem to have everything well in hand," Octavia said. "I'm going to get forty winks."

"You can sleep now?" Colette asked, incredulous.

"No worse than a quiet day in a St. Giles pub." She slid the window shut.

Colette gave the reins another snap and the horses sped up. Farmers pulling carts of vegetables rushed to get out of their way. Colette shouted at an old woman with a blood-stained poultry sack over her shoulder. The grizzled woman stepped off the road a moment before she would have been trampled by the horses and made a rude gesture.

"The horses will tire soon," Colette said. They were already slick with sweat, their manes drenched.

"Then we'll steal other horses!" Modo stared hard at the horizon as if he could will his enemies to show themselves. He assumed Lime had a carriage. If they were on horseback they would travel faster, but it would be more difficult to hold their struggling prisoner—his mother. Unless, of course, they had taken measures to stop her struggling. He didn't want to imagine that.

It was also possible that they had taken one of the many side roads.

Ten minutes passed. Then twenty. The horses' breathing was ragged. Just as Modo was beginning to lose hope, he caught sight of a distant carriage.

"There! There!"

"I see it!" Colette flicked the whip and the horses whinnied angrily, but responded with greater speed.

The driver of the other carriage was coming into focus: a thin, tall man.

"That is Lime, I am certain," Colette said.

"Then hand me the reins." Modo grabbed for them.

At first she wouldn't give them up. "Why?"

"Only men drive carriages here. Besides, Lime will recognize you. Get down into the cabin."

"You do not give the orders, Modo. This is a partnership!" she said, though she relinquished the reins. "At least hold them correctly. You must feel the horses' mouth from this distance. So, do you have a plan?"

"To smash right into them and knock Lime off his perch."

"Will your mother survive the collision?"

Modo had no response. He wasn't thinking clearly.

"Your plan will fail. The horses will not charge directly into another wagon and, besides, they are exhausted. Better to approach from behind slowly and not let them know who we are. And we should wake Octavia."

Modo heaved a sigh, pulled on the reins, and pounded on the roof until the window slid aside.

"Yes?"

"They are just ahead of us," he said.

"Do you have a plan?" she asked.

"What is it with you two?" he snapped. "Of course I have a plan! We are going to catch up with them. Slowly. From there we'll have to adjust as the situation develops."

"Ah, we're winging it, then," Octavia said.

Before Modo could protest, Colette said, "If you can pull up alongside them, I will jump across to the back of their carriage and get your mother out of that monster's clutches and, if possible, get her back into our wagon. Lime won't even see me."

"You won't go alone," Octavia said. "I'll help steal the poor woman from under their noses. Let's hope your driving skills are up to it, Modo."

"Then that is our plan," he agreed. It seemed impossible to pull off, but he couldn't think of a better idea. They were both extremely brave for offering to do it.

Colette climbed along the side of the carriage, her dress flapping in the air. Octavia opened a door and followed her around until both were hanging off the back. Having these two on his side was like having ten good men. Modo felt a surge of hope. Lime and his partner wouldn't know what hit them.

He brushed sweat from his brow. His features were slipping back to ugliness; exertion had sped up the process. What did he care? He'd frighten Lime half to death, then he'd break him like a twig. *Do not let anger drive your decisions*, Tharpa had told him many times. Well, then he'd use it to overpower his enemies instead.

Modo eased his carriage closer and closer, until he was only twenty feet behind Lime's. They were now traveling on a winding road towards a town. étaples, Colette had called it. Modo could see a port in the distance.

Lime glanced back at them, then lifted a pistol. Modo prepared to swerve out of the way if he turned to shoot. Instead, Lime aimed straight up and fired, sending a flare arcing through the darkening sky.

A few seconds later there was an answering flare from a large steamship anchored near the coast. Lime was much more prepared than Modo had expected; there'd be swarms of Guild soldiers on that ship.

He urged the sweating horses on, and within a minute he was alongside his enemy. The carriage curtains were drawn and that behemoth of a man was in there with his mother. It was all he could do not to jump over there himself.

Remember the plan! He slowed the horses, trying to match the other carriage's speed, hoping to make it easier for Colette and Octavia to make it over to the back of Lime's.

"Nous sommes pressés!" he spat out. He'd nearly shouted "in a hurry" in English. *"Passagers importants!"*

Lime turned and glared. His skin was so pale it was almost luminescent now that dusk was upon them. "Fools rush in," he said, "where angels fear to tread. Nay, fly to Altars; there they'll talk you dead."

Colette had been right. He thought himself a poet, and was quoting Alexander Pope, of all people, and not even accurately! Modo pointed at his ear and shrugged as if to say he didn't understand. He edged his carriage over as close as possible, so close that his horses nearly rubbed sweating shoulders with Lime's. He felt a lift in the weight of his carriage as Octavia and Colette leapt off.

"Passagers importants!" Modo said, jerking his thumb over his shoulder at his cargo. That's when he realized that it would be too difficult to pull his mother into a moving carriage. Modo could more easily hop across and knock the

poetic teeth out of Lime's mouth, along with his conscious-
ness. Then he'd yank on the reins and bring the carriage to
a stop.

But how to stop Typhon from hurting his mother?

"Why, dear lass, are you taking so long to pass?" Lime
shouted.

Modo shrugged and said, *"Je ne parle pas anglais."*

"How do you know I'm speaking English?"

"Je ne parle pas anglais!" Modo repeated.

Lime chuckled. "The little mocking bird doth sing."

Had Lime seen through his ruse? Modo gave the horses
another snap of the reins, and then, once he was a few yards
ahead of the other wagon, he jerked his reins to the left,
forcing his horses to cut across the path of the other
carriage. At the same time he cracked his whip at Lime,
hoping to knock him off his bench.

As if it were a well-rehearsed feat, Lime caught the end
of the whip and pulled so sharply that it flew out of Modo's
hand. Lime then used his own whip to attack Modo, the
leather flying with such precision that it caught Modo below
the eye. Modo raised both hands to protect his eyes, but the
whip laid open the flesh on his cheek. He screamed in rage,
but even through that he could hear Lime's high-pitched
cackle.

"Better to reign in Hell than to serve in Heaven!" Lime
yelled.

Another *crack* and Modo's left ear stung with pain.
Modo released his reins and leapt, hoping he was soaring
towards Lime.

A shot rang out.

22

A HOLE IN YOUR SKULL

It had unravelled far more quickly than Colette had imagined possible—*a poor plan falls apart like a house of cards*, her father had drilled into her.

She'd leapt across to the back of the other carriage and swung around the far side, all without Lime noticing. Octavia was only a few handholds behind her. Colette gave her a smile and Octavia grinned back.

After a hand signal to Octavia, Colette had pushed aside the window, revealing red plush curtains. A stench like dead meat assailed her nostrils.

She moved the curtain back slightly and peaked in. The side of the monster's head was inches away. She moved the curtain a little farther. He was staring down at Madame Hébert. Her bonnet was in disarray, her face ghostly pale and eyes downcast as if she did not dare even look at her captor.

Colette noted Typhon's matted, dark hair, the greenish ear stitched into place on the monster's skull. It was as if this man were not born of a woman but sewn together by a tailor. Was it possible? Is that why she couldn't kill him with bullets? He might not have a heart, but whatever his making, she was certain he had a brain—and most men preferred to keep their brains in their skulls.

With one hand gripping the wagon she brought her derringer up, used it to thrust the curtain aside and then placed it against the side of his head, saying in a low voice, "Don't move or I'll blast a hole in your head."

She nodded to Octavia, who had to crawl over Colette to get to the carriage door.

The hulking thing made no reply. Was he deaf? Colette dug her derringer harder into his temple. That would get his attention. He turned his head ever so slightly, the pale skin wrinkling, his dull eyes measuring her. They held no intelligence. No pity. Nothing human.

"Do not move," she repeated.

Octavia opened the door and climbed in, then scrambled over the monster's legs and rammed open the opposite door. It would be a short leap to the other carriage. She then turned her attention to Madame Hébert, grabbing her arm and trying to yank her out of this prison on wheels. But the woman wouldn't budge or even open her eyes. Was she drugged?

"Madame Hébert! We are here to help you," Colette whispered in French.

Before Colette could react, he smashed his fist through the thin carriage wall and grabbed her wrist, squeezing her arm so tightly that she felt as if the bones would break. She pulled the trigger, firing her derringer, and at the same moment the wagon lurched to one side. The monstrous man was still squeezing her arm. Had she missed his head? How was that possible? He was less than an inch away from the barrel of her gun! She pulled the hammer back again with her teeth. She wouldn't miss a second time!

Before she could finger the trigger she was yanked into the cabin through the window, glass breaking around her, and landed on the floor beside Hébert. The wagons crashed together, tearing off their door. Octavia fell out, nearly pulling Madame Hébert with her.

"Octavia!" Colette shouted. She couldn't survive such a fall!

Then, to her relief, she saw a flapping dress. Octavia had found a handhold on the other carriage and was pulling herself inside. Colette grabbed Madame Hébert's hand, intending to pull her across to the opening.

"Woman, stay," Typhon grunted. He pulled Hébert out of her grip and sat her, almost gently, across from him. He turned to Colette, who was reaching for her stiletto. "Woman, go."

She raised her arms but he smacked her so hard that she flew out the opening, and miraculously Octavia caught her and dragged her into the other carriage.

"Anything broken?" Octavia asked.

"No." Though Colette wasn't certain. "We need an elephant gun to kill that thing. A cannon!"

Then there was a great crash and the carriage disintegrated around them.

23

A MOMENT OF BEAUTY

Modo was wrestling with a human eel. Every time he thought he had a firm grip, Lime slipped out of his hands and landed another blow. And all the while Lime was laughing and shouting, "Tra-la-la!"

He was absolutely cracked.

Modo did manage to knock a knife from the man's hand, but he was rewarded with a fist right to his throat.

They had reached the outskirts of étaples when the carriage veered off the road and struck a post and then the side of an inn. Modo was thrown face first to the ground and managed to scramble to his feet.

Both horses had broken free and were charging madly down the street, dragging their harness behind them. Lime's carriage had landed with the front jammed into the ground. The back wheels still spun in the air. A moment of silence had passed, enough time for Modo to turn and see that his carriage was on its side a hundred yards back, the two horses struggling to pull themselves out of their harnesses and away from the wreckage.

The door to Lime's carriage smashed open and Typhon

leapt out, clutching Madame Hébert. She was flopped over and Modo couldn't see her face.

But this was Modo's first good look at the giant. Nearly twice as tall as Modo, he had legs like the trunks of trees. Modo felt for a weapon, but his stiletto had fallen out of its sheath. He had no gun, but Colette had said bullets were useless against the monster anyway, and now Modo believed her. Typhon didn't move, but he was searching around, for Lime perhaps.

And now, more horrible than this monster, rising in the air over Typhon's shoulder was what Modo first took to be a dark cloud. Then he realized that an airship was approaching, scudding earthward. It had probably come from the deck of the steamship. It was armour-plated and would be heavily armed. Typhon began lumbering towards the dock.

Modo ran and jumped, aiming squarely at the monster's back, but in mid-air a whip wrapped around his throat. He was jerked backwards and flipped hard onto his spine, knocking the breath from his lungs. He grabbed the whip and pulled. Lime came tumbling off the roof of the carriage. Modo struck him with his palm, knocking him to the side. Then he ripped the coils of the whip from around his neck, charged towards Typhon and head-butted him in the spine. The airship was getting closer and Typhon kept going, the woman now across both his arms. Modo struck him again and this time the giant turned, gently set the woman down, and faced Modo.

For such a massive creature, Typhon moved with great speed. Modo dodged his first blow and came in under his arms, planning to execute a body throw, but the thing countered quickly and locked hands with him. Modo had never met a man stronger than himself; he had lifted wagons, even an airship's boiler with his bare hands, but he couldn't budge Typhon. He was lifted like a sack and held in the air. The beast's eyes were empty, his face a map of scars and stitches.

"Woman to skyship," Typhon grunted. "Must get her."

"Don't talk him to death," Lime shouted. He walked underneath the struggling Modo, rubbing blood from his nose. "Break the bastard's spine, Typhon," Lime spat, grabbing Madame Hébert by both arms and dragging her to the ropes dangling from the airship.

Modo was lifted higher, and now had a clear view of the airship. No sign of Miss Hakkandottir, though a black Clockwork Guild flag flapped at the bottom of the airship. Along its side was the name *Erebos*. Six soldiers in grey uniforms were now rappelling to the ground. He recognized the same short hair and look of obedience in their eyes—Guild soldiers.

"Let me go!" Modo shouted.

"Break spine." Typhon lifted Modo even higher and manoeuvred him so that he was hanging over a stone fountain next to the inn. Then the monster let out a small huff and Modo fell to the cobblestones.

"Leave him alone!"

Colette was between them now, her stiletto buried deep in the creature's chest. Typhon yanked the stiletto out and stared at the black sludge clinging to it. Colette swung a piece of the carriage, but it broke on Typhon's arm. He dropped the knife, grabbed her by the arms and spun her wildly as one might a child in a playful game. But then he released her. She flew several yards through the air, out of Modo's line of sight. A moment later there was a *crash* and a cry of pain.

Typhon lumbered back and glared down at Modo.

Modo could only raise his arms, like some upturned

insect flailing on his back. Was his spine broken? Typhon leaned over and stared directly into Modo's eyes. There were stitches across his cheeks and he had a hideously ugly face. His eyes were two different colours.

Modo tried to shift his own face, to go back to his ugliness. Perhaps that would shock the creature.

Typhon held his massive hand a few feet above Modo's chest. Oddly it had a disproportionately small little finger. Modo was briefly mesmerized by it and his own finger suddenly itched.

Typhon poked him hard in the chest. Modo groaned.

"You broken," he announced, then lumbered over to the airship.

For several moments Modo couldn't move. He heard the *pop pop* of pistol fire. He gritted his teeth and forced himself to roll onto his side. Octavia was crouching behind a statue of a man on horseback and firing her derringer at the airship. Modo still couldn't catch his breath, couldn't get up. He turned his head to see the airship rising, soldiers on it aiming rifles at them. A bullet struck the ground near Modo's head, spraying him with stinging chips of cobblestone. A bell rang in a nearby church, and Modo blacked out, for how long he couldn't have said. When he opened his eyes again, his head was in Octavia's lap.

"Modo! Modo! Wake up! Wake up!"

With great effort, and her help, he was able to sit up.

"Don't move too quickly," Octavia said. "You look like hell. Your face has some rather wicked gashes."

Modo nodded. Townspeople had gathered and he could hear the buzz of their astonishment.

"Where's my mother?" he asked.

"I'm sorry, Modo. I tried to stop Lime, but he's got her."

"And Colette?"

"She's . . ." Octavia averted her eyes. "She's over there. She's not doing well."

Octavia helped him to his feet and he limped to where Colette had been thrown.

"It's really bad," Octavia warned him.

And it was. Colette had struck her head and was bleeding from several scalp wounds; a trickle of blood leaked from her nose. Her body was crumpled on the cobblestones, her left arm obviously broken. Her eyes were open and full of pain.

They crouched over her.

"Colette," Modo said.

She raised a hand as if to wave. "Did you . . . did you save your mother?"

"No."

She squeezed her eyes shut. "I am so sorry, Modo. This is what happens when you do not have a proper plan." She bit her lip in agony. "I—I am not long . . ."

"I won't hear of it," Octavia said. "Someone's gone for the doctor." She squeezed Colette's hand and tears came to her eyes. "We still have too much to argue about."

Colette managed a smile. Modo pulled out a handkerchief and dabbed at the blood on her face.

"Tavia—may I call you that?" said Colette.

"Please."

"May I . . ." She coughed, and her voice was weak. ". . . have t-time alone with Modo?"

"Of course," Octavia said.

She moved away, and Modo could hear her trying to keep the townspeople back, saying, *"Non! Non!"* The total of her French vocabulary.

"Modo," Colette said in a faltering voice. "I have failed you."

"No, you haven't." But to himself he said: *we failed, failed, failed*.

"I ask . . ." She took a sharp breath and it was several moments before she sucked in another. "Will you show me your face? Just once more."

"No."

"Please, Modo. Don't deny me this. I must see it."

It was easy to shift his shape as he was completely exhausted. He let his features slide, his face blossoming back into ugliness. A few moments later it was as deformed as it had been at birth. His hair began to fall out in clumps. Modo prepared for her reaction.

She looked up with red-veined eyes, blinked. "It is beautiful," she whispered, so sincerely that he wondered if she were delirious. "*Merci*, my *bonne chance* friend." She closed her eyes and breathed one last broken breath.

He brushed her dark hair back behind her ear and began to sob. She was, despite her wounds, still so perfectly elegant. So much lost. His sob turned to a low howl, his body shaking.

After several moments he felt Octavia's hands on his shoulder, pulling him away.

"We have to go, Modo. Gendarmes will soon be here."

He stood and turned around to see that a very large noisy crowd. A few braver townspeople were exploring the wreckage, perhaps looking for more victims. Others, more wary, had gathered at the edge of the scene. Some backed away from him when they saw his face.

"She was Colette Brunet!" Modo shouted. "She served your country well. Her name was Colette Brunet."

And then Octavia led him away.

24

THE BOY WITH THE IRON SHOULDERS

A young man named Oppie slept restlessly on a cot in a military tent he shared with several other soldiers. He dreamed of his home far, far away in London.

Over a year earlier he had been inside a giant that walked across London and swung its metal fists at the Parliament Buildings. He was one of many children chained to the giant to make it work, and he had only blurred memories of those events. If he didn't know better he would've said that none of it had happened. It had been a nightmare—a horrible flight of imagination.

But the bolts that stuck out through the skin of his shoulders proved otherwise, as did memories of a redheaded witch with a metal hand and an evil white-haired doctor who had poked and prodded and made him drink potions that had changed him. When he closed his eyes at night he saw the hideous pair lurking in the darkness, so he rarely slept well.

He had been removed from the broken body of the giant, set on the ground and given chocolate. He recalled talking to Mr. W, a detective-type who'd had a room at the

Red Boar, Oppie's place of employment. Oppie had been taken away in a carriage to be poked and prodded some more, then questioned by men in black uniforms and an old, gruff man named Mr. Sockrats, or some such name. And later, Oppie was poked and prodded by other, friendlier doctors. Within a week they had cut the tops from his bolts, patched him up and sent him home to his mum.

He enjoyed six weeks of bliss and magic. His mum suddenly didn't have to work because of something she called "shush money." So she stayed home and Oppie went to school—actually went to school—the place Mr. W had said he should attend. He'd started to read his first words. And the best part was that his father was growing stronger each day. His father had been yellow with some sickness that had crawled down his throat, but his mother could now buy medicines and pay a doctor.

Within a week his dad got up and walked and laughed and rubbed Oppie's head and said, "My boy, my boy." And Mum had told Oppie that he had a brother or sister who would be delivered by a stork. A stork of all things! He didn't understand exactly where the stork was from, but his mother kept rubbing her tummy.

One morning he awoke to his mother shouting for the doctor, but his dad was already cold and yellow and dead. Then Oppie got sick too. His shoulders grew bulkier. His feet and his hands outgrew the rest of his body. Then the rest of his body began to catch up. Sometimes he'd grow an inch in height overnight! And his temper grew, too. He wouldn't remember his tantrums, but would awake up to broken chairs or dishes or pots lying all around him, his mum huddled like a frightened bird in the corner.

The men in black uniforms returned, along with Mr. Sokrats, who told Mum that he was changing because of the potion Britain's enemies gave him. It was affecting his body and his mind. Making him age. He didn't understand but he had to go with the men to a secret fortress. His mum hugged him and said she'd see him again when he was all better.

They put him in the back of a carriage, and thus began a journey that would take him away, far, far over the ocean.

25

VALUABLE CARGO ARRIVES

M iss Hakkandottir was the first to see the airship *Erebos* descend from the heavens. She was standing on a rocky plateau looking out over the cliffs when she spotted the dark oval in the sky.

She marched down to the dock as the *Erebos* flew lower. A squadron of Guild soldiers had been on guard there all morning, piquing her curiosity. She knew the airship had been on a mission in France and, judging by the torn straps and the trailing smoke, it had returned at full speed. Its armour was frosted, a sign that they had been travelling dangerously high in the atmosphere, catching strong air currents. The outer balloon looked worn.

Soldiers grabbed the landing ropes and the ship descended gracefully until it was floating only a few feet from the sandy ground. The squadron lined either side of the airship and the side gates opened.

Stepping haughtily down the gangplank was Lime, a triumphant light in his eyes, a buffalo coat wrapped around his thin frame. Behind him trudged Typhon. The monster still amazed her. She had watched as Dr. Hyde brought it back from the dead. She wondered if the doctor would do the same to her one day.

She had hoped to see one of the Association's spies— Mr. Socrates or Modo—all trussed-up and stumbling down the gangplank, so she was disappointed when instead a frightened woman, crossing herself, was led down by soldiers. She was short, haggard, and several years older than Miss Hakkandottir, her hair protruding wildly from under a torn bonnet. She had the strong-shouldered build of a peasant, of someone who worked with the earth. And so plain! Lime gave Miss Hakkandottir a leering smile, then followed the soldiers and the woman to the entrance of the Crystal Palace.

What had she just witnessed? Who could be so important? She stood watching until they had entered the palace gates. The woman matched no one in Miss Hakkandottir's files.

Only an hour later, sitting alone at a table in the mess tent eating rabbit stew, did she put it together. She dropped her spoon with a clatter and immediately went to the doctor's cave.

She found Dr. Hyde arranging his collection of needles.

"I would like to see her," she said gently.

He turned. "Ingrid, you know that is not possible. She has just arrived. We need her to be in perfect condition for our tests. She must rest."

"Did the Guild Master expressly forbid me visiting her?" She waited as he paused to think that through. Perhaps because his brain was steeped in formulas and calculations, she found him easy to manipulate. "I would never harm her," she promised. She put her metal hand on his shoulder. "I am only curious."

She did have some affection for him, or something

resembling affection. He had, after all, constructed her metal hand. She would never want her weak skin and bone hand back again; the metal one was perfect. It struck fear in the hearts of her enemies and it never wore down.

He stroked her metal hand. "Perhaps your hand needs adjusting. Though, it did not rust with the altitude and humidity of your airship adventures."

He was trying to change the subject.

He found a small lever in his pocket and used it to adjust her index finger. "Ah," he said. "Better?"

"Yes, much. Could you one day replace my arms? My legs? My body?"

His eyes widened, magnified by his odd glasses. "If required. I would turn you into a goddess."

"*More* of a goddess," she said with a hard laugh. "And we would rule the world together."

He laughed, too. She knew he was picturing them side by side. Perhaps he would have his own gleaming metal body.

"Please, Cornelius, let me see her."

"I—I suppose there is no harm in it." He paused. "She will be extremely valuable to us."

He led Miss Hakkandottir to a stone door, which he opened with a key from his pocket. The room was one of the many recent additions on the island. She followed him inside. He turned another key and an electric light buzzed to life. A perfectly clear quartz wall cut the chamber in half. On the other side was the woman, sitting on a stone slab, her expression terrified, gazing at the floor. She looked as though she had just awakened.

Hakkandottir stared at her. How tiresome and weak some humans were. But from this woman had come such a powerful child.

"She can hear me clearly?" she asked.

"Yes." He gestured at sound holes drilled into the quartz. "But please don't upset her. I need her to be as relaxed as possible for my tests. Fear and anger may alter the blood chemistry."

The woman looked up and Miss Hakkandottir was taken aback by her proud eyes, the way she fixed them on her and did not turn away. There was a bandage on her arm, but no bruises. A bible sat on the table. Perhaps the Guild Master had given it to her. To what end, Miss Hakkandottir couldn't guess.

"So you are the mother of Modo?" Miss Hakkandottir said in French.

The woman shook her head.

"But indeed you are. Lime is an unerring fox and he sniffed you out. You are the mother of a most interesting creature."

"I have no children."

"You had one. Of that we are certain."

"No. I have none. I did not give birth to that abomination."

That term made Hakkandottir smile. "Yes, an abomination. You did give birth to one. And perhaps you will be the birth mother of even more."

"Please, Ingrid," Dr. Hyde said. "We are not to upset her."

"I am nearly done, my dear," Miss Hakkandottir said without moving her gaze from Modo's mother.

She didn't know exactly why she wanted to see her writhe. Was it because Modo had bested her? Modo had battled Fuhr, her friend, and dragged him to his drowning death in the Thames. Modo had been in the submarine *Ictíneo* when it stabbed her ship from below, sinking the unsinkable *Griffon*. And he had turned his horrific face upon her at the Egyptian temple in Queensland and forced her to flee. Three times he had defeated her. Defeated the Guild.

Was she just here then to taunt Modo's mother? She shrugged. Or maybe there was something she could learn about such a powerful adversary. Was the Guild Master using the mother as bait, hoping to lure Modo here?

"I shall tear your son into pieces and feed him to my hound," Miss Hakkandottir said. The woman met her eyes, then picked up her bible and began reading aloud.

"We must leave her," Dr. Hyde said. "Please."

"I have seen enough. Words will not save you," she said over her shoulder as they left and Dr. Hyde pulled the door closed behind them.

A BETTER WOMAN THAN ME

The return voyage to Canada was not one Octavia would ever want to repeat. They had reported by telegram to Mr. Socrates; within hours they received commands to return home, home now being Montreal, of course.

She and Modo first sailed to Liverpool, stopping tantalizingly close to London. She wanted to flee to the rugged and ragged streets of Seven Dials where she had grown up. She'd be safe in any of those rat holes they called pubs. Even the Clockwork Guild wouldn't poke their noses in there. Instead, she and Modo booked a second-class cabin on the SS *Montreal,* playing husband and wife for the third time.

Modo was a dark and quiet stone sitting at the end of his deck chair or, more often, could be found in their cabin staring out the porthole with that blasted netting mask covering his face, and his emotions. The bruises and cuts on his face were healing quickly; inside his heart she doubted things were going as well. But Octavia did not pry.

Besides, she was not in much of a mood to talk. She had spent fewer than three days with Colette, had quarrelled with her, and yet her death was like losing a close friend, a mate. Such a blow. She had been an equal. *No,* Octavia had to admit, *she was a better woman than me.* Colette could speak several languages, had risen to the top of the ranks in her Bureau despite fellow agents trying to undermine her because she was a woman and half-Japanese. Even half-mad, she had been formidable.

And Colette was broken by that bull, Typhon, as though she were a doll. The sight and sound of that would haunt Octavia. There'd been nothing she could do to prevent it. She'd been crawling from the wreckage of their carriage when Typhon lifted Colette over his head.

"It looks like it'll be another boring day," she said, pouring her tea. "But only four more to go before we're back in Canada."

She could only imagine how all of this was affecting Modo; he had given her little more than short sentences since their departure. She so missed the Modo she'd once known.

"Yes," Modo answered, "same as the last."

"What do you suppose Mr. Socrates has in store for us?"

"It doesn't matter."

"What do you mean?"

"With or without him I'll find my mother and save her from those . . ." He shook his head as though he couldn't find any words to describe the Clockwork Guild.

"Just like that?"

"I'll find the hiding place of the Guild and I'll break them." He was bending the teaspoon like a child in a tantrum.

"Modo, the best way to do that is to work with Mr. Socrates." She was surprised by her own words and yet, as she spoke them she knew they were the truth. "You know it too. After all, you're on a ship returning to him."

"It was the only course I could take." He sighed. "I'm confused, Tavia. I am French. I am English. I was orphaned. I have parents. One is dead and the other doesn't know me. They abandoned me and yet I must save my mother. And Colette is dead. Dead. Dead. My mind bounces from one dark moment to another. It's all too much."

"Nothing is too much for you, Modo."

He looked up at her. Was this another jibe? But she returned his gaze.

"Why are you being so kind?" he asked.

"I cared for Colette too."

"You did?"

"She was a beautiful, remarkable young woman. Truly heroic. I've come to think of her as a sister."

"A sister?"

"Yes. She was an incredibly annoying and strong-willed she-devil. I would've been honoured to call her sister."

"Aye, she was strong. I am heartsick," he admitted. He shook his head and smiled, looking out at the sea. "She would be laughing now if she could hear us."

"We'll go back to Montreal, Modo. You never know what Ol' Mr. S will have up his sleeve."

"I hope you're right."

"I'm always right," she said.

What was she doing? She was thankful to Mr. Socrates for taking her from a life of pickpocketing, but he often got on her nerves and always put the needs of Britain before the needs of his spies. Now she was actually talking him up to Modo. To Modo! This was how bad things had become.

"And if he doesn't have a plan for us, Modo, one that involves rescuing your mother, I'll go with you. If she is that important to you then she is that important to me. We'll make certain Colette did not sacrifice her life for nothing. Through hell or high water, together, we'll find your mother."

He stared at her for a long time. He was so hard to read with that mask on, but she thought she saw disbelief in his eyes. Or bewilderment.

"We will," she added, "I swear this to you."

He nodded. "Then the Clockwork Guild and whoever else stands in our way had better be ready to run."

27

STEPPING OUT OF THE TRENCHES

Mr. Socrates had been part of the great siege of Sevastopol during the Crimean War. He remembered the backbreaking labour of digging trenches on one side of the Russian port city while their comrades, the French, dug trenches on the opposite side. Summer passed, Fall, Winter, Spring. Then another Summer, Fall and Winter. The harsh weather and the long months had been horrible for morale. And then, when they felt Sevastapol had been truly weakened by shelling and starvation, they rose up from their trenches and charged the city.

Now he would rise again. Hiding in Montreal had been necessary, but the time had come to act. Step out of the trench he had dug around himself and charge into the unknown.

He was beginning to feel at home in Montreal: the food, the newness of the buildings; the energy of a colony. He could comfortably spend his last years here, away from the hurly-burly of London. But being comfortable was wrong. He had to live with the heart of a soldier, moving from camp to camp, and be ready to charge the enemy at a moment's notice.

And, above all, it was time to follow his instinct.

And so he sent out several telegrams, packed a kit bag and luggage, and had Tharpa order a carriage to the docks. He left Mrs. Finchley to keep Montreal House in good order. "Guard it with your life," he said. "You're the last bastion of our part of the Association."

She nodded and smiled sardonically. "I shall fight the cobwebs and the mice until my final breath."

They looked at each other, smiling grimly. How many years had he known her? Twenty? Then she said, almost defiantly, "You give Modo and Octavia my love."

"I most certainly will not," he said. "They are agents, not our children. Your children."

Her smile was curious. "They belong to us, either way. And you know that."

He stomped away from her. Women! He could not fathom the pathways of their minds.

Minutes later he and Tharpa were in their carriage, rolling towards the docks.

He took the wireless telegraph and folders of reports with him. He had received updates from Cook and Footman, and the latest was the most exciting: a telegram saying that they'd discovered a mysterious shipyard hidden on the coast of China. It had no flags of any country and most of the workers were European. It was most likely a Clockwork Guild shipyard.

But how to give the Guild a hammer blow? He did have one ace in his deck, an experiment that, from all reports, was coming to fruition. It was waiting on Vancouver Island on a patch of land deeded to the Association by a retired general. It had been part of Mr. Socrates' long-term plan.

Intuition told him he was making the right decision. This new weapon—these new weapons—would be a sabre to the heart of the Guild.

He thought again of the siege of Sevastopol. Of how he and his regiment had charged those walls under harrowing cannon and rifle fire. It had been a failure on the British side, he remembered with a bitter laugh, but the French broke through on the other side and, by nightfall, they were all in the quarters of a dead Russian general, drinking his vodka.

28

WESTWARD HO!

Modo was so impatient to get his feet on land that he was standing by the gangplank with their luggage long before they finally docked in Montreal, next to several tall-masted ships. Octavia stood beside him, using her umbrella to shade the sun. It was colder here in Canada: the early October wind chilled him. Or was he shivering with nervousness? He was using the Doctor persona again.

The moment the sailors lowered the gangplank he scurried down. He and Octavia were the first to have their papers stamped at Customs House. He strode quickly up a ramp to the street.

"Wait, Modo! I'm not a gazelle!" Octavia blurted. He slowed down and, once she had caught up, she hissed, "You should try running in a dress. It's abominable!"

"I'll leave that to my imagination."

He was just about to wave down a *calèche,* when he saw Tharpa standing outside an ornate carriage, waving them over. Modo placed their luggage in the carrier on the back and shook Tharpa's hand. He wanted to hug his weapons master. He hadn't done that since he was a child, but he needed to feel that connection now. Instead, he held onto Tharpa's hand a little longer than usual.

"You have returned, young Sahib, and young Miss Milkweed," Tharpa said, slapping Modo's back. "Old Sahib awaits you inside, as you have likely surmised."

"I have. It . . . it's good to see you, Tharpa," Modo said. A well of emotion was rising up in him, so he bit the inside of his cheek.

"Mrs. Finchley sends her regards to both of you," Tharpa said.

Modo nodded, a little confused. Wouldn't he be seeing her in a few minutes? He reached to open the carriage door for himself.

"Modo! You help the lady in first!" Octavia reminded him.

"My apologies." He bowed in front of her, then with a flourish opened the door, took her hand and helped her step into the compartment.

He followed, seating himself across from Mr. Socrates, who wore a long coat trimmed with fur. Modo was surprised at how happy he was to see his master again. How he wished he could lay all of his problems at Mr. Socrates' feet and have them solved.

"Welcome to your home away from home, both of you," Mr. Socrates said as the carriage began to roll down the street. Tharpa was riding with the driver. "I hope you rested well on your journey." He leaned back in his chair, his walking stick across his legs. "We're about to travel west by train all the way to the coast."

"We won't be stopping at Montreal House?" Octavia asked. "I need a bath. And my clothing needs a wash."

"There's no time. We'll have the clothing, and you, laundered along the way."

Octavia frowned and turned to stare out the window with a huff.

"And what of Mrs. Finchley?" Modo asked.

"She's in charge of Montreal House." Mr. Socrates raised an eyebrow. "You'll see her when this next phase of our battle is over, Modo. If that is your worry."

It was. He had wanted to tell her about what he'd seen, to be held in the safety and comfort of her arms like a child. Of all his teachers, she would be the one to understand his pain. There was no point in mentioning this to Mr. Socrates. Perhaps, Modo decided, he could write to her.

He felt time pressing in on him. Thirteen days had already passed since his mother's capture. She could very well be dead. He couldn't help imagining how she must have cowered in the car of the airship.

"Where are we going?" he asked.

"First, Modo, I need to hear in your own words what happened in France. Every detail. Of course, I'll want your version, too, Octavia."

Reporting was a skill he had perfected in his years of training as a child at Ravenscroft, so he spoke calmly from that place in his mind where he remembered every pertinent detail. He didn't even tear up as he described Colette's death and his mother being hauled away. Octavia followed with her own observations.

"I've read files on this Lime," Mr. Socrates said. "Several agents have fallen to his blade. Typhon is someone new."

"Larger than any man I have seen," Octavia said. "And he smelled."

"Smelled?"

"I was in the carriage with him. He stunk like rotting flesh and formaldehyde. And he had stitches along his neck and face and arms."

"From wounds?"

"No. The pattern was more like a surgeon had, well, stitched him together."

"Curious," Mr. Socrates said.

"He was impressively strong, too," Modo added, "but he was cold, sir."

"Cold?"

"His bare flesh was like ice. And he was impervious to bullets and Colette's blade. Which struck his heart."

"You are certain she hit him there?"

"Yes." Modo remembered it so perfectly. Colette, his saviour, standing between him and the monster. She had paused in disbelief when he didn't fall.

"Do you know the origin of the name *Typhon*, Modo?"

"I . . . I hadn't thought about it, sir."

"Come now. You know the Guild has a penchant for Greek names. Who was Typhon?"

Because Mr. Socrates' teachings had focused on military tactics and history, Modo had not spent much of his time on mythologies, though he had memorized everything he'd read. The Greek and Norse stories of how gods and Titans had walked the earth were too fanciful for Mr. Socrates. But Modo was pleased to be able to dredge up the answer from his memory.

"Typhon was the father of all monsters in Greek mythology," Modo said. "His hands reached east and west. He had a hundred dragon heads and snake coils. He had wings and fire flashed from his eyes. Even Zeus feared him."

"Your brain is a great big book, ain't it, Modo?" Octavia said. "If we cracked open your skull we'd just find pages and pages of words."

"I'm glad I impressed you."

"Oh, I didn't say that."

But he could tell that he had.

"The Guild picks certain names for a reason," Mr. Socrates said, "and in those names we'll perhaps discover something about their plans. Why this name for this man? You said he had stitches."

"And a very tiny little finger on his right hand," Modo added, having almost forgotten that detail. His own finger tingled when he spoke of it. "It was pink, like normal flesh."

"What kind of man survives so many wounds? So many surgeries? Who knows what they've done to make him this resilient, this powerful. They must see the man as being very important. Any sign of his cerebration?"

"His what?" Octavia asked.

"How smart he is," Modo explained. Octavia stuck her tongue out at him and he nearly laughed—how he needed a good laugh. "He spoke in short sentences. Very gruff. He seemed to do whatever Lime asked of him. But there's one order he didn't obey. He was told to break me and could easily have snapped my spine. But he only dropped me."

"Very curious," Mr. Socrates said. He took his walking stick and leaned forward. "But we haven't asked the important question. Why do you think the Clockwork Guild wants Madame Hébert? What do you suppose they will do with her?"

"I . . . I can't . . ."

"Don't hold back, Modo. This is of utmost importance."

"It has been a long journey, Mr. Socrates," Octavia said.

Modo gritted his teeth; he didn't need her to defend him.

"I don't even want to imagine what they want with her, sir," he snapped. "Don't you think I haven't been running through a hundred horrific scenarios? How can you ask me to speak of this? You know what the Guild is capable of.

Your guess is as good as mine. Don't make me speak of my mother this way."

"Don't be weak—weakness will be used by the enemy to break you."

That sharp tone! After years of hearing it, Modo involuntarily straightened. He thought hard and finally he drew in a deep breath. "Okay, I can think of two reasons. One, they want to get to me. They would dearly like to capture me. So this suggests they are using her to draw me to them."

"A doubtful scenario," Mr. Socrates said. "They would have to communicate with you again in order to give you the location to which they want to lead you."

"Exactly, sir. My second conclusion is that there's something in her, in her biology or her . . . her body . . . her blood . . . something they can use. In the past they've applied drugs and metal enhancements to modify and strengthen hounds and children. For what exact purpose they'll use my mother, I do not know."

"We must look into the abyss, Modo," Mr. Socrates said. "It's the only way to defeat such blackguards. It is becoming obvious to me that they intend to bring at least one more Typhon into the world."

"That makes sense," Modo whispered.

"Then what is the connection between Typhon and Modo's mother?" Octavia asked.

"There isn't one," Modo said. "There can't be."

"No, Octavia has a valid point," Mr. Socrates said. "Excellent rational thinking. If this Typhon has been somehow strengthened by . . . by stitching parts of other men together, then he would be well served by the ability to regenerate. And, Modo, no one is stronger nor heals more quickly than you. Think of how your finger grew back."

"No. The Guild can't be aware of my regenerative abilities. We didn't even know ourselves until Miss Hakkandottir cut off my finger." He stared at his hand. She had sliced the little finger off while he was hanging from her airship and he'd fallen to the earth, leaving his finger behind.

Mr. Socrates tapped Modo's hand with his walking stick. Modo drew his hand back.

"It would not be beyond Miss Hakkandottir to keep a trophy of her battle with you. And, once that trophy was in their lab, for Dr. Hyde to experiment with it."

"It can't be." Modo recoiled in shock, and Octavia gasped.

But his finger had itched when he'd seen Typhon's little finger. As though even his body had recognized the truth. "Typhon did have a proportionately small little finger," Modo said. He shuddered, though he knew it was better to face facts without emotion, as Mr. Socrates had always taught him.

"Then it is possible that there's a connection between you and Typhon as well. Ah, we have learned a lot in a short while. We'll have plenty of time to think upon these riddles and others as we travel."

The carriage stopped in front of Bonaventure Station, a grand stone building that reminded Modo a little of Notre Dame Cathedral. There were rows of carriages waiting out front, loading and unloading passengers.

Modo was the last to get out and Mr. Socrates pulled him aside and said quietly, "I'm sorry about Monsieur Hébert and the girl." Then he patted his arm and said, "Come along."

Modo paused. His master had actually sensed that Modo was feeling some pain. *Perhaps the old man has grown a heart.* It was curious, he noted, that Mr. Socrates only referred to his parents by their last names. Not as *your mother and father.*

Tharpa tossed half the luggage to Modo and carried the rest himself. Modo followed the others into the train station, almost running across the intricate marble floors. Within minutes they were on a westbound train leaving the island of Montreal.

"Where are we going?" Modo asked.

"Westward ho!" Mr. Socrates said jauntily. "We're travelling through Ontario, then taking the Grand Trunk Railway. We'll follow the North Pacific route through the United States, since the laggardly Canadian government has not yet figured out how to build their own national rail line. This band of metal that crosses the United States is quite the accomplishment. And all done without the British. I guess the old colony is growing up."

"I'm sure they'd be pleased to know they have your approval," Octavia said.

"Indeed they would," Mr. Socrates said.

Modo wasn't certain if he was joking or not.

"Are the Clockwork Guild located in the American West?" Modo asked. "How soon will we lock horns with them?"

"No, no," Mr. Socrates said. "The Guild is somewhere in the Pacific Ocean, I am certain. I'm following my intuition on this one."

"You mean we may be going through all this trouble and end up in the middle of nowhere?" Modo asked.

"Be assured, I know their general whereabouts. The real difficulty will be in locating their base."

"And what will our assignments be?" Octavia asked.

"To deal with events as they unfold. Enough about work. Let us enjoy our trip."

Modo and Octavia exchanged glances. No plan? His intuition? Who was this man?

The hours passed. The car didn't have the first-class cabins Modo had come to admire in England and France. Instead there were two rows of seats on either side of the train. They did have beautiful wide windows and above them, in the curve of the ceiling, elaborate stained glass windows. Dressing rooms and lavatories were at the far end of the car.

The lack of cabins would make for an uncomfortable trip. Modo wouldn't be able to hide his disfigurement without privacy, but for some reason, he found he didn't care. His mask would have to be enough to protect the passengers from seeing his face. And if they were put off by the mask, too bad.

He and Octavia were delighted to explore saloon cars, balcony cars, dining cars and refreshment cars. Modo bought a copy of *The Moonstone* by Wilkie Collins from a boy with a basket of books for sale. He loved a good detective story.

They had taken seats at the front of their car so they could not easily be gawked at, and Modo sat nearest the window. They passed into Ontario and through the city of Toronto, and crossed at Sarnia into Michigan. At eight o'clock a steward announced, "It's bedtime, folks." In the space of a few minutes the seats were lowered and beds and red curtains gave everyone some privacy. Tharpa was across from them sharing with a stranger. Octavia had a seat to herself.

Modo had never slept in the same room with Mr. Socrates, never mind inches away from him.

"Good night, Modo," he said, pulling his nightcap on tight.

Mr. Socrates fell asleep almost instantly, but Modo's mind was still aching from all that had happened. Unbidden, Colette's face filled his vision. She had asked to see his brutal features before she died, had actually wanted it to be the last image she saw. His face!

There had been other deaths in his life, but not someone he . . . he . . . loved. That was it. He had loved her. Not in the same way he did Octavia, but under different circumstances they might have spent a lifetime together. She had tried to save him from the monstrous Typhon and had given him a gift by looking at his face. By saying he was beautiful. Would a dying woman lie?

Such were his thoughts for a very long time before he finally drifted off to the rhythm of a train chugging westward.

29

EXPERIENCING ELOCUTION

Typhon was sitting on a stone gazing in wonder at the Pacific Ocean. They had named him Typhon but he didn't feel as though the name truly belonged to him. He wasn't Typhon; he was several people at once. There were voices in his head, bubbling like a brew, but this voice, the one that was thinking at this moment, was his own. Wasn't it?

His thoughts had come to him slowly, as though he were waking from a deep sleep. For so long the only other voices he heard were those of his masters; their commands would rattle around in his skull until he obeyed them. As time passed, more of his own thoughts sprouted up between those commands. And, occasionally, he would even have memories. They were dark names and feelings. A mother. Yes, he remembered a mother who had held him as a child. And the feeling of coarse, itchy rope around his neck. Then darkness. Did the memories belong to him or someone else? And he remembered, too, the emotions of those moments. The comfort, the uncertainty.

They had tried to turn him into a labourer, but someone

had to be there constantly to give him instructions. So they let him wander the island. They fed him when he was hungry, but the soldiers and even the mechanical hounds kept their distance.

Every night he would visit Dr. Hyde to be examined. Occasionally there was a stitch that had broken and needed mending. "Your flesh will eventually grow together," the doctor said one day, "like the regeneration of a lizard's tail. A very exciting scientific discovery, Typhon."

The monster nodded.

"And Lime tells me you've learned more words. You speak well, at times."

"I speak well."

"Yes, yes, I've heard you speak before. But it's great news that you've retained those faculties. Communicating will be much easier."

"I experience elocution."

"Ah." The doctor stared at him dumbfounded, his eyes behind his gold-rimmed glasses so big they were comical. Typhon nearly laughed. "You use such sophisticated words."

"Yes. I can . . . I am cognizant of that."

"Marvellous, simply marvellous," the doctor said.

Perhaps, Typhon mused, he would crush the doctor's skull. This was the man who had brought him to life—the first face he had seen when his eyes opened. This old, tiny, frail-boned man. Typhon lifted his hands, then lowered them. He chose not to commit the act. It would be an interesting experience, but he had a curious affection for the old man.

"I am very proud of you," the doctor said. "So very proud."

Typhon nodded. "Who was I?"

"Who were you?" the doctor said. "Oh, I see. You have

some questions all children ask: *Who am I? Why am I here?* Very interesting. I didn't expect that. Do you have memories of—how shall I put it—another time? Another you?"

"Sometimes, yes."

"Oh, now that is *very* interesting. You see, you were not one person, but several. Your brain is an amalgamation. From the grey matter of a man named William Middleton. He was a prospector and a murderer. And another named Duncan McTavish. He was a writer and a murderer. Other brains were required, though I only used smaller portions of those. Do these names mean anything to you?"

"They sound familiar." But he couldn't picture either of them.

"Well, do tell me if you experience any more memories. Curious that they can live on after the electric charge of life has been snuffed out and reignited. I have more good news, Typhon." The doctor gestured to the walls around him with a palsied hand. "Soon you won't be alone."

Typhon looked around the room at the others, frozen in coffins of ice. Would they be his brothers? His sisters? His friends? Or his enemies? He should destroy the bodies now. Then he wouldn't have to risk *being* destroyed.

"You are dismissed, Typhon," Dr. Hyde said.

He walked out of the cave and along the wet stony ground. There were always soldiers around, and sometimes that woman with the red hair. And he had once stood before someone called the Guild Master. A tiny man with a powerful voice. He could not find any older memories of such people inside his head. He did have memories, though, of a wife with a reedy voice. Had he been married? Had he children?

Sometimes he would see Lime. The man with the metal teeth had barked at him and treated him like a dog. He would snuff him out for that. He imagined the event, the glee he would feel. He could do it now, but the hounds and the soldiers would tear him apart. It would not be wise to kill him at this juncture. He would wait.

Besides, Typhon was beginning to understand how small Lime really was. He had not built a palace on this island. He had not given the orders that created Typhon.

He walked where the seagulls flew along the edge of the island. He watched the other little birds flit through the air. So pretty. He sat under a palm tree and held out his hand.

He held it perfectly still for three hours, his breathing shallow and quiet. Finally a bird with pretty yellow wings landed on it. He watched the bird. It watched him. He couldn't think of the name of the bird. He should know that.

Then, with a quick squeeze, he crushed it.

"Canary," he said.

30

AN OLD BUT YOUNG FRIEND

Though the trip across the American West was one beautiful landscape after another—each could be a giant painting like those in the National Gallery at Trafalgar Square—Modo wished the train would chug faster. He'd shovel the coal himself if it'd help. Their travels took them from Wisconsin to Minnesota and onward. Sometimes the stations were the only signs of civilization.

This was a country that had survived a massive and horrible civil war; he'd read about tragic battles, desperate charges, countercharges and hand-to-hand combat. This was also the land of adventure, according to the penny dreadfuls—six-gun shooters, sheriffs and gangs of unruly cattle thieves. And the savage Indians, too.

No, *savage* was the wrong word. He remembered the native Rain People of Australia. In the short time he'd spent with them, he'd realized they were far from savage. He'd long since decided it was best to judge who was savage by their actions.

Every second stop was a fort: Fort Clark in the Dakotas, Fort Alexander in Montana. Outposts surrounded by nothingness as far as he could tell. There was little to do but wander from car to car. Read. Wait. Mr. Socrates had predicted that it would take four nights and four days. Impossible to imagine crossing such a large continent in such a short time, but he knew an airship would cross it at twice the speed.

The close quarters of the train made it particularly hard to hide his deformities and only by acting the invalid were they allowed to keep his bed down and the curtains closed. Invalid? He could outwrestle any man on the train, except perhaps Tharpa. But playing an invalid gave him time to read.

When he did change into the Doctor, he would dress and stroll up and down the aisle or play chess against Tharpa.

"You've tramped this train from beginning to end at least a hundred times," Octavia said. They were in the observation car watching the green hills of Montana pass by.

"I have to do something. I'm clamped in, trapped and angry."

"Anything else? A sore toe perhaps?" She clapped his shoulder. "Ah, Modo, we are all trapped. Though Mr. Socrates seems to have a light in his eyes. He's enjoying this."

"The man has no plan."

"Then no one can predict his actions."

Modo shook his head. "You sound like him. I had no plan when we attacked Lime's wagon and Colette died."

"Do not carry her death on your shoulders, Modo. All three of us accepted the risks and we came up with the best plan possible in such a short time. You didn't ask her to stand toe to toe with that monster. She chose to."

"You're right. But I'd feel better if our master were plotting everything out carefully."

"He hasn't led us wrong before. Perhaps we're better off without a plan this time. And at least we're on the move. We could be stifled in Montreal House reading Plato to each other."

"Now, don't you poke fun at Plato." He put his hand against the window. "I—I keep wishing I had said something more to my father. I don't even know if he heard me. Who was he, Tavia?"

"Maybe when we have more time you could . . . we could return to Montreuil and ask some questions."

She wanted to go there with him! He couldn't help smiling.

"I have to confess something to you, Modo," she said.

"You do?"

"I once said I didn't care about my parents. Didn't want to meet them. It's a lie. I . . . I'd like to set eyes on them once. To see what they look like. I know it sounds odd, but I now envy you that you saw your father. My dad was likely strung up by the hangman or is sleeping in Davy Jones' locker."

"I hadn't thought of that, Tavia. I'm sorry."

"Oh, don't be sorry. Once I got over the first glance I'd tear a strip off 'em. After all, how dare those louts abandon me?"

"I feel the same way," Modo said, "but it's harder to be angry now that I've seen them."

"Well, we'll rescue your mother. And you can jabber with her 'til your tongue falls out."

"It seems impossible," Modo said. "There are just four of us. Against the Clockwork Guild. What are we thinking?"

"Like I said before, perhaps Mr. Socrates has a trick up his sleeve, or hidden in his walking stick."

"I sure hope he does."

They took in the view for a while, until Modo said, "I just don't understand exactly who I am. What country I belong to."

"You're Modo," she said, as though it explained everything. "We don't belong to countries, Modo. We belong to friends."

"I belong to you?" he asked.

"Well . . . Yes, of course. You're my mate." She gave him a friendly punch in the arm. "And you're such a bore when you're a sourpuss. Don't trouble yourself about what'll happen. I live in the moment."

"That's one of your many wonderful traits."

"It's the only way, Modo. I told you about Garret once, didn't I? My mate who was hanged for stealing a watch. He's the one who taught me to live by the day, the hour, the moment." She paused. "It's best not to think about him. Gets me teared up."

The vast mountains of Montana and Idaho—the Rockies—were stunning. And someone had cut a path through all that rock so this band of steel could wind through the mountains. How much dynamite had been used? The whistle blew as they passed a town called Hellgate.

"They do have particularly clever names for their towns," Octavia said.

The final stop was a small station near the coast. Modo leapt out into the fresh air, clutching his bag and Octavia's. The four agents loaded everything into a canvas-covered wagon with a driver who was, to Modo's great disappointment, wearing a conductor's cap. He'd expected a cowboy hat. They began rolling towards Seattle. He was glad for the canvas as clouds scudded over them; thunder sounded and just like that, it began to pour rain. The horses snorted and struggled, kicking up mud as they dragged the wagon down the sludgy First Avenue past square wooden buildings that looked as though a good wind would knock them over. Every second building was a saloon.

"This really is the Wild West," Octavia said. She had opened her umbrella and was hiding underneath it because the rain was soaking through the canvas. "They don't even have cobblestone streets."

They slogged their way to the port and, after Mr. Socrates had paid for tickets, loaded their soaked selves onto a sternwheel steamboat named *Alexandra*. It was not the largest Modo had ever seen, but it fit thirty passengers comfortably and chugged across the Juan de Fuca Strait to Victoria. How many cities, rivers, lakes and mountains had been named after the Queen? They passed an island and docked near what looked to be government buildings, small by comparison to the Parliament Buildings of London, but still impressive.

"This is the farthest edge of the British Empire in North America," Mr. Socrates explained after they'd debarked the paddleship.

The city's newness and size reminded Modo of Sydney. The familiar buildings and bridges were British in style. Civilization! He nearly sighed. Within minutes Mr. Socrates had summoned a small black carriage. The ride took them through the streets and under a vined archway with the sign God Save The Queen. They passed the Bank of British Columbia and beside it was the Victoria Boot and Shoe Manufactory.

"It's all so very quaint," Octavia said. "It's like they've made a tiny copy of everything in England. Which reminds me, my boots need mending."

"There's no time," Mr. Socrates said. "We're less than an hour from our destination."

Soon they were pulling up to a military establishment. "Esquimalt, the headquarters of the British Pacific Fleet," Mr. Socrates said.

Seeing the ships and marines, Modo wondered if his master had formed a plan as they were travelling. Why else come to a military base?

A marine opened the carriage door and Mr. Socrates produced papers from his pocket. The marine squinted at the passengers, his eyes on Octavia so long that Modo felt like giving him a bop on the nose. The marine nodded and said gruffly, "Your transportation will be here soon enough." He motioned to the driver. "The civilian is not allowed any farther."

They got out and pulled their luggage down. An uncovered wagon, the box stained with some black substance—blood?—pulled up. They threw their luggage on and climbed into their seats. Their driver was another marine. At a flick of the reins the horses began to trot down the main road of the naval base.

"They added more docks," Mr. Socrates said. "Good. Good." There were docks, of course, and sailors standing outside wooden barracks. "I was invalided here during the Crimean escapade." Mr. Socrates looked at the barracks. "Fir trees and coal make this a valuable area. And it's within easy striking distance of the United States, if need be."

"Are we going to war with them?" Octavia said. "Did they dump our tea in the sea again? Outrageous."

"One must prepare for all possible outcomes," he said. "You can trust an individual, but never trust the country."

"And does that include England?" Modo asked.

"Especially not England," he replied with a smile. "Empires are not created by accident."

The HMS *Shah*—an iron-hulled, wooden-sheathed frigate—waited in the dock, the metal glistening in the dull sunlight. Three masts towered above the deck and two steam funnels puffed smoke. The warship looked brand new. It was a sword, Modo decided, sharp and powerful. Meant to cut through the ocean and the ships of the enemy.

They were soon past the docks and encountering fewer buildings, though there were massive stores of coal. Several men were shooting at a practice targets and charging straw dummies. Ah, the life of a marine, Modo thought. It would be so simple.

They arrived at a guard post and were stopped by men in black uniforms. Modo recognized the uniform— members of Mr. Socrates Permanent Association. The exact position of these soldiers in the hierarchy of the British army had never been made clear to Modo. It was likely that they weren't accounted for on any records.

Their driver climbed down, saluted, then began walking back to the naval base.

"It's good to see you again, sir," the Association soldier said. "I'll take you the rest of the way." He climbed into the driver's seat.

"Where are we going?" Modo asked Octavia.

"The outback, I guess," she said. "Mr. Socrates really is unpredictable. Or he's lost his faculties."

"I haven't lost my hearing, Octavia," Mr. Socrates said.

They drove through two more checkpoints. Modo was intrigued: What secret were they about to see that needed three separate security checks? Even the marines weren't allowed beyond the gate. They entered a camp around which stood a ten-foot-tall thorny fence. A secret within a secret on a distant military base.

They passed through a copse of pine trees that opened up into a large clearing. Before them stood at least twenty white tents, circling a tall pole flying a British flag. The wagon lurched to a stop before the largest tent.

"First we dine," Mr. Socrates said.

"I can only imagine what we'll be dining on," Octavia whispered.

Mr. Socrates led them into a mess tent with wooden tables set with metal plates. It stank of smoke and burnt food. "Sit, sit," Mr. Socrates commanded, and as they did, two cooks scooped piles of an unrecognizable goulash onto their plates.

"What's this?" Octavia asked.

A grizzled cook waved his spoon at her. "Food. Plain and simple."

Plain and grey was more like it, and glued together by a gravy dotted with globules of fat. Modo poked at what he believed were white potatoes. The gruel tasted peppery, with the slightest hint of lime. He couldn't identify what animal the stringy meat came from. Venison? Beef?

"It has everything you need in it," Mr. Socrates said.

"Oh. Is this pleasant loblolly your recipe?" Octavia asked. Even Tharpa was looking at it twice.

"No. I am good at making tea, but little else in the kitchen. I approved it. It's made our soldiers strong."

Another experiment? Modo wondered. He finished the food on his plate.

"You were all hungry," Mr. Socrates said, looking satisfied. "I'm glad you enjoyed that; you'll be getting your fill of it here. Now, come along. I have a squadron of soldiers I'd like you to meet."

He knew his way around the camp. He led them past a series of empty tents, each with five cots.

"So where are we?" Modo asked.

"Welcome to Camp Cobra, a base for the Permanent Association," Mr. Socrates replied. "This is where we train and plan and, when the time is right, strike."

Beyond the tents was a field littered with straw dummies that had been torn in half. It looked like a battlefield.

"But who are you training? The Association soldiers?" said Octavia.

Mr. Socrates' eyes twinkled. "Your question will be answered momentarily. Listen."

As if on cue, a low rumble emanated from the north. At first Modo thought it was thunder, but the ground began to shake under his feet like an earthquake. Mr. Socrates gave the slightest hint of a smile. He was enjoying this! The rumbling grew to a pounding and Modo's heart pounded in response. Then came a deep, monstrous roar. He met Octavia's eyes; she looked nervous. Tharpa was calm as ever, and it occurred to Modo that he'd been here before.

The roaring was closer now. Was it bison? He'd read about how large they were. He fully expected to see a herd stampede over the rise and trample them.

To Modo's shock a giant charged over the rise, followed by another and another—twelve feet tall, metal creatures with massive gleaming helmeted heads and arms and legs that hissed. A dozen pounded along in formation, holding what looked to be multi-chambered elephant guns. The armour on their chests was dented, yet glittered. They yelled in unison and Modo nearly wet his britches.

Right behind them was an Association soldier, holding a speaking trumpet. He gave a command and the giants split into two groups, drew massive wooden clubs from their backs and began fighting one another.

Octavia's mouth was hanging open. Mr. Socrates grinned, ear to ear, obviously pleased and proud. "These men are the most elite fighting unit in all the world."

"There are men inside all that metal?" Modo asked.

"Of course," Mr. Socrates answered. "Very large men standing on steam-powered legs and strapped and bolted into an armoured torso. See how smoothly they move?"

The dragoons continued to battle, arms hissing with steam. After several minutes of exchanging blows they were given a sharp order and they retreated back into formation. They stood motionless as the Association soldier shouted at the top of his voice about their laziness.

When the diatribe was over, Mr. Socrates commanded, "Sergeant Beatty, send me Trooper Entwistle!"

The sergeant barked another order and one of the giants turned, saluted with a huge metal hand and lumbered across the field towards them.

"You are about to get a good close look at a secret weapon about which neither the Prime Minister nor the Queen is aware," Mr. Socrates said. "A member of our 7th Dragoons Regiment, or the Lucky Sevens as we call them."

Modo remembered that dragoons were part of the cavalry, trained in lance and rifle warfare. But these men were riding metal machines instead of horses. When the giant stopped a few feet away from them, Modo strained his neck to look up at its face. Behind the slit in the visor were two glowing eyes.

"Remove your helmet," Mr. Socrates commanded.

"Yes, sir, Mr. Socrates," the man replied. He unlocked the golden helmet, which was adorned with a small image of the crown and topped with a horsehair plume.

Modo had expected to see some grizzled veteran inside, but instead the soldier was young. His eyes were confident, his face tanned by hours of outdoor training. There was a familiar cut to his jaw. And he was freckled.

Recognition struck Modo. He hadn't seen this face for over a year. He had once peered at it through a keyhole in a London inn. The face was much younger then.

"Oppie," Modo said incredulously, "is that really you?"

31

BOLTS OF ANGER

The boy was much changed—larger, older and scarred —but Modo knew him. Oppie was ten years old the last time he'd seen him, just a year and a half ago. Yet today he looked sixteen, if not twenty. By what little Modo could see of his body in all that metal, he guessed Oppie was at least six feet tall.

"Do I know you, sir?" the dragoon asked. Such politeness seemed odd coming out of something so large and powerful.

"Oppie, it's me," Modo said, then nearly smacked himself for being such a dunderhead. Modo had been wearing a mask the only time they'd met face to face, after the Association had brought down the Clockwork Guild's giant constructed of children. Before that, Modo had rented a room at the Red Boar and Oppie had brought his meals to his door. Modo had not wanted to show his face, so he had entertained the boy by reading to him through the keyhole. What name had he been using back then? Ah, yes! "It's Mr. Wellington," Modo said. "I'm Mr. Wellington! But my real name is Modo."

The man was silent, measuring. "I've never seen your face before, sir."

"I wouldn't pull your leg, Oppie. You brought me pork buttons and ale, every night. Don't you remember?"

"I think I recognize your voice. It's a pleasure to see you, sir."

His lower-class accent was gone. He'd changed so very much in such a short time.

"I—I don't understand . . ." Modo said to Mr. Socrates.

"Oppie is a dragoon now," he said. "You may return to your duties, Trooper Entwistle."

"Thank you, sir." With a clanking of gears he saluted, clicked his helmet into place, then strode smoothly away, his metal suit hissing. His back was protected by several plates.

"We added to the Guild design," Mr. Socrates explained, "stealing the pattern from their giant. We also dredged up Fuhr's body from the Thames. There wasn't much left of his flesh after the fish'd had their way, but his coal-fired arms and legs were intact—a true marvel."

"It really is astonishing," Modo said.

"The dragoons can travel absolutely silently for short periods, using their electric batteries. But once their steam engines are fired up they can burst through brick walls or scale the highest cliffs. They are bolted to the structure using the shoulder bolts Dr. Hyde had already inserted into the children. We had to extend them again, of course."

"You extended the bolts?" Modo echoed. "I thought you'd find a way to cut them off."

"For the others we did, but not the dragoons. It was the only logical thing to do."

"Good Lord," Octavia said, "is that Ester?" One of the cavalry soldiers had removed her helmet to reveal short red hair. Octavia, too, had known one of the children in the Clockwork Guild's giant.

"Yes," Mr. Socrates said. "Lance Corporal Esther McGravin."

"I thought you were going to return them to their parents!" Modo said.

"We did." Mr. Socrates leaned on his walking stick. "At least to those parents we could find. And when we couldn't find parents, some of the children became robust enough that they could work on farms in Canada or Australia. They are doing well. Others died, within a few months. Failed livers and such. We discovered the causes through autopsies. There were fifty-seven children who made up the giant. Twelve of them were altered permanently by the tincture they'd been given and could not adapt to civilian life."

Modo watched the dragoons march in formation, felt their metal feet shaking the ground.

"Altered in what way?" Octavia asked.

"It accelerated their growth and their age. Each of those soldiers is over six feet tall. They're all aging before their time. A week is the equivalent of a month for them."

"So how long before they die of old age?" Modo asked.

Mr. Socrates sighed. "We don't know. They also have some deep physiological problems. They are unpredictable and possibly dangerous. Oppie, for example, twice attacked his mother. They need constant supervision and extremely clear goals to keep them focused. It became clear that only the Association could care for him and the others."

"This is caring for them?" Modo asked. "You've turned them into—into war machines!"

"I don't like your tone, Modo. Each of them chose to come here."

"How long have they been at this camp?" Octavia asked.

"For eight months. We couldn't keep them in England; there are too many prying eyes and squeamish hearts. And this is absolutely top secret. Even those soldiers in Esquimalt are not allowed on this base."

"And why are you showing them to us?" Modo asked.

"Because they will strike the blow that shatters the Clockwork Guild."

Of course. So Mr. Socrates did have a plan. But what a plan! Modo's mind could not process what he was seeing.

Mr. Socrates led them back to the tents. Had the child soldiers stayed here through the winter? Modo wondered. The tents had little more than cots and a brazier. He could only imagine how harsh the winters would be; it seemed almost cruel. As cruel as Ravenscroft.

"These will be our lodgings for the remainder of October and likely November, too," Mr. Socrates said, pointing at four separate tents.

"We're going to just sit here?" Modo asked.

"Do you have a better suggestion?" Mr. Socrates asked. "Shall we jump on a raft and paddle off in search of the Clockwork Guild? Have you any idea exactly how big the Pacific is?"

"You said you aren't certain that they're even in the Pacific."

Mr. Socrates grabbed Modo by his lapels and pulled him into a tent.

"Your insubordination is becoming rather tiring," he said quietly. "I did not raise you to be a thorn in my side."

"Mrs. Finchley raised me."

"Modo." There was a sadness in his master's eyes. "I am not your father. I know you want to find your mother and perhaps you seek to avenge that French girl's death. But believe me, anger only leads to rash decisions. I learned that the hard way. Allow me to do my job and you will be able to do yours."

"Yes, sir."

Mr. Socrates let go of Modo's lapels. "And, Modo, don't feel you have to hide your face here. The soldiers have been prepared. No one will stare at you. You are to feel at home and conserve your energy. Very soon we will be going to war."

32

A STATUE STANDS

Several weeks earlier Footman and Cook had crossed the United States by train and taken a steamship to Hong Kong. There the real work had begun. It'd taken several bribes and days of scouting before they discovered the entrance to the secret shipyard along China's coast on the Yellow Sea. And now they sat on the green mountainside above it, squirrelled away behind a cypress tree, drinking cold tea and eating hard tack and dried rice. Footman surveyed the scene below with a spyglass, his eyes still unbelieving.

It was a massive shipyard in a perfectly protected cove, and hundreds of workers, mostly European, were labouring with hammers, hauling coal, or tending to various other duties while heavy cranes moved giant beams of steel and metal plates into position. It was ingeniously hidden; from the ocean it was almost impossible to spot the entrance because of the way it fit into the folds of the mountains. Moreover, the Guild had disguised the access with a wooden flotilla that looked from a distance like rocks.

There were at least a thousand men working on a multi-tude of projects. Three enormous warships were in various states of construction: the *Hydra,* the *Gorgon,* and the *Medusa.* The first two were nearly ready to launch; the third looked like the skeleton of a giant beached whale. It was months, if not a good year away from completion.

Footman couldn't help watching in wonder as smaller boats raced at impossible speeds through the waters.

"Stunning, ain't it, mate." Cook chewed a dried plum. "A whopping big operation. You see the little boats? *Tritons* they're called. I've never seen anything go that fast on the water."

"Yes, they are impressive."

"They take them out in groups of two, but they're going straight out into the Pacific. Not hugging the mainland. Wherever those little ships go, that's where our mutual enemy resides."

"So we must steal a boat," Footman said. "And follow them."

"I like the way you think, Footman. The question is how?"

"I have a plan."

"I'm all ears," Cook said.

Footman led him back towards the entrance to the bay. It was guarded by sentries in an old pagoda-style tower that perhaps once had been home to monks. It took Footman and Cook two hours to make their way down there. The door to the pagoda was closed and Footman had no idea how many soldiers would be inside.

"I go, you wait," he said. "You're clumsy."

"All too true, Footie. Just shout if you need help."

Footman stole through a line of shrubs and up to the

door. It was unlocked: so they weren't expecting an attacker. He opened the door slowly and crept up the stone stairs. The lookout guards were at the top and judging by their voices there were at least two. Soldiers, even the well-trained ones, could not always be focused after hours of staring and waiting. And it was very likely that no one had ever trespassed here. He padded to the top floor and peeked in the door. One soldier was staring over the water. The second played solitaire on a table.

He struck the first in the temple with his palm; the second received a kick to the side of the skull. They both fell, unconscious.

"Shall I come up now?" Cook asked from the bottom of the pagoda.

"Yes."

Cook was not exactly quiet coming up the stairs and he clapped his hands when he saw Footman's handiwork. "Bravo! Wasn't sure if you needed my help or not. They sounded like a bit of trouble."

"No trouble." Footman had already undressed the shorter man and was pulling on the soldier's grey uniform.

Cook changed too and they waited, briefly debating how long the shifts might be.

First one hour, then another passed.

"Cards?" Cook asked.

Footman shook his head.

"What's your real name?" Cook said.

"Footman," he answered.

"No, your Chinese one. Singsongy, innit?"

"I am Footman, that is all."

"Funny thing, Footie. My real name's Cook. Albert Cook. And I became a cook. Destiny, eh?"

Footman shrugged. "Names are never who you are."

When he first arrived in London he'd soon noticed that the higher class in England often called their servants by their occupation, not their name, so he took the name Footman. Mr. Socrates had not disagreed, for they knew others would make assumptions about him if that was his name. Assumptions could always be used against the people who made them.

Footman had worked for Mr. Socrates for over twenty years. He'd first met his employer in Shanghai and had been hired at the age of eighteen. Then his name had been Gong Le, and he'd trained under the Shaolin masters, warrior monks. He'd completed his years of chi kung, of long runs and combat by carrying a red-hot cauldron down a long alley, balancing the great pot on his forearms. Seals on the cauldron burned a tiger on one arm and a dragon on the other. They still sat there, symbols of his time, training and beliefs. He had wanted to see the world, so turned his back on the monks. Mr. Socrates had opened up the world for him.

Footman jumped to attention when two of the boats sped towards the exit of the bay. Earlier, they'd seen the lookout soldiers run out and open a section of the camouflaged flotilla, so Footman and Cook knew they should do that. They scurried down and let the first boat pass. It was large enough for ten men and was steered using a round wheel with two handholds. *Triton 12* was painted on its side.

When the second boat arrived, Cook put out his hand and signalled: *stop*. The boat, *Triton 13,* pulled up to the small dock. There were two Guild soldiers inside, both wearing goggles.

"You want me to handle them?" Cook whispered. Footman nodded.

"What are you stopping us for?" the driver asked.

"Paperwork," Cook said. "Got it right here."

He stepped onto the boat and gave the first one a punch to the skull that dropped him. The second swung, making contact with Cook's shoulder, and was knocked out by Cook's left hand. Cook stripped the men of their goggles, then casually tossed them onto the dock.

"That was a little sloppy," Cook admitted. "But we haven't all been trained in a Shaolin temple, now have we?"

Footman shrugged and jumped on board.

"I'll take the wheel," Cook said. He needed a few moments of experimentation to learn the controls of the ship and then they were out on the water, keeping the first boat within sight. The vessel's speed was amazing. It seemed faster than a train as it jumped over each wave. They put on the goggles to protect their eyes from the spray.

Footman pointed at the pack of food and bottles of water. There were several boxes of coal next to the firebox, but the coal had been compressed and, he guessed, would last a long time.

"They were expecting a long trip," Cook said. "Not certain I like taking such a small craft out on such a great big ocean, good as its engine is, but I guess we have no choice."

"We don't," Footman agreed.

Cook spun the wheel like he'd piloted the boat his whole life.

As the sun set, the lead boat moved farther and farther ahead until it was out of sight. They kept a straight course, following the compass next to the wheel.

"We'll keep following these bearings," Cook said. "They were going straight and there's enough coal and food for a few days."

They had a wireless telegraph, but since there were no telegraph cables in the Pacific, it was useless. The only way to get a message to their master would be to take it to him themselves. They had received one last communication giving them coordinates for where they could flee to, if necessary.

After four hours of travelling in the dark, a slight glow appeared on the horizon and grew gradually brighter.

"There she be, mate," Cook said.

In another half hour they were close enough to see an island with a large central building that seemed to be made from glass. Footman had seen the Crystal Palace in London and recognized this replica. Cook slowed the engine.

"We know the coordinates of the enemy now," Footman said. "We should leave."

"We could take a closer look," Cook answered. "This boat's got an anchor. How's your swimming these days?"

"I swim well," Footman said, "but I think we should get back to Mr. Socrates."

"I'm the senior officer."

"Leadership was not delineated."

"Delineated?" Cook laughed. "Where'd you learn such fancy words?"

Cook pushed the anchor over the side, tied his shoes together, hung them around his neck and jumped into the water. Footman sighed. Cook had been in the house for the last five years; perhaps he had grown tired of boiling carrots for Mr. Socrates. He knew that the boat wouldn't be easy to find, so Footman followed him moments later.

With his strong strokes he easily caught up with Cook and passed him. The island had a beach and docks that were well lit and well guarded, so they swam around to the north, where rocky crags pushed out of the water. They swam for half an hour. The cold water was beginning to get into his bones, but the tiger and the dragon on his arms would keep him warm. Cook was huffing and puffing; he should have been trained more often.

Footman led Cook to a protruding rock and they clung to it to rest. The tide was at its lowest, the moon bright, showing that the rock walls were almost as smooth as glass. Perhaps they'd even been blasted to make them so smooth. They would be impossible to climb with bare hands.

"Looks like we'll have to go back to the boat," Cook said. "Too bad."

"Wait!" Footman pointed at a dark spot on the wall. "I think there is a cave over there."

They swam several yards until they were just below the mouth of the cave, then climbed up and into it. They had to crouch and crawl alternately to make their way inside. It had been pure luck that they'd seen it, Footman realized. An hour later and the tide would have covered the entrance. He turned on his pocket lucifer and followed the cave thirty or so feet into the island. It gradually sloped up and became drier. In time they came upon a man-made tunnel.

"We will not be able to leave this way when the tide rises," Footman said, wringing the last of the salt water from his shirt-tail.

"Then let's not dilly-dally, mate." Cook was shaking with cold.

Footman climbed a ladder to another tunnel that led to several more tunnels. They chose one to follow, and found that with each step they took it stank more of decay, and of vinegar.

But they continued to work their way towards the surface, covering their noses with their hands.

At the end of one tunnel Cook found a trap door and pushed it up. "Land ahoy," he whispered, poking his head up. Then, after a quick glance around, he crawled out. Footman followed and they both sucked in fresh air.

They were near the cliffs, looking down the island at a massive dock, a line of cannons pointing to the sea.

"They are sixteen-pounders at least," Cook said. "Twelve of them. It would take an armada to storm this place."

The glass building at the centre of the island glowed red, as though it were a living thing. Soldiers were walking to and fro in front of the gates, several pulling wagons of wood and brick. Even in the dead of night there was work to be done.

Footman spotted several huge hounds and guessed that these were the half-mechanical hounds Mr. Socrates had spoken about. One sniff of his or Cook's scent and the hounds would be on them, but the breeze was working in their favour and they were far enough away to be safe.

"Quite the set-up," Cook whispered. "Guns, hounds—I've counted at least a hundred soldiers. If that's the night shift, then it must be like an anthill when the sun rises."

"You talk too much," Footman said.

"I'll keep me smackers closed."

As they explored the island they stayed close to the huge rocks, and were hidden by the surrounding shrubbery. They were about to step around a large rock formation when Footman noticed a cave mouth emitting light. He put his arm back to stop Cook, and peeked around the rim of the cave entrance. Inside, a white-haired man stood at a table, his back to Footman, measuring liquids into several flasks.

Footman knew immediately that this was Dr. Hyde; he'd been briefed on all the enemies they might encounter.

The doctor stood next to a long operating table. And was that an arm lying on it? And a torso? What horror was this?

He poked his head farther around the rock and gasped. Along the back wall were hung half-finished men who looked stitched together. Tall, strong men, their eyes closed. A green fog gathered around them, a gas emitted from several pipes. Footman pulled Cook in front of him so he could see.

"Good Lord," Cook whispered, "let's get the seven hells out of here."

They slowly worked their way back towards the trap door. As he crept along, Footman took a measure of the place. The glass palace was at least a hundred feet tall and two thousand feet long. The logistics of transporting the materials to create it were mind-boggling. The massive dock, with its cranes and airship tower, could resupply the largest of warships. The entire island slanted down towards the dock on the east side so that all armaments could be fired towards the enemy. The cliffs protected them from the west.

Cook led them around the central mountain of rocks, but as they approached the trap door, he stopped. A huge man was sitting on a stone, staring up at the moon. He turned his gaze to Footman and Cook.

"I saw you climb out of this hole," he said. His voice was ragged. "I waited for you to return."

The monster was expressionless, as though his face had frozen. His eyes glimmered with moonlight, but not much else. Footman had never been superstitious, but standing here under the moon he believed he was looking at the undead.

"You are intruders," the thing said.

"Intruders?" Cook said. "We're delivering coal, mate. That's all. We're lost."

The man stood. It was like watching a stone statue move. "No. You are too clever to be one of the soldiers. They all drink of some pacifying tincture. And they wouldn't say 'mate.' Therefore, you are from off-island and an enemy. If you run, the hounds will shred you to pieces. I haven't told anyone you're here. Just get past me and you'll be free."

"So it's a game for you, is it?" Cook asked.

The man nodded. "A momentary entertainment."

Cook gave Footman a glance and raised his eyebrows.

Footman saw the glint of daring in his friend's eyes. "Do not try—"

Cook charged. He lowered his head and butted the man squarely in the chest, a move he had perhaps used in a hundred brawls. The monster lifted him with a huge hand, flipped him over and smashed him head-first against a boulder.

He was clearly dead. Footman never would have dreamed a man as strong as Cook could be swatted down like a fly.

"You are smaller," the creature said. "Perhaps not easier to kill. Please prove entertaining."

Footman had a knife in his pant leg, but knew it would be useless. He reached inside his shirt and let out a small battle cry as he dashed towards his enemy. The man opened his arms as though to embrace him. At the last second, Footman flipped open the pocket lucifer, blinding him. At the same time he leapt to one side and tried to race past. But he wasn't fast enough, and the monster struck him in the ribs a glancing blow that threw Footman several feet. He rolled along the stones, which cut into his skin, and leapt up, ignoring the pain.

Trap door ahead! He measured the distance with his eyes.

The monster pursued him with a bull-like speed. No time to think. He'd be crushed. So he ran past the trap door towards the sound of the crashing waves, the rocks under his feet slick from the mist. He glanced back to see the monster at his heels. His own death at his heels.

Footman ran to the edge of the cliff and dove into the Pacific.

33

OVER THE FALLS

"I'm not going to have to rescue you from drowning, am I?" Octavia asked.

They were north of their camp, staring down from the edge of a small cliff at the river below. There was a waterfall and she would have thought it rather beautiful if she weren't dreading the next step.

This was their first day of what Mr. Socrates had suggested would be weeks of training. They were to cut their way through rough bush using a compass, working as a team. A prize was waiting at the end of the "map" Mr. Socrates had given them. He hadn't said what it would be.

"I'm a much better swimmer than I used to be," Modo said. "Are you just worried about your hair?"

Hair? That was the last thing Octavia was concerned about. She'd tied it back with black ribbon to keep it out of her eyes and hadn't worn a dress since her arrival two days ago—only black military fatigues. A slimming colour, she noted, making her look all the more boyish. Good! She wasn't one of those overdressed plump ladies who spent their lifetimes lounging on velvet chairs. Her accessories were a utilitarian brown belt and a razor-sharp sabre that Tharpa was teaching her how to use.

After a week on a boat and days on a train, it was glorious to be active again, even if it meant tramping through the bush. She preferred city streets, of course.

They had crawled, run and cut their way to this location, only to find the river blocking their way. Going around it might take days and the idea of spending the night out here didn't appeal to her.

"One of us should see if it's deep enough," she said. "I nominate you."

"Ladies first," he said.

"But you're the gentleman."

"You're more a gentleman than me."

"What's that supposed to mean?" It was the closest thing to a joke she'd heard from Modo in weeks. "Well, Modo, if I stick around you're going to talk me to death." With that she stood up, ran and jumped into the air, aiming close to the waterfall. She hoped the water had carved a deep enough well that she wouldn't break her legs! It must be all right— after all, Mr. Socrates wouldn't have sent them here unless it was possible. Halfway down she wondered if she'd made a mistake; maybe they were supposed to use their rope to cross.

The water was shockingly cold and she sank much deeper than she'd expected to; at any moment her legs would strike the bottom and snap like twigs. Instead, she came to a stop and began kicking, climbing for the surface, and was soon splashing in the open water.

"It's toasty warm," she shouted, then swam for the opposite shore as Modo, doing his best impression of a cannon-ball, struck the water nearby. Not the smoothest dive she'd seen. But Modo had only recently learned how to swim.

"You splash around like a mad dog," she said. "You'll scare the beavers, the ducks and the whatnots for miles around." She had taken to swimming in the Thames when she was a street child, but had never enjoyed taking a bath. It wasn't until she became an agent and had her first hot bath that she understood why the aristocrats spent half their lives in bathhouses.

"At least I can float." His wet netting mask clung to his face, showing his deformities and making him look like a sea monster. Despite wishing it could be otherwise, she still shuddered. But she had sworn to herself that she wouldn't show any weakness.

They climbed onto the bank.

"The compass still works," he said.

They made their way up the ravine, following the coordinates Mr. Socrates had provided. Soon they were tramping through the bush again.

"Maybe that was our toughest test," she said.

"Not so loud," Modo replied, "you're snapping every twig."

"I'm going to snap you." But he was right. She could move quietly in the street, but in the forest she wasn't certain where to step. Modo, on the other hand, moved as though born in the forest. He was a peasant's son, after all. Maybe that was it.

"What do you think the point of all this is?" Octavia asked.

"I don't know. Maybe Mr. Socrates just wants us out of his hair. He—wait . . ." Modo grabbed her shoulder and yanked her back a step. He pointed at the ground. "A trap." He lifted a branch of leaves. Below was a hole.

"How did you see it?"

"Fresh leaves on the forest floor alerted me."

"Since when did you become Robin Hood?" she asked.

"Are you Maid Marion?"

"No. I'm always Richard the Lionheart. But I see Mr. Socrates doesn't want this to be just a gallivant around the forest. At least there aren't as many insects and snakes here as Australia."

They took another compass reading and Modo checked his watch. "We're about an hour behind," he said. "We've maybe travelled two miles."

It was the first time they'd been alone in two days, so Octavia decided to bring up a question she'd wanted to ask the day before. "I'm curious, Modo," she began. "How do you feel about the dragoons?"

He shrugged. "I don't completely trust Mr. Socrates' motives. I can't help wondering if there was something else that could have been done besides turning them into soldiers."

"I talked to Ester. She's very happy with her position—says she was made for it, in fact! And she's eager to stick a poker in the eye of the rotters who tortured her."

"But they've been turned into weapons. Again. Oppie wanted to read and become a detective. That's all he wanted when I met him."

"Do you think Mr. Socrates gave them more of the potion?" Saying it made Octavia go cold. The birds seemed to grow quiet. Modo was taking a long time to answer.

"No," he said finally. "I—I think he's made some hard choices for Queen and Country, but he wouldn't do that."

"How can you be sure?"

"Because if he had, he'd have kept every one of the children, not just a dozen of them. Can you imagine fifty dragoons?"

She didn't want to point out that maybe there were other

bases where dragoons were being trained. No, she told herself, Mr. Socrates sometimes had a chunk of ice for a heart, but he wouldn't go that far.

"The dragoons want to hit back at the Clockwork Guild, I have no doubt of that," Modo said. "And they seem to be mature enough to make their own decisions. And . . . wait." He stopped next to a tree. "I hear something. It was like—"

Men in grey uniforms thudded from the trees around them.

Guild soldiers! How'd they find us? Modo blocked a blow, then twisted and threw one soldier against another. Octavia ducked under the club of yet another soldier and struck the man in his midsection. Well, lower than the midsection. He collapsed, and she smiled to herself. They never expect a lady to do that. Octavia was never a lady.

When all of the men were unconscious, Octavia said, "How did they find us?"

Modo peeled away the uniform of one man to find a black shirt. "Our men! Why, they were just posing! I wondered why they had no pistols. This is another part of our training, I see."

"What'll we do with them?"

"Just leave them," Modo replied. "They'll be up and around soon enough."

Following the coordinates they broke through the forest. On a stump of a pine tree in the middle of a clearing they discovered an envelope. Octavia snapped it up. Inside were a pair of tickets. Each said: *This ticket good for one hot bath at the Officer's Tent.*

"So the old man has a sense of humour after all," Modo said, and they burst out laughing.

34

CONTENTMENT UNDER ADVERSE CIRCUMSTANCES

For Modo, a hot bath seemed an indulgence that he could not afford—after all, he needed every moment to perfect his martial skills. But after Octavia said that he smelled like an old dead dog, he found himself in a steam-filled tent, sitting comfortably in a claw-footed tub that looked far too fancy to be out in the middle of the bush. It had probably been used by officers for several years, maybe even Mr. Socrates himself.

He relaxed, letting his face return to its natural shape and his hump protrude. It was his first rest and first proper bath since he'd departed for Paris, a trip that felt as if it were years ago. When was the last time he'd had a hot bath? A year ago? Certainly not on the submarine *Ictíneo*. Or in the jungles of Australia, or on any ships or airships he'd been on. Even in Montreal House the hot water was intermittent.

On a shelf in the bath tent he found a red-covered book called *Roughing It in the Bush*. He flipped through the account of a woman living in the bushland of eastern Canada. He stopped when he read, "IT IS DELIGHTFUL to observe a feeling of contentment under adverse circumstances." He read the sentence several times. It *was* a delight to be in this bath in the middle of Camp Cobra. But should he be partaking of delight?

That was the problem with rest. Any time he stopped to take a breath, thoughts rose up like Macbeth's ghosts. Colette's broken body, her look of joy as she gazed upon his face. Had she been delirious with death? Then he thought of his father, crushed by the same monster. He must avenge their deaths. But Typhon had spared his life.

He remembered the creature's odd look as it showed its pinky finger to him. As though giving a secret signal. His own little finger had tingled. Had a part of his body really brought that monster to life?

He was out of the bath before the water was cold. He dried his bits of red hair and stared in the mirror for several moments. He hadn't looked in a mirror for ages. He examined his face, tracing the sunken nose and lopsided features. It wasn't as ugly as he remembered. In fact he thought he saw a hint of distinction. He laughed at himself and slipped the mask on. Distinguished or not, it'd scare the living daylights out of the soldiers.

Despite Mr. Socrates' promise that he could walk around unmasked here, he didn't want to test it.

He dressed and returned to his tent in the centre of Camp Cobra. He presumed the name was a reference was to a trained cobra coming out of a basket. It was curious how military men chose the toughest, most frightening names for their ships and their camps, but often named their guns after girls.

The battle cry of the dragoons startled him. He walked over the hill where he could see that a training course had been set up overnight, complete with coils of thorny wire and mud holes, and a fifty-foot wooden climbing wall. The dragoons stood in formation across from it, about to conduct their first charge.

"Boys and their toys," Octavia said.

She'd snuck up on him! He needed to be more alert.

"A tough course," he told her, hoping his voice hadn't given away his surprise. "I'm curious how they'll do."

The dragoons began to clank ahead, forcing their way through snapping wires. One stepped into a mud hole and had to struggle to extricate himself, but the others charged on, yelling in unison. The mysterious cacophony made Modo stiffen, even though they were charging away from him. There was something about the noise that reminded him of the horrible potions the children had ingested. He shuddered to recall how they'd looked strapped to the iron giant and attacking the Parliament Building. Absolutely monstrous.

"I just know Mr. S is going to want us to run through all that muck, too," Octavia said. "He enjoys seeing me suffer."

"If he really wants you to suffer he'll make you wear a dress while you do it."

He found it difficult to keep his eyes off her while she was wearing the Permanent Association uniform. When she caught him staring at her, he glanced away and said, "The wall will be the real test for them."

As the squadron moved on, their arrowhead formation remained intact. The first dragoon climbed the wall, using iron fingers to grip the wooden slats. Holes had been cut into the wall and soldiers were shoving large posts through them, slamming them into the armoured man. He clung to the wall, continuing his ascent. A second dragoon climbed and a third followed, the rest firing above their heads. Live rounds! They were practising covering fire, blowing the heads off dummies at the top of the wall.

"This is what Odysseus must have felt first looking upon the cyclops Polyphemus," Modo said.

"Good Lord, you are so full of fantastical bosh, sometimes. Stop quoting mythology as if it were real life."

"It was an observation. This is a quote: 'He was a horrid creature, not like a human being at all, but resembling rather some crag that stands out boldly against the sky on the top of a high mountain.' That's the first description of the cyclops."

She put her hands on her hips. "It's a good thing Mr. Socrates raised you in the country. You'd have been pummelled senseless at my orphanage."

He was searching for a retort when the engine on a dragoon near the top of the wall made a loud *bang*. The dragoon fell forty feet to the mud and began to sink. Association soldiers swarmed around him within seconds, but they couldn't pull him up.

Modo dashed to the dragoon's side. The man was struggling, face sunk into the mud, and would soon drown. Modo grabbed a metal-encased arm and, grunting hard, helped pull him to a sitting position. His nose and mouth were plugged up with sludge and straw, but he couldn't use his metal hands to clear it. He began flailing his metal arms in panic.

"Stay calm!" the sergeant shouted. He ducked under the arms and pulled soil and mud from the man's nose and mouth, and finally the dragoon was able to suck in a breath. Then he took another and another, wheezing and coughing repeatedly.

"Now, now, calm down."

Modo realized the dragoon wasn't even a man, but Ester.

Her face was hardened and chiseled like a man's from the effects of the tincture. Tears ran down her cheeks.

"Now, now," the sergeant repeated, his voice soothing, and he actually patted her cheek. "Calm down, Lance Corporal McGravin. Calm down. That's an order."

"I—I will, Sergeant," she said. She gritted her teeth.

"Are you injured?"

"Yes, Sergeant." She nodded down towards her right arm.

He delicately removed a steel plate and they could clearly see that the bone below her shoulder was broken.

"It's not so bad, Lance Corporal," Sergeant Beatty said. "We'll fix you up. Now, get on your feet, unless your legs are hurt."

"They aren't, Sergeant." She slowly stood, and everyone took a few steps back because she was wobbling on her feet.

"Report to the medical tent. Sawbones will put you back together."

She lumbered away, carrying her helmet in the crook of her good arm.

"Form ranks!" the sergeant shouted, nearly rupturing Modo's eardrum. "Resume your positions!"

Modo ran back up the hill to Octavia. "Will Ester be all right?"

Modo nodded. "She's certainly tough as nails."

He and Octavia watched the drill for another hour, until lunch was served. By then Modo was famished. He made his way to the mess tent; it was already crowded with the enormous dragoons, each with special sections cut out of their uniforms for their shoulder bolts. They were talking jovially. Even Ester was at a table, a metal brace on her arm. Modo wondered if the tincture made them more immune to pain. Did they heal faster, too?

He stood in line and received the same grey food they'd

had for breakfast, lunch and dinner. Modo took a seat beside Oppie.

"Mr. W," he said. "Pleasure to have your company."

"Please, just Modo. I don't have a surname."

"One name is all you need?" Oppie was quickly eating his food. "You travel light."

"I guess you could say that." Modo's eyes strayed to Oppie's nearest shoulder bolt. He tried not to stare at it.

"I've learned to read, a bit," Oppie said. "I remember you telling me to learn. Sergeant Beatty reads to us at night. He teaches us the words."

"He sounds like a good man. What do you read?"

"Oh, I can't read much on me—*my* own," he admitted. "Just fairy tales and some of *Alice's Adventures in Wonderland*."

"Good!" Modo rubbed his hands together. "I love that book!" And then he quoted: "'I almost wish I hadn't gone down that rabbit-hole—and yet—and yet—it's rather curious, you know, this sort of life! I do wonder what *can* have happened to me! When I used to read fairy-tales, I fancied that kind of thing never happened, and now here I am in the middle of one!'" Modo laughed, a little embarrassed for having let his performance get away on him.

"Yes, that's it!" Oppie said, excited. "You know it by heart!"

"Just that speech and a few others; I'm extremely fond of the book."

"Sergeant Beatty will be reading the last chapter to us tonight. It's good for us to learn to read. It helps with tactics and the manuals they give us."

Modo raised an eyebrow. They were being read to like children at bedtime, then trained to kill in the morning. They really had gone down the rabbit hole.

"How do you feel about your training?" he asked quietly. "About being here?"

Oppie's eyes narrowed. "It's a good place. I love being part of the 7th Dragoons. We're the Lucky Sevens! They feed us. And if I get a chance to strike back at the Guild I'll be happy."

"Is that all this is about?" Modo asked.

Oppie's eyes were fierce. It was hard for Modo to remember the child Oppie had been only a year earlier.

"Have you had your flesh cut into, your childhood plucked out?" Oppie asked. Modo nearly answered that he had. "Where else do I go? The army has given me a home, companions and a purpose. I'll destroy the ones who created me. Destroy them." He jabbed the fork into the table. A few dragoons glanced their way.

Perhaps Oppie hadn't completely grown up, Modo thought. "Did you ever see your parents again?"

"Yes." At this Oppie's eyes grew gentle again. "My dad died. My mum, she tried to care for me, but she didn't know what to do. I wasn't *Little Oppie,* any more. I broke things. And outgrew my clothes so quickly. She was given money."

"Money?"

"Yes. For her to live and to look after my sister, or my brother, I don't know which the stork brought."

"I see," Modo said. "Was she paid for her silence?"

"Paid to tell others I'd run away. Paid compensation for the loss of my wages. I understand. Me being here keeps my family in bread, keeps a roof over their heads." He looked down at Modo. "Your questions . . . bother me. You think I'm the boy that you once knew. I am. But I'm not. I have grown up. I've found a place where I belong."

"I'm happy for you, Oppie," Modo said. But . . . was that the truth?

It was complicated. Part of Modo felt that what these children had been twisted into was horrible. And yet, without these monstrous men there was no chance of defeating the Clockwork Guild, not to mention rescuing his mother.

My mother, Modo thought. My. Mother.

Perhaps he too had gone down the rabbit hole.

35

A PECULIAR BOAT WITH A PECULIAR CARGO

It was a dark, cold and stupid night, according to Sergeant Booker. Stupid, he thought, because he had lost his day patrol shift in a card game and was now in the observation tower on Macaulay Point, swinging the port light back and forth across the empty waters, shivering and staring out at the Pacific; the perfect, natural harbour of Esquimalt stretched out before him.

It wasn't like there was anyone who would attack the home base of the British Navy's Pacific Squadron. They had enough six-pounder guns to ward off the Russians, if they had a fleet worth considering. And the Chinese were in stone-age junks. Laughable, really. In any case, Britain already controlled the Chinese. The Americans, now they might make noise. He had been eye to eye with the Americans during the San Juan Islands Pig War, but they hadn't shown any sign of aggression for twenty years now.

It began to spit rain, so it was now a useless, stupid, *wet* night. No one would be entering their harbour tonight.

Which was why he was stunned to see a motored boat enter the bay and begin to circle in the open water. It was a type of craft he hadn't seen before, and there was no captain at the helm! He rang the warning bell and seven marines appeared within a minute.

"Gloucester, you take the light, keep it on the boat," he commanded. "The rest of you come with me. Let's see who our visitor is."

He climbed into a rowboat and stood at the stern as four marines rowed and two pointed their rifles at the target. The mysterious boat circled, slower and slower, and the motor gurgled as though it would die at any moment.

"Ahoy, there!" Booker shouted. "Stop your engines! Ahoy!"

The craft continued on. It took some hard rowing, but they were soon able to pull up to it, close enough to jump. Booker was the first over. The fumes were strong, thanks to the coal that burned in the smallest steam engine he'd ever seen.

Lying across the bottom of the boat was a Chinese man, his breathing laboured. He opened his eyes and said, "T— take my sock rates."

"What?" Booker said. "Speak English, man! What was that?"

"Mr. Socrates," the man said. "Take me to him. I am his footman."

36

ELEMENT OF SURPRISE

Octavia awoke and looked at the clock in her tent. A quarter of six exactly. After two days of heavy training her muscles ached. Tonight she would turn in her ticket and take her bath, an hour of heaven that would keep her going through another day of sabre fights, body throws, calisthenics and long runs.

A soldier stepped into her tent without knocking. "Report to Mr. Socrates' tent at zero-six-hundred hours." He turned and marched out.

"Good morning to you, too, bufflehead," she said.

It wasn't shocking to have him enter unannounced. She was considered a regular member of the Association forces and the soldiers only knocked if a tent belonged to a commissioned officer. She'd learned to dress quickly. She'd been sleeping in her uniform for the last few days anyway, to save time. She dropped to the ground and did twenty-five push-ups and when she was done her brain was fully awake. All the hand-to-hand combat training with Tharpa had sharpened her skills; several times she'd taken down Association soldiers, to their great surprise and embarrassment.

"I'm a real prizefighter," she told herself. "A slasher, no less."

At a minute before six-hundred hours she crossed to her master's tent. It was four times the size of her own and bright with oil lamps. Mr. Socrates sat at a table, maps spread across it. Tharpa was there, too, with Modo sitting across from him in his Association uniform and his black mask. Anticipation shone in his eyes.

The she recognized the man sitting beside Mr. Socrates: Footman! She had only ever seen him answering the door or serving food at the many Association safe houses, but here he was, at Camp Cobra! All this time that he'd been fetching tea and answering the door, he'd actually been one of Mr. Socrates' agents. Footman's arm was in a sling, his face bruised, and he looked like he hadn't eaten for days. Tharpa set a cup of tea in front of him.

"So, last to the table, Octavia," Mr. Socrates said.

"Fashionably late, sir," she said. "It's a woman's prerogative."

"But not a soldier's. Please have a seat." He waited until she had done so. "As you can see, Footman has returned. He's brought valuable intelligence about the Clockwork Guild. He and Cook even managed to steal one of their *Triton* boats."

So Cook was an agent, too? How could someone so good with pastry and beef also be an agent? What next? Mrs. Finchley proclaimed as the true master of the Permanent Association? "Where is Cook?" Octavia asked.

"He's dead," Mr. Socrates said matter-of-factly, "We'll get to the events that led to his death in a moment."

Octavia felt her chest tighten and she exchanged glances with Modo. With his mask on it was hard to read his reaction. She had been so fond of Cook.

"Footman has provided us with the exact location of the Clockwork Guild's island." He tapped the map with his finger indicating what looked like open water in the Pacific.

She noted that it was northwest of Hawaii, the only islands she recognized on the map. "They've been hiding there all this time, building up their armaments. They have even assembled a replica of the Crystal Palace and use it as the centre of their operations."

"Why the 'Crystal Palace'?" Modo asked. "They hate all things British."

"There must be some symbolic message for us in that choice, but it doesn't matter. What does matter is that we've uncovered the fact that the Guild is very close to completing three massive warships, even larger than the *Wyvern*. With those ships manned and armed the Guild would become very difficult to defeat. Footman also discovered that they seem to be working on what I can only describe as a horrible cadaver project; our fears about another Typhon were correct. Footman, please tell them what you saw."

Footman nodded. "Bodies. We discovered a laboratory with many bodies. And Dr. Hyde was sewing them together."

"You mean dissecting them, don't you?" Modo asked.

"No. Reconstructing them. Later on we had to fight one of those dead men. He killed Cook, and broke my ribs and arm."

"What Footman's describing is an encounter with Typhon or another creature," Mr. Socrates said. "They have somehow animated the dead. Neither Footman nor Cook could injure him. The Clockwork Guild's science in this realm is well beyond our own. If they're creating more Typhons, then that would be a powerful advantage in any battle. Imagine ten Typhons leading an infantry charge." He let this image sink in. "Remember, Modo, what his name means? Typhon was the father of all monsters in Greek mythology. This is a message to us from the Guild."

Mr. Socrates stopped to sip his tea. His hand was steady as he set the cup down. Octavia thought he even looked younger—he loved this part of his life!

"We must strike now, before those ships arrive." He looked around the table, gauging everyone's reaction.

Octavia remained solemn and unreadable. She liked sneaking in and out of houses or alleys, but full-force attacks on enemy islands were not on her list of enjoyable activities.

"Footman's keen eye has taken a measure of their island," Mr. Socrates said. "Through the night I designed a map with details of their defences." He unfolded another small map, this one drawn in ink. It looked rather messy to Octavia. "Here is the palace; below it, the port, well guarded by guns. There is an observation tower here along with an airship dock. Tall cliffs on the three other sides of the island make it unassailable from those directions. But Footman discovered water caves in the cliffs that took them to the surface. They may even lead into the fortress."

"The dragoons are too big for the tunnels," Footman pointed out.

"Yes, but they're designed for a frontal assault. The number of guns will make it a very difficult task."

"With the full strength of the British Navy behind us," Modo said, "it shouldn't be so difficult."

"We'll not have the full force of the navy," Mr. Socrates said. "We are a small but elite force. And we'll have the element of surprise on our side."

"I do hope that we'll have more than surprise," Octavia said. "Maybe a few howitzers. Just a suggestion."

"We'll have plenty enough military muscle," Mr. Socrates said. "Trust me when I say that a full frontal assault with the navy would require months of planning, requisition forms and having to convince certain implacable admirals. If only Lord Nelson were still with us. There was a man who could make quick decisions." He paused and pointed at the map. "If we strike now we can destroy them with one blow. If we wait, they could get wind of our plans, pack up their island and slither away."

"But what is the plan?" Modo asked.

"It will be unveiled the night of the invasion. Until then, only I will know what it is."

"And when will the invasion begin?" Octavia asked.

"We leave tomorrow night."

So soon! she wanted to shout. How could they possibly organize troops and armaments and supplies?

She looked at Modo to see how he was taking all this. His eyes shone with excitement.

37

ABOARD THE HMS SHAH

Early morning fog stretched its tendrils across the docks of Esquimalt and seemed to reach right inside Modo, through his clothes, under his mask, making him shiver. He and Octavia would be the last in line to board the HMS *Shah*. Ahead of them on the gangplank were the twelve dragoons in their green uniforms, their hair cut short, kit bags hanging from their arms. They were led by their sergeant and followed by twenty Association soldiers, bayonetted rifles slung across their backs.

Not a bugle or a drum was heard. In fact the base seemed deserted. Everyone but the necessary seamen and soldiers had been ordered to their quarters. It was, after all, a secret mission.

Mr. Socrates was on deck beside the captain, watching the arrival of his troops. The armoured suits were being hauled up by crane and placed on the deck under Tharpa's supervision. And there were marines already on board, lined up to silently welcome their comrades-in-arms. Modo guessed that Mr. Socrates needed some extra muscle and marksmanship. Several marines looked stunned at the size of the dragoons.

"There are fifty of us," Octavia said.

Modo counted quickly. "You're right. Plus the sailors, of course. Fifty against . . . what? Three hundred Guild soldiers? How many mechanical hounds?"

"Ten at least," she said, "and there's Typhon, and it sounds like there are more creatures just like him."

"They'll have airships and those *Triton* boats. Imagine those with cannons."

"It's quite a list. Are you nervous?" Octavia asked.

"No," he lied, adding, "I'm eager." That, at least, was the truth. He desperately wanted to get there. He must strike back at the Guild, rescue his mother. Or, if it was too late, exact revenge.

They were given officers' cabins. The HMS *Shah* began to shudder, a whale awaking from slumber, as they unpacked.

They travelled without stopping, four days and nights of steaming southwest, the air growing hotter and more humid, so that by the third day Modo wished he were dressed in tropical khaki, not the damnably hot black uniform.

They trained on the deck every day, soldiers running back and forth, doing their best to march and drill, and three times a day they ate the grey gruel. And still Mr. Socrates gave no hint of his plans. Modo began to wonder if there was any sort of strategy at all, other than a full frontal assault? How many of them would live through that?

On the fourth evening a command was shouted along the deck and lights were put out. Not even a cigarette could be seen. All was silent, except for the clanking and creaking of the ship. The thudding of the steam engines far below echoed like war drums.

He met Octavia at the bow and stood staring into the dark. The breeze was cooling, and he wished he could lift his mask to feel it full upon his face. It was far warmer here than in London at this time of year. Several sailors were manning the guns. He braced himself for flares, cannon fire, and explosions to light up the sky.

But nothing happened and an hour passed as he and Octavia stared forward at the dark ocean and their dubious futures. At some point he realized she was holding his hand. He didn't remember when she had taken it, but he held tight and wished for this moment to never end.

"Do you think we'll still be alive tomorrow?" she asked quietly, with more seriousness than he'd ever heard in her voice.

"Yes," Modo said, trying to sound as confident as possible.

"How can you be certain?"

"I guess you won't get to tell me that I was wrong." He let out a forced laugh.

"I feel as though I've known you my whole life, Modo," Octavia whispered. "Somehow I was meant to know you. We are supposed to be standing here together, right now. Do you believe that?"

"I don't know. Fate is . . . it's not rational."

"Well, feelings aren't rational. So what! It's a feeling I happen to have. That I was meant to know you. To be your friend."

"Friend?" he asked.

"We are more than friends, Modo. You know what I mean."

No, he didn't, actually. Once again she was speaking in

riddles. He looked away from her. "Don't talk as if we're about to die. It's bad luck."

"You don't believe in luck, Modo."

"I don't. Nor do I want to think about our deaths or about life beyond tomorrow. I only want to think about our duty."

"And what is our duty? Queen and Country?"

"To Colette's memory. To my mother. To put an end to this Guild once and for all."

Her hand tightened on his. "But, what's the point if we don't succeed?"

"We have to."

The engine noise rumbled, then stopped, but the *Shah* was still moving. The masts creaked above them.

"We've switched to sails," Modo said. He took a deep breath in an effort to calm his now-racing heart.

"We are closing in on our destination," Mr. Socrates said from behind them. Modo quickly released Octavia's hand. "Come and receive your orders."

They followed him to a cabin, passing the dragoons who were getting into their armour with the help of the Association soldiers. They looked like black ants scurrying around wasps.

It was a small cabin lit by a single lamp. The porthole was covered with black cloth. "Quick, the door," Mr. Socrates said.

Modo shut it.

Their master handed them two maps: one of the island, the second of a series of tunnels. "Memorize these," he said. After they had both studied the images he took them back. "You two will have tasks that best suit your skill sets," he explained, pointing at the tunnel map. "While the dragoons attack, you'll be entering the sea cave. By my calculations the tides will be at a sufficiently low level by 4 a.m., an hour from now. If possible, you'll first free Madame Hébert. Given how valuable she is to their experiments, my best guess is that she's in the cave near the centre of the island. Hand her over as soon as possible to the protection of the Association soldiers."

"And what's the other assignment?" Modo asked.

"To capture the master of the Guild. It will be a tricky job, since a full-out battle will be underway."

"Assuming we can find him, that is."

"Assuming he's a man," Octavia pointed out. "He could be a woman."

"Perhaps," Mr. Socrates said, "but doubtful. If it's unworkable for you to take him prisoner, then I expect you to eliminate him."

"Kill him?"

"This isn't a game, Modo. This is how our business is done. If he escapes, then many more Britons will die, perhaps thousands." The ship shuddered to a stop. "The *Shah* has orders to begin shelling the island at sunrise, which will be 6 a.m. Or earlier if targets become clearly visible. You'll have to work fast." He paused. "We have arrived. Prepare yourselves."

He flicked off the light and opened the door to the dark.

38

SOUNDING THE ALARM

It was only chance and sleeplessness that had taken Miss Hakkandottir to the docks so late that night. She had traversed the island and was now standing at the end of the pier looking out at the Pacific. She had just visited Dr. Hyde, still hard at work on his creations.

They were ugly creatures; it was an ugly business, but necessary. She still did not understand the intentions of the Guild Master, but she felt better when she walked. And her presence kept the soldiers alert. She'd caught one guard sleeping and dealt him such a blow with her metal hand that he was now in the medical tent. That would keep the rest of them on their toes.

She missed the *Wyvern* and how strong she'd felt standing on the deck of such an incredible warship. It had been a part of her, and when it went down she felt that part of her sink into the ocean, too. The airship *Hera* had been another part of her, almost like her metal hand. She had failed far too many times.

The Crystal Palace glowed dimly behind her. The Guild Master would still be working. It was nighttime here but it would be daytime in other countries. He had myriad agents around the world who reported to him.

She stroked Grace's large skull. The mechanical hound was silent because she had no vocal cords, a design of the good Dr. Hyde. Grace had been a valuable companion for years now. The dog made that familiar clicking sound from the back of her throat that meant she was happy.

"Yes, you always stand with me," Miss Hakkandottir said.

She stared at the dark horizon. How much of her life had been spent as a pirate on those waters? That had been her first introduction to the Guild Master. Even then he'd had no name. She would work hard to get into his good graces again. Then she laughed. "Good graces?" she said. "And you are my good Grace."

The dog clicked in agreement, then lifted her ears and looked towards the west. She made a rasping sound, as close to a bark as she could get.

"What do you hear, Grace?"

A moment later Miss Hakkandottir heard something too, a distant droning. It was not familiar, though sometimes she discerned a mechanical whine. There were no shipments that she knew of arriving at this hour.

She saw the bow of a craft glinting in the moonlight a fair distance away. Behind it were two other boats. She squinted. They were square-shaped boats with gates at the front. British flags flapped in the moonlight.

"Sound the alarm!" she shouted, and sprinted back across the dock, Grace pounding the boards beside her. "Now! Sound the alarm!"

Klaxons began to scream. Guild soldiers took their positions, and orders were shouted as bright electric lights came to life, pointing out to sea. She raced up the circular stairs to the top of the observation tower and watched the boats draw closer. The clear outline of helmeted heads. Soldiers! Rifles on their shoulders.

"Fire!" she hollered. "Fire, now!"

The field guns let loose their first volleys—*boom, boom, boom!* The sound shook the very tower itself but it was not easy to bring the big fourteen-pounders to bear on moving targets, and the shots landed well past the boats. The enemy gained speed as they approached, engines buzzing like wasps. The first craft hit the shore and skidded several feet onto the beach. Someone jumped off the back and began swimming out to sea.

The gate of the boat dropped open. The Guild soldiers, who had gathered along their trenches, fired. The enemy was standing in the boat, guns at the ready but not charging her men. No matter how many shots they fired, the enemy didn't fall but rocked back and forth, taking hits here and there. Helmets flew off and still they just stood in the harrowing fire.

Then it dawned on her. They were dummies! At that same moment the second boat struck next to a stanchion on the pier. The third landed near the base of the observation tower. The gates flipped open and more dummies were revealed.

"Cease fire!" she shouted. "Cease fire!"

It took a full minute before her orders were relayed. When they finally stopped firing, all she could hear was the ringing in her ears from the booming of the big guns. The dummies continued to sway, many of them torn in two by rifle fire. What did all this mean?

"Board the vessels!" she commanded.

A group of six Guild soldiers approached the first of the landing craft.

The boat exploded, sending a cloud of shrapnel through

the approaching soldiers, knocking them into the sand. Then the second boat blew up. She watched in disbelief as the pillar on the pier was smashed to pieces. The third boat, which had beached itself directly below the observation tower, burst into flames like a giant Roman candle.

The tower she stood on began to sway gently and then, as though tired, it gave way.

39

THE ISLAND ASSAULT

Modo sat in a boat that was cutting silently through the waves. He shivered when he heard the cannon fire begin. They were approaching the opposite, rocky cliffs of the island. Octavia put her hand on his shoulder; it was comforting to feel her touch at that moment. Each boom seemed to shake the island; it certainly shook his confidence. He'd heard smaller cannons before, but these ones sounded like hammers of the gods.

The operation was underway and there was no turning back. To his left and right were six other boats, each transporting Association soldiers and the fully armoured dragoons, metal glinting in the moonlight. He was glad for his mask, so none of the other soldiers or Octavia would know how frightened he was. As for them, their grim faces seemed carved in stone. The soldiers were silent but for the occasional hissed command. The boats were surprisingly silent, magically gliding along thanks to their electric engines. "A trick we stole from your friends in the *Ictíneo*," Mr. Socrates had explained. "Electric boats provide a swift, inaudible attack."

With all the rifle fire and cannons going off at the docks, no one would hear the slight humming of the boats from such a distance away. As they approached, no alarms sounded on this side of the island. It seemed deserted above them. Had the attack on the docks drawn all the sentries to the battle? One could only hope.

At the moment his master would be back on the deck of the HMS *Shah,* watching the mission unfold through his spyglass. Tharpa would be at his side. Modo wished Tharpa were going into battle alongside him. Maybe he'd feel more confident. He patted himself to be sure his Colt pocket revolver was in its holster and his knife still in its sheath.

They glided right up to the rocky cliffs, fully a hundred feet tall, slick with spray, unassailable by ordinary men. Even Modo, an expert and natural climber, wouldn't risk it. But given what he'd seen of the dragoons, he was fairly certain they could ascend the rocks with little difficulty.

"Do you see any caves?" Octavia whispered. "Footman said they'd be on this side."

"It's a big island."

He squinted, wishing for a bit more moonlight. No cave that he could see. It was so dark it'd be difficult to find it.

"The entrance is here somewhere," he said. "We just have to keep searching."

Modo watched as the dragoons stood in their boats, reached up and found holds with their metal hands, then began to scale the cliffs. One by one, they climbed like insects. It was a glorious sight, seeing them move in perfect unison. Mr. Socrates had long ago spoken theoretically about soldiers in mechanized suits of armour, and now here they were as promised, and about to strike the Clockwork Guild.

Several stones hit the water and they looked up to see

that a dragoon was hanging by one arm, scrambling for another handhold. Moments later he plummeted and, without so much as a squawk, splashed into the ocean and sank.

There was no rescue attempt, not even a pause in the operation.

"Could it be Ester?" Octavia said. "Or Oppie?"

"We won't know until later," Modo said, surprised at how steady his voice sounded.

The lead dragoons were already reaching the summit. He expected them to be pushed back, but the last of them reached the top without incident. The cannons went on booming. Ropes were lowered and Sergeant Beatty and the remaining Association soldiers climbed up.

"I do wish we were going with them," Modo said. "I don't much like crawling into holes."

"I'm part sewer rat!" Octavia said. "Anyway we'd better find this cave quickly!" She flicked on her pocket lucifer.

"Put that out!" Modo hissed.

"If no one saw the dragoons, no one'll notice us."

Modo took out his own light and shone the beam on the rock walls. After a few minutes, he spotted a hole, barely large enough for a grown man. "There it is!"

"You climb up first, since you're part monkey," Octavia said.

He directed the sailor to manoeuvre the boat closer, then jumped up, grabbing at the lip of the cave. It took some effort but he climbed in and lowered a short rope. Octavia was soon beside him and they pulled out their compasses.

They crouched and crab-walked their way deeper into the cave. At times Modo had to squeeze his shoulders together to shove himself through narrow passages. Thankfully the tunnel eventually widened. When he slipped and splashed into a pool of water, he kicked and found the floor, then carried on, pushing against the water, holding his pocket lucifer high.

"It's deep," he said. "Be careful."

"Yes, sir," Octavia answered, splashing in behind him.

It wasn't long before the map they'd memorized became useless. There were several fresh tunnels, which only seemed to confuse them both. In time they found themselves in a small chamber surrounded by numerous openings. A smidgen of light could be seen at the end of a few of the tunnels.

"This way," Octavia whispered, pointing at one of the partially lit openings.

"Are you certain?"

"Yes."

They followed the tunnel to a dead end where a ladder was fastened to the stone wall. The light source was somewhere above them. Modo climbed up first. Footman had warned them of the stench but it was beyond anything Modo had imagined: a mix of carcasses and sulphur and other foul odours. The higher he climbed the worse it stank. He was close to retching, so when he reached the top he covered his nose and mouth with one hand, and helped Octavia up with the other. When she emerged she took a deep breath like she needed a gulp of fresh air. Modo wrinkled his nose in disgust.

"How can you stand the stench?" he asked.

"Oh, no worse than the cabbage soup the headmistress used to feed us every day," Octavia joked, but she looked pale.

There was a sputtering lamp above them. The tunnel in front of them was partially collapsed, but his lucifer light revealed enough room for them to squeeze through.

Octavia glanced at her compass. "That tunnel goes west towards the beach. The cave that we're supposed to be entering is in that direction."

"Then let's take it, but we'll have to do it in the dark," he said.

They both put out their lights, but after a minute, Octavia flicked hers back on.

"This is madness, Modo. We could fall into a pit or be sucked into slime. I won't look good dead, Modo."

"That's for certain," he said glibly, and then an image of Colette flashed through his mind, how she'd looked after her death. He didn't want to so much as imagine losing Octavia that way.

He flicked on his light and led the way. With each step the air grew colder, as though they were walking into winter. The stink was subsiding. When they reached a chamber lit by gaslight, he peeked around the corner. No one around— but along the wall were stacks of crates. Modo and Octavia crept into the room, shivering. Big square chunks of ice stuck out of a blanket of straw. The crates were labelled with Roman numerals.

"Do we dare look inside?" Octavia asked.

"What would they keep at such a blood-numbing temperature?" he wondered aloud as he lifted the lid on a small crate. The wood creaked as Modo worked it back and forth till it finally popped off. He grimaced and Octavia clutched her chest.

There, looking up at them, were about fifty eyeballs, each neatly tucked into felt holders like they were eggs. They could only be human eyes, plucked out and waiting for . . . for what? He quickly closed the lid.

"Well, that's me done," he said. "I certainly don't intend to look in any more crates."

"I'm with you," Octavia said, her own eyes wide and uncertain.

They crept out and along another tunnel. Once again a putrid smell assaulted their noses. He paused at the entrance of the next chamber and motioned Octavia to stay still. He could hear shuffling, and when he peeked around the rock he saw men in white coats setting down a crate. Then they got into a lift. One pressed a button and they ascended silently.

Modo cautiously entered the chamber. The room was humid and he began to sweat, drops running down into his mask, his eyes burning. In the middle were two vast brass cauldrons boiling over a coal fire. Glass tubes led from one to the other, a blood-red substance inside. He peeked over the edge of a cauldron and saw a burbling red liquid with pinkish streaks. It smelled horrible.

"That's definitely worse than boiled cabbage," Octavia said.

"I can't imagine its purpose."

"Best not to."

A grating noise came from behind them. They turned to see the lift was on its way down, and quickly hid behind a stack of barrels along the wall.

A man stepped out of the lift, his back to them, and began to pick ice from the top of a barrel and crunch it in his mouth. Modo signalled to Octavia his intention, counted to three using his fingers, then leapt. She jumped at the same time.

But as Modo flew through the air, the man pivoted, gave a glittering metal smile and darted out of the way. Lime!

He stopped some distance away and turned. "So, a couple of Alices have tumbled down the rabbit hole." He drew long knives and waved them. "I came down here to escape the booming booms. *Boom boom boom.* I'm not much of a military man. A little too noisy for my taste."

"You're hiding, you mean," Modo said.

"I'm being selectively brave. And thank you for making an appearance. I'm happy to have you to entertain me."

Modo triumphantly drew his pistol and was pleased to see Lime stop smiling. Aiming to wound, he pulled the trigger. All he got in reply was a *click* of the hammer. He pulled it again and again. The gun was dripping water.

"Ah, so grievously sad," Lime said, taking a step towards them, twirling his blades. *"One, two! One, two! And through and through / The vorpal blade went snicker-snack."*

40

APPLAUDING THE DESIGNER

By the time Oppie and the other dragoons had crested the top of the cliff, there were only eleven of them and a small team of regular soldiers. The noise of their ascent had been covered by the gun battle on the beaches, but now the guns had stopped firing.

"Form ranks!" Sergeant Beatty commanded, and they split into two groups.

At that moment Oppie knew for certain that Edmund had been the one who'd drowned, as he'd always been on Oppie's left in his squadron. A horrible way to go. He'd miss him; they'd played with toys together in those first months at a place called Ravenscroft. Then later, when they'd been shipped to Esquimalt, they'd played with guns and axes.

"Squadron A, take the point! Full speed!" Beatty commanded.

Ester's squadron chugged forward, their mechanized arms and legs hissing. Oppie was in the second group of five, bringing up the rear. He pushed all thoughts of Edmund from his mind.

This is what he had trained for! The crimes of Oppie's

enemies had grown and festered in his heart since the day they'd kidnapped him as a boy. How he had been longing for this moment! And now that it was here, oddly, he found himself thinking of his mother: her face before him.

Such thoughts would only cloud his mind. He banished them.

"Squadron B! Forward! March!" His troop pounded down the path towards the beach, hundreds of yards away. The beach was lit in such a way that he could clearly see a redheaded woman waving her arms, directing the Guild soldiers. Miss Hakkandottir! He had seen her when he was a child. Her face was burned in his memory.

Silencing the massive field guns was their first objective. Ester's troop had almost reached them. The Guild soldiers tried to hold their position, but their lines were split in two by the juggernauts.

His squadron began their charge, but Oppie slowed down as they passed the glowing mouth of a cave. Inside, an old man with stringy, long white hair was watching the unfolding battle. Ah yes, Dr. Hyde.

"Sergeant Beatty!" Oppie yelled, but his sergeant was out of earshot and Oppie was at the rear of the squadron. Oppie brought himself to a stop, motor burning, steam hissing, his chest heaving as there was more than a little exertion required on his part to keep his armour in motion. One of his squadron's objectives was to capture the doctor. He'd do his best not to kill him in the process.

The doctor was much smaller and older than Oppie remembered. He was a child when this man had forced his tinctures on him. He didn't give his fellow soldiers a glance; they would be able to take the beach.

Dr. Hyde met his gaze and then his eyes took in the spectacle of Oppie's armour. "You are beautiful," the old man said. "You are so very beautiful."

It had been a lifetime since this man had administered Oppie the potion and promised him he'd become something extraordinary. "You don't recognize me?" he said, flipping back a section of armour protecting his shoulder.

The doctor looked at the bolt that protruded from Oppie's shoulder. "Your bolt. Shoulder bolts! I . . . remember . . . you are mine."

"Yes," Oppie said. "I am yours. Your creation. And I have come for you."

One blow and he could crush the old sawbones into pieces. How easy and satisfying—destroy the old man as he had destroyed Oppie. But his orders had been to capture, not kill.

"Come with me," he said.

"Young man," replied Dr. Hyde, "I cannot leave my work. It is the most important work of all. And it is very nearly done."

"I have orders. I must follow them."

He grabbed the doctor's shoulder with his iron hand, which moved as though it were his real hand. He had worked so hard to perfect it, had practised picking up eggs without breaking them.

The doctor looked at Oppie's metal hand, examining all the gears. "Marvellous work," he said. "I can see how it can be improved, but still I applaud your designer."

"You'll meet him soon enough."

"I cannot leave. My creations wait for me. They are close to life. It has been so very good to see you again."

"You will—"

Then, without warning, Oppie found himself flying sideways and the doctor slipped out of his hand. He rolled, the armour protecting him from breaking his back on the stones. Standing up quickly, his pistons whining, he turned to face his enemy.

A massive man stood before him as the doctor limped slowly back into the cave.

"My master requested your departure," Typhon grunted.

They had been warned about this man, too. But he was larger than Oppie had imagined—nearly as big as Oppie. His skin had a mottled greenish pallor that seemed to glow in the moonlight. Their orders had been to destroy him.

Oppie unsnapped the axe from his back and charged.

41

ONE MORE DIE TO CAST

The Guild Master watched from the observation deck of the Crystal Palace. He heard the klaxons first, tearing him away from his work with telegrams and calculations. He strode to the eastern windows from which much of the island was visible to him.

There was a light in Dr. Hyde's cave. Flares filled the air around the docks. And the gunnery soldiers were firing at targets in the dark ocean. Boats. Then a great explosion, a second, a third. The destruction of the observation tower and the crashing of the flaming airship to the ground had been particularly bothersome. The metal shell had protected it from rifle fire but not from an explosion of that magnitude. A design flaw?

This raid had not been a major part of his calculations. There had been such a small chance they'd ever find him so he'd only dug a few trenches and put up barricades. This was a well-planned attack. How had they discovered the island? There was that one small *Triton* ship lost at sea. He had assumed they were swamped. Maybe not.

No matter, the enemy was here, had hunted down his

Guild. No need for panic. It wasn't as though this scenario hadn't occurred to him. It was part of the risk. He just hadn't foreseen the metal juggernaut soldiers that were currently routing his own troops. Had the British advanced so much in such a short time?

But they had come at a time when his forces were weak. He'd lost so many men when the *Wyvern* went down. They had recruited more, but they weren't yet well trained.

What was Britain's ambition? Kill or capture?

How to make either of these goals more difficult was the question. He had often thought of himself as a tortoise, slowly making his plans for the world. What did a tortoise do when attacked? Withdrew into itself.

First, he had one more die to cast.

42

CAULDRON BOILS

Octavia watched Modo throw his useless revolver at Lime. The man ducked and gave them another broad smile as he clashed his knives together.

"Beware the Jabberwock, my son!" Lime taunted. *"The jaws that bite, the claws that catch!"*

"Jabberwock?" Modo said, drawing his own knife. "Quoting poetry at me?"

If that was poetry, Octavia wanted no part of it. Modo's knife was much smaller than Lime's, and though Modo was strong, he hadn't grown up in Seven Dials to fine-tune his knife-fighting technique. Octavia drew her sabre, brushed by Modo and rushed Lime. When he raised his knives, intent on slicing her from gullet to belly, she dropped to the floor and blocked them both with her own blade, striking him directly in the knee with her foot. It was a move Tharpa had taught her.

He let out a shout and tripped backwards, and she gave him another good kick. He fell back into one of the boiling caldrons. It was almost comical. He let out a muffled scream as the pink smelly substance wrapped around him. He flailed his legs.

"I suppose we should drag him out," Modo said.

They yanked on his boots, now still, and he was surprisingly light as they pulled him to the floor.

"My Lord," squeaked Octavia.

All that remained of Lime was a skeleton, which quickly fell to pieces. His metal teeth rattled across the rocks towards Modo, who booted them away.

"Acid," Octavia said, taking a few steps back. The sight of Lime's bones was enough to make her want to vomit. The acid sloshed around on the floor as though it had a mind of its own.

"Let's get out of here," Modo said.

They ran to the lift and got on. He pressed a button and they rose up thirty or forty feet, passing other tunnels. She caught a glimpse of more crates and containers.

"Should we stop?" she asked, but Modo shook his head.

"To the top. Dr. Hyde's cave must be above us somewhere."

With a *clunk* they reached the highest floor. It was made of smooth stone that led down a long tunnel to the south. That tunnel gradually grew wider and opened into three tunnels.

"Modo, we are cursed by tunnels."

"At least it's not London's sewers, eh?"

They took the middle tunnel and, after a few minutes, for the first time found themselves at an actual door. The lock was no problem for Modo. He simply pulled on it hard and it snapped. Octavia had always been impressed by his strength.

Beyond the door the room was brightly lit by several gas

lamps hanging from the ceiling. A small bench sat just inside the entrance. Modo stopped in the centre of the room, putting his hands on a wall of glass. A step later, Octavia saw what had taken his attention.

"Mother," he said softly.

43

A HORRIBLE WHISTLING

It took all of Oppie's concentration to deflect blow after powerful blow. His countless hours of training, of swinging clubs and fists against the other dragoons, made each move natural. But how could his monstrous opponent, who was just flesh and blood, unleash such staggering hits? Oppie had even used an axe to deflect Typhon, but the handle broke in half like a toothpick.

The sun was rising, the light showing how ugly his opponent was. He punched Typhon in the temple, a wallop that would have taken off another man's head, but the monster didn't even blink.

"You are a worthy combatant," Typhon said.

"Such fancy words." Oppie had wanted to say something clever, but failed. He struggled, pushing his body and his mechanical armour to its limit. His anger made him stronger.

He landed a kick in the middle of Typhon's chest, knocking him into a barricade strewn with wires and breaking it into pieces. The creature was up again in a heartbeat, smiling lopsidedly.

"Very impressive."

Typhon lifted a stray beam and swung, taking Oppie out at the legs. As he pushed himself onto his knees, Typhon hit his head. Oppie's helmet broke in two and flew off, exposing his skull.

The monster was toying with him! But Oppie rose, shoving the beast ten yards back. There was a great *boom* in the distance.

"Let's have at it, as they say," Typhon grunted.

A horrible whistling filled Oppie's ears. He thought Typhon's punch had done something to his hearing, but the screeching grew louder. Even Typhon paused.

A shell landed several feet away, blasting Oppie against a bin that collapsed, dumping coal on him. Could he drown in coal? He was suffocating under the weight of it. He kicked and dug his way to the surface, coughing up coal dust. The world was completely silent now. This time he knew his ears had been damaged.

He got to his feet, his machine legs steady, his vision clouded with smoke. As it cleared he saw Typhon on his back. Oppie limped over to him. The monster was fully intact, despite how close he had been to the shell blast. He wore a peaceful expression, though he looked quite dead.

A small movement caught Oppie's eye. It was the strangest thing: the monster's little finger was curling and uncurling, as if inviting Oppie to come closer.

44

SHELLING AT SUNRISE

M r. Socrates stood on the deck of the HMS *Shah* and watched through his spyglass. Amid the darkness and smoke it was hard to make sense of the morning's events, but he'd known early on that the explosive boats and the feint for the beaches had worked. The three perfectly timed explosions had caught the enemy unaware and brought down the dock and the observation tower. He had been particularly satisfied to see the airship burst into a series of flames. It had lit up the beach, making the assault that much easier to observe.

They'd been able to rescue two of the three soldiers who had piloted the dummy boats and set the charges. The third might still be somewhere in the water.

The official sunrise was at half past six, but a full hour before that the sky grew light enough that their targets became visible, so they began pressing them with fire.

The dragoons drove the Guild soldiers back. It was like watching Titans battle humans. Then they ripped the firing pins from the enemy's field guns, so the HMS *Shah* was now safe from the long-range guns and the beaches were open for the third phase of their attack.

He counted. He'd lost three of the dragoons. From this distance it was impossible to tell which ones, only that two lay on the beach immobile. Perhaps they were not past medical attention.

At his command, the ship's guns began to fire again, smashing the trenches where the enemy was trapped. Then, satisfied that the volley of shells had softened their targets, he and Tharpa climbed down a rope ladder and led a flotilla of electric boats jammed with marines and sailors towards the shore.

Five minutes later he was striding up the beach to the front line.

45

BED OF STONE

Modo's mother lay on a stone bed covered with a thin mattress. Her red hair had been combed, but clumps had fallen out. She was gaunt and her skin unnaturally pale so that her veins made a spiderweb pattern over her arms and neck. Her forearms were freckled with needle marks. Clearly they had been stealing from her, blood and perhaps more. She was not a beautiful woman, and he found himself surprised by that. He had imagined her to be handsome, though he, of all people, should not have expected to have an attractive mother.

The quartz that separated them was clear as glass. He pounded on it, slamming his fist again and again. She stirred but didn't awaken.

"We must get her out of there!" he shouted, and pounded even harder.

"Yes. Yes," Octavia said. "Calm down. There must be another way."

"Yes, there must be. We . . ." His voice trailed off.

His mother had opened her eyes and was looking at him for the first time since she and his father had left him at

Notre Dame. Of course, there was no sign of recognition on her face—after all he was wearing a mask—but surely she must realize that he and Octavia were not part of the Guild.

The woman blinked, looking drowsy.

"We're here to take you home," Modo said in French. He had no idea if she could hear him. "We are friends."

She didn't speak. What incredible pain had she already endured? What torture at the hands of this horrid Guild? He placed his open palm against the quartz, a sign of peace. Of love, perhaps.

Then a section of the floor inside her chamber slid aside. A nearly bald man rose up through the hole on a lift. He paused, not quite startled, and stared at Modo and Octavia. He rubbed his chin for a moment.

"Dr. Hyde," Octavia said.

He was only a few inches taller than Modo. The doctor examined him through the glass without any hint of fear. Then he nodded, turned, and lifted Modo's mother from the slab of stone.

"Where are you taking her?" Modo shouted. "Where?"

The man didn't respond as he carried her back to the lift, then disappeared into the floor, leaving the room empty.

Modo slammed his fists against the quartz.

"Come," Octavia said, pulling him back towards the door, "we'll find another way."

A bullet struck the wall and the room echoed with the shot. A Guild soldier blocked the doorway, pulling back the hammer on his rifle. Modo lifted the wooden bench and threw it, knocking him to the floor so hard that he didn't get up again.

"Let's go!" Modo said, leading Octavia through the door. "We will find her. We will."

46

THE POWER VESTED IN ME

When the barrage arrived, Miss Hakkandottir watched it cut through her ranks and she screamed with rage as the Guild soldiers scattered. The tincture that had been used to bind them also weakened their brains, sometimes in unpredictable ways. Despite the training, they were now like mice fleeing from some discovered hidey-hole.

"Form ranks!" she shouted, to no avail. She instructed Grace to herd them like cattle, so the dog snapped at their heels. "Form ranks!"

She began to chase them and pull them into formation, smacking several with her metal hand. The moment she let one go, he ran. Panic had set in. She didn't have time to execute each and every one of them.

A hasty retreat was her only option. She leapt from the trench and ran from the oncoming enemy, Grace at her heels. Wagons and barricades had been blown to pieces by the attack and the farther she went, the thicker was the smoke. Guns fired from behind her, a good sign; she was at least going in the right direction.

She jumped a dead horse and landed in an open crater. It had been cleared by a shell blast. Something large was moving in front of her and when the wind blew the smoke away, she saw one of the giant metal soldiers looking down at the body of Typhon.

He had bested Typhon! The man's helmet was off and she was shocked to see his face, so childlike, on the body of an adult enclosed in a giant suit of armour. Seeing her, he raised his head.

"You," he said. "I know you! I remember you!" He pointed his metal finger at her as though he'd caught a mischievous child. "Miss Hakkandottir, by the power vested in me I declare you under arrest!"

It was the oddest thing she'd heard all day. The boy-thing actually recognized her and he was . . . was arresting her? She laughed, almost uncontrollably, then drew her pistol and shot. The bullet ricocheted off his shoulder. She fired again. Another ricochet.

"Put down your weapon!" he commanded. He lumbered towards her, gaining speed.

"Get him, Grace," she hissed. Her hound leapt, but he swatted the dog aside with his metal arm. "Grace!" Hakkandottir screamed, but the hound hit the rocky ground hard and didn't move again.

She was about to charge at the soldier, but drew up short. There was only one way out. She fled. Straight for the Crystal Palace.

47

A GAME WELL PLAYED

M r. Socrates watched from the beach with a sense of pleasure and confidence as the HMS *Shah* sent a barrage of shells towards the Crystal Palace. The first phase had unfolded with relative ease. And this second phase had gone equally well.

The ship's doctor had assured him that the two wounded dragoons would live, but five of the Association soldiers and three marines were dead. In exchange the enemy forces had been scattered and a collection of prisoners had been taken on a boat back to the HMS *Shah* for questioning. The enemy's guns and airships had been destroyed. Typhon, the odd monstrous creature, was dead; Mr. Socrates had inspected the corpse himself. Impressive, that one. He had not seen Modo and Octavia yet, but he was convinced they'd soon emerge from the tunnels.

The only detail that irked him was the Crystal Palace itself. From a distance it had looked like one shot from the *Shah*'s nine-inch muzzle-loaders would shatter it, but apparently not. So it couldn't be glass. It was some sort of impervious material, thick enough to withstand their heaviest guns. Through his spyglass he could see that they'd succeeded in breaking off a few chips, but it seemed structurally sound. An astounding architectural feat!

They had scored one direct hit at the top of the building, shearing off the airship landing tower. At least they could be sure their enemies wouldn't be fleeing that way.

In short order his snipers silenced the last of the rifle fire. Now the enemy could only retreat to the palace. They'd be trapped in their shell.

How to bust the shell open was the problem. He hadn't counted on a siege. He had enough supplies for a week, but there might be months of supplies stored away inside those walls. A siege would require that he got a message back to Esquimalt, and it would be weeks before reinforcements arrived.

He raised his hand, sending a signal to one of his lieutenants, who in turn made a sign to a flagman on the beach who waved *cease fire*. The *Shah*'s guns fell silent.

Mr. Socrates stepped out from his cover. Only a gifted marksman could hit him at this distance from the palace; it was worth the risk. He raised his speaking trumpet and shouted, *"Clockwork Guild agents! It would be best for all concerned if you were to surrender now."*

The Crystal Palace was quiet. The quartz was clear, but he couldn't actually see inside. Tharpa stood a few yards behind him, his rifle trained on possible sniper nests.

"It would be best for all concerned if you *surrender,*" a woman answered, using an even louder speaking trumpet.

There was no way to detect her actual location, other than the general direction of the palace. He knew her voice, of course. Miss Hakkandottir. He'd hoped a shell or a bullet had removed her from this earth, but, alas, no such luck.

"Ingrid, how lovely to hear your voice again." His

trumpet made him feel as though he could blow their walls down by merely speaking. *"Your Swedish accent is a joy to my ears."*

"Ha! Intelligence has failed you. This is what comes of mediocre agents," she retorted. *"I'm Icelandic."*

He was amused. Had his sources actually been so far off? *"Are we to settle this with swords again?"* he asked.

"It would be less than gentlemanly of me to duel with such a doddering old fool."

"Enough," he snapped. *"I will address your master."*

"I am the master of all you see," she replied.

"No," Mr. Socrates said. *"You are not capable of such visionary thinking. Send him out. Ingrid, I'm growing tired of this charade and it's such a lovely palace. Do not force us to destroy it and all who remain inside."*

He expected her to shout a defiant answer, or take a shot at him. Instead a male voice spoke into the trumpet.

"You have done well, Alan Reeve," he said. *"I salute you. A clever plan executed with great precision."*

"With whom am I speaking?"

"You may call me *Prometheus*." His tone was flat. Disinterested.

He'd named himself after a Titan. Was the man mad? Of course, Mr. Socrates himself had taken on a last name of distinction, but that was only to hide his past. This man, on the other hand, might well believe himself to be a Titan.

"Well, Prometheus, I also salute you. Let us chat, shall we? Face to face, over tea and sweet biscuits. On the deck of my ship."

"I have analyzed our situation and there is no other choice for us but surrender. It was a game well played. I shall open the gates for you conquering heroes."

Immediately the main doors at the front of the palace

began to part. The dragoons raised their elephant guns, the soldiers and marines raised their rifles. It was still dark inside the palace, but something large was sliding out.

"It is an offering of surrender," the man said, a smile now in his voice.

About a dozen Guild soldiers were heaving against a giant wooden crate, rolling it across wooden poles towards them. What odd sort of gesture was this? How was this a surrender? The rolling crate slowly descended the paved road from the palace. It had air holes and was so large that it easily could contain twenty horses.

Horses! The Trojan horse! *"Fire! Fire at the crate!"* he commanded and his men obeyed. The Guild soldiers stopped and fled back into the palace, and the gates slammed shut after them.

The box collapsed, revealing five monstrous hulking men, eyes dead. Each was much larger than Typhon and they had been redesigned more than Mr. Socrates had dreamed possible. One had four arms, another had large horns, a third had ten-foot-long tentacles. The final creature was part metal and part human, plate armour fastened like scales to his flesh. His arms were clearly steam-powered, ending in huge crablike claws. The machines of war, the cannons and Maxim guns that tore men apart, were civilized compared to these creatures. Their appearance shook him to the core.

There was something else. A small wave of silver ran across the ground in front of the monsters. He squinted. Metal spiders!

He retreated behind their barricade and took stock of his soldiers. Behind their helmets, the dragoons were hard to read, but helmetless Trooper Entwistle was staring, wide-eyed. The Association soldiers and the marines fired automatically, but he knew they had to be unnerved. They'd faced cavalry charges and cannon fire, but none had seen an enemy as terrible as this. It was too late to call down a barrage; it would hit his own men, too. That could only be a final option. One of the signallers ran screaming onto the beach and into the water.

Mr. Socrates thought of Sun Tzu and his Art of War: *He who knows when he can fight and when he cannot, will be victorious.* Was it time to flee? They could be off this beach and back in the boats in minutes, leaving only a few to cover their retreat. Those men would die, undoubtedly.

No. They had not sacrificed this much only to be driven back. This is what the Guild had created; what they ultimately wanted to unleash upon Britain. Their new ships would make the invasion possible, carrying these beasts across the Pacific.

Sun Tzu had also said: *Look on them as your own beloved sons, and they will stand by you even unto death.*

"Hold your positions," he commanded. "I'm right here, men. Standing beside you."

The monsters began lumbering towards them, but first, a hundred little spiders scurried over the lip of their trenches and up the legs and arms of the men and began biting. Most of the marines shook them off, but one cried out when he felt the bite, then fell over. After a few short convulsions he was dead. Poison! The other soldiers were quick to smash at the spiders with the butts of their guns, but one ran up a dragoon's leg, found flesh, and the dragoon fell over, waving his arms and thrashing around.

Four sailors fled into the water. Mr. Socrates couldn't blame them. They might have held their position if they'd been on a ship, but not here, faced with something so outside their understanding. He, too, felt an overpowering revulsion at the melding of human and animal parts, metal and gears.

It took a full minute of stomping and crushing to kill the spiders. By then the monstrous squadron was nearly upon them. The elephant guns only slowed the beasts down; nothing could stop them. And they wouldn't die. They just would not die.

They were already dead.

48

A TIMELY BURST OF ANGER

It was clear to Octavia that they were very lost. They'd climbed back down into the tunnels hoping to find the route Dr. Hyde had taken, but the tunnels underneath the cave went off in every direction, except back towards anything that might be below the quartz prison room. And the longer it took, the more intensely she could feel Modo's growing anger.

When he slammed his fist into a beam, she said, "You are a trained agent. Calm yourself!" Part of her wanted to laugh; she sounded just like old Mr. Socrates. But Modo was becoming unhinged with rage.

"I am calm!" he spat, but when they came upon three white-coated men, he chased them down and began throwing them around. It was like watching a hound tear into cornered rabbits.

"Stop!" she shouted. Within seconds they were all unconscious on the floor.

"Take a moment and think!" Octavia said, pushing him into a corner. "We could've questioned them."

"What am I doing?" He looked at his fists. "How do we find Hyde?"

"Maybe these tunnels don't join up with any routes below the cave. We could go back to the surface and look for another entrance."

"But I'm certain we are close!" He pulled out his compass and stared at it. "This is west. The tunnel led west. We must be right next to it." He slipped the compass back in his pocket and slammed his fists against the wall until he fell, exhausted, against it. "No!" he said, and began bashing at it again.

He had lost all discipline. She grabbed him by his shoulder and said urgently, "Modo! Modo! We're doing the best that we can," as earth and stone fell around them. "Getting all bullish won't help."

"I'm sorry, Tavia. I'm just so tired of holding back. All these thoughts running around in my head." He let out what might have been a sob and slumped against the wall.

There was a rumble and a *crack*, then a *swoosh* of damp dirt as the stone wall collapsed under his weight.

Modo fell right through it onto his side, but Octavia jumped over him and through the hole, her hand on her sabre. Bright light burned her eyes. They were in a hallway lined with marble walls, ceiling and floors. It was lit by electric lights and, thankfully, was deserted.

"See? It pays to get really angry once in a while!" Modo stood up and began jogging down the hall, Octavia a few feet behind him. She checked her compass. They were travelling towards the palace, were perhaps already beneath it.

In a few minutes the marble walls turned to wooden panels covered with paintings of scenes incorporating mythological heroes and monsters. One was of a man tied to a rock. Another of a giant holding up the world. A third depicted a man clenching the severed head of a woman with snakes for hair.

The next chamber was populated with an army of bronze and marble statues; men were throwing discs, sitting on thrones, holding spears, while women grasped vases or children, or fixed their hair. Most were naked. If Octavia hadn't grown up in Seven Dials she might have blushed.

Modo rushed up to a wide door covered with ornate carvings.

"Don't just yank it open!" she whispered.

He peeked through the keyhole. "Another hallway," he said. "No sign of—uh-oh— Hide!"

The door slowly swung open.

49

HOW HANNIBAL WAS DEFEATED

Mr. Socrates was nearly out of bullets as the monstrous brigade advanced. They now stood in the midst of his front line. The marines and Association soldiers were reduced to swinging sabres and stabbing bayonets. It was like pricking giants with pins.

The creatures sent soldiers flying, kicked aside marines and were able to topple five of the dragoons. Those dragoons that kept their feet exchanged blows with them, but were only half as strong.

Mr. Socrates dropped his rifle and drew his pistol, but it wasn't long before that was empty. Not one monster had fallen. All his manpower wasted!

He reloaded his pistol, leaned around his barricade and fired at the armoured monster, the bullets ricocheted off. It was becoming difficult to suppress his fear and revulsion. What had Hyde done? And how did the little peasant woman, Modo's mother, fit into it? Or Modo's finger, for that matter?

There was a great *crash* and he saw that the armoured monster had cut the barricade in half with a metal claw. Mr.

Socrates looked for Tharpa among the slain as he fired his last bullet and unsheathed his sabre. No retreat! No, not before these mindless creatures! If this was the end, so be it. He'd go down fighting, like a true Briton.

"Come on," he snarled, "I've got British steel for your innards!"

Another monster came at him from the side, swinging a club, but something else knocked Mr. Socrates down just before the blow arrived. He hit the ground hard, his vision blurring. When he raised his head, blinking, colours swirled around him. But what was that? Music? He squinted hard, shook his head until he could see.

And there stood Tharpa, alone, in front of the creatures and blowing a trumpet like a madman. He had taken it from one of the sergeants. The Indian had gone barmy.

The monstrosities covered their ears, glaring at Tharpa as he advanced, step by step. One let out an odd yelp of pain and fled, diving into the water. He was followed by another, then another, until all of them had stampeded into the water and disappeared below the waves. He waited for them to rise again, saw a massive waving hand break the surface, then fall. There was thrashing in the water for a few seconds, then nothing.

Mr. Socrates ran to Tharpa and clapped him on the back. "My man, my man, you're brilliant!" The surviving soldiers cheered. Tharpa beamed.

"It was you, Sahib, who once told me the story of how Hannibal and his great elephant army were defeated by Roman trumpeters who let out one big blast of sound. It was worth a try."

"Indeed it was! Though, you were horribly out of tune. Perhaps trumpeting lessons are in order."

"It may be best to be out of tune, master. Britain has yet

to explore horrific noise as a weapon. Perhaps the right frequencies will be more effective than one hundred guns!"

"I will take that under consideration, my friend," Mr. Socrates said, thumping Tharpa on the back again.

Then he rallied what remained of his army and turned to the Crystal Palace. It was silent and, he was quite certain, now undefended.

50

TO FIGHT AGAIN ANOTHER DAY

"It is finished," the Guild Master said.

Miss Hakkandottir looked down from the observation deck and nodded. "Yes, I am afraid the battle is lost."

"But not the war. Like the phoenix, we will rise again," her master said. "One must know when to retreat. It will take a few years, but I can see my mistakes and I will correct them. Madagascar will be a good home. I have land there for this very eventuality."

"Yes, our future plans are important, but we don't have much time to discuss them right now, sir," she said.

He took one last look around the ruins of his communications centre. "You are right, Miss Hakkandottir. I put myself in your capable hands."

She led him to the elevator and they took it down to the basement floor. There, waiting for them, was Dr. Hyde, and three of her most trusted Guild officers, one of them carrying a limp Madame Hébert. Miss Hakkandottir was tempted to suggest leaving Madame Hébert behind, dead of course—Modo finding the body would be a nice blow for her enemies—but she knew that the old woman's chemistry was far too valuable.

She armed herself with one of their pistols, loosened her sword in its scabbard and led them down the hall. It would take Mr. Socrates and his men at least an hour to break into the palace. By that time they would have boarded the *Triton* boat waiting in an underground cave and would be well on their way to Madagascar.

At the end of the first hall she opened a wide door, urging them on into the great room that the Guild Master used for meditation; he called it his temple. All she could see were some useless statues. Why had he wasted money on these when he could have bought more armaments?

A *chirp* stopped her. She couldn't place where it was coming from, but knew it was not from a bird. She signalled the officers, who raised their rifles.

"Who is there?" she asked.

The forest of statues did not answer.

Another *chirp*, this time to her left. She spun, her pistol at the ready. "Show yourself!"

One of the officers fired, chipping the ear off a statue. The report of the gun nearly deafened her.

"What was it?" she asked.

"Someone moved over there."

"Don't shoot until you have a target."

"Please don't harm the statues," the Guild Master pleaded, looking rather pathetic.

Miss Hakkandottir nearly cuffed him.

Then a statue fell over on the opposite side of the room. Feeling a drop of moisture on her face, she touched it, confused, and looked up.

There, clinging to the chandelier, was a man wearing a mask.

51

A BATTLE AMID THE GODS

Modo did what he had been trained to do.

Without hesitation, he dropped to the floor in the middle of his enemies, yanked the rifle from one soldier and knocked him out with the butt end, then broke the gun over the head of another soldier. He threw the pieces at Miss Hakkandottir, striking the aimed pistol out of her hand.

Octavia took care of the third soldier and then grabbed Dr. Hyde and held her sabre to his throat. Modo's mother fell to the floor.

He was face to face with Miss Hakkandottir.

"Modo," she said, "how I have longed for this." She swung her metal fist at him, but he deflected the blow and she knocked the head off a statue of Zeus.

"That's a Polykleitos!" the man with glasses shouted.

Modo had lost his balance and Miss Hakkandottir now delivered a kick to his midsection, sending him tumbling into another statue. She drew her sabre. All he had was his knife. In desperation, he threw it and watched it speed end over end towards her heart, but with her metal hand she batted it aside.

"This time I'll take more than your finger," she said. "I'm not leaving without your head."

"Give it your best shot," he said.

As she swung, he lifted a broken arm from a statue and parried the blow. He was surprised at how fearless he felt. She lunged to stab his stomach and he knocked the blade aside, driving it into the wall. It stuck there, and as she tried to pull it out, he smashed the sabre with the arm of the statue, breaking the blade.

She smacked him in the head with her metal fist, and he staggered, swinging blindly. Catching his fist with her metal hand she squeezed, crushing his bones together. She gritted her teeth as she brought him to his knees. Octavia ran towards them, sabre raised to slash her, but with amazing speed his enemy knocked Octavia aside with her other arm.

"*This* is for destroying my ship."

She tightened her grip; Modo let out a yell. He tried to get up, to push back against her, but the pain was unbearable.

Then he saw his mother lying on the floor behind Miss Hakkandottir. She was coming to, fear in her eyes. His heart caught in his throat and he gathered every last ounce strength and got to his feet, despite his crushed hand. Miss Hakkandottir refused to let go so he swung his arm with all his might, slamming her into the wall. She still wouldn't let go—perhaps couldn't. Her hand seemed to be locked. He swung her again and again, smashing over statues.

Dr. Hyde was shouting, "Leave her be!"

Modo swung her a third time and she flew through the air, screaming obscenities.

Her metal hand was still attached to him, her blood dripping from it.

He pried at the fingers until they loosened and the hand

fell off, not daring to look at his own throbbing, mangled fist.

Miss Hakkandottir shrieked. "Damn you!" and tried to stand, but couldn't. Dr. Hyde ran and wrapped her stub with a piece of cloth torn from his shirt.

Octavia had grabbed a pistol from a fallen soldier. "No one move," she commanded, sweeping the room with it.

Everyone was still. Silent.

Then the man with the glasses fled. She fired two rounds, missing him by inches, then he was out the door and gone.

52

TAKING THE LIFT

The doors to the palace wouldn't budge, so they blew a jagged hole in them with dynamite and the dragoons thrust the remaining pieces open.

Mr. Socrates sent the dragoons in first, then the soldiers and marines. When they weren't met with gunfire, he entered. Several dead Guild soldiers lay on the floor; the rest of the palace was deserted.

As his men explored the interior, Mr. Socrates stopped to look up at the giant clock, the symbol of the Clockwork Guild. Beside it was a massive fountain spouting fresh water. Such magnificence, and all from one man's mind. But why a *guild*? After all, it was a collective, several minds working together, wasn't it? So once they destroyed this island fortress, would other cells pop up?

If so, the Association would have to silence them all, one by one.

Some forty yards away, a trap door was flung open, and a small man leapt from the hole and slammed the door shut again. He wore glasses and grey clothing—he looked like a clerk, one of many the Guild must employ. Near the door was a spiral staircase, and without a glance at Mr. Socrates or his men, the clerk raced up the stairs.

The trap door opened again and a short, bulky figure leapt out and sped up the stairs in hot pursuit.

Modo!

"Should I stop the little man?" Tharpa raised his rifle.

Mr. Socrates shook his head. "No. Modo wouldn't chase this man for no reason. We take the lift to the top. We'll want to know what this fellow has to say."

CLEANUP DUTY

While the other dragoons cleared the palace, Oppie was assigned cleanup duty around the island. He combed the wreckage with one of the other dragoons and three soldiers, and rounded up all the surviving Guild soldiers. They would be sent on boats to the *Shah* for imprisonment in the hold.

Finding himself in the area of the battlefield where he'd left Typhon's body, he realized there was now no sign of the creature. He looked back at the *Shah,* anchored in the bay. One of the ship's cranes was working, heaving a large crate from a boat over to the deck of the ship.

There we go, he thought. The marines had already transported the monstrosity to the *Shah.*

"And good riddance," he shouted at the crate before carrying on with his rounds.

MISCALCULATIONS

Modo pursued the man up to the highest room in the tower. It was a mess: telegraph machines smashed by the blows of the *Shah*'s guns, shattered glass and burning paper littered the floor. The west wall was in ruins, one section open to the air.

This odd man had to be important, might even be the Guild Master. Why else would he have been with Hakkandottir? Did he still have a trick up his sleeve? A means of escape? A hot air balloon, perhaps? Nothing was impossible, but if a balloon had been tethered to the broken landing post, it was gone now.

"There's no way out of here," Modo said, facing him.

The breeze was warm, rustling and separating the burning papers. The man stood at the far side of the room, blinking as though what was happening was beyond his comprehension.

"So, you are Modo," he said, coming out of his trance.

"Yes."

"A very curious, determined creature."

"I'll take that as a compliment."

"I'm afraid I miscalculated. I failed to foresee this outcome. Plato would be ashamed."

"Who's Plato?"

The man cocked his head. "A philosopher."

"I know, I know. I thought you were using a code name."

He heard a noise behind him. Modo turned to see Mr. Socrates, Tharpa and several Association soldiers enter the room.

"Ah, your master comes." To Mr. Socrates he said, "A well-played hand."

"Thank you," Mr. Socrates replied. "Would you do me the courtesy of stating your name?"

"I am no one," the man said. "Prometheus one day. Midas the next. Yes, that would be a good name for me. A foolish king who could make everything turn to gold, but could never eat."

"Come now, the game is done," Mr. Socrates said. "I know a little about you at least. You were once the Dragon Master of the Red Fish Triad, weren't you? Or should I say 489?"

The man nodded and grinned.

So this *was* the Guild Master! Modo shook his head at the thought. This little bespectacled fellow?

"Marvellous! I didn't imagine you or your allies got that close to my old life. You're much more effective than I believed you to be. Another miscalculation. But yes, that number was once me and I was once that number."

Mr. Socrates said, "Please return to my ship. We won't mistreat you. In fact, I'll give you your choice of tea."

"Such kindness," the Guild Master replied.

Modo studied him. Sarcasm? He really seemed cavalier.

"I suppose logic dictates that I offer up my arms for manacles and bow down to your might."

"There won't be any need for manacles," Mr. Socrates said. "We're all gentlemen here."

"I am more than that. And I have more names than you will ever know. My father named me Douglas, for one." Then he began dancing around in a circle, flapping his arms like wings, looking every bit the lunatic, until he said, "But I truly am Daedalus."

Daedalus—the Greek scientist who created wings from wax and feathers to escape a prison, along with his son Icarus. Did the Guild Master really believe he could just up and fly away? As the man began to giggle, Modo glanced out at the airship docking station just to reassure himself it was indeed broken. Then something over his head caught his eye and he looked up: white, ragged, man-sized wings hung from the shattered ceiling.

"To the sun!" the Guild Master yelled, leaping onto an upturned desk and grabbing the wings.

Modo sprang after him but the distance was too great. As the Guild Master ran towards the hole blasted in the side of the observation deck, he slid the wings on and leapt into the sky.

An impossibly large hand shot up from outside the palace, catching the Guild Master in mid-air and sending his glasses flying. He was thrown back into the room, where he landed on his broken wings.

Typhon climbed in and stood over him, a boot on the small man's chest as he writhed around. If the roof hadn't been blown off, the towering creature wouldn't have been able to stand up straight. Typhon grabbed the Guild Master by his lapels and lifted him.

"So it is the master of the masters," Typhon said. "Are we standing inside your broken dreams?"

Put me down, monster!" the Guild Master ordered.

"Correct. I am a monster. But it was you who ordered my creation. You set your doctor and your minions to the task of piecing me together." He paused. "So, tell me again, who is the real monster?"

"Put him on the floor," Mr. Socrates demanded. "That man is *my* prisoner." Tharpa and the soldiers raised their guns.

Typhon tilted his head. "Your bullets won't harm me. You cannot wound flesh that is already dead."

"Release me!" The Guild Master was now shouting. "Release me at once! I command you, Typhon."

"I reject that name. And your tinctures and commands no longer work on me. Beg, beg for my forgiveness. Tell me that you accept me as your child."

"I shall not."

"Then are you Daedalus or Icarus?" he asked.

Modo didn't like the direction this was going. Icarus, after all, had flown too close to the sun, melting his waxen wings and crashing to his death.

"I am Daedalus," the Guild Master cried. "I am Daedalus!"

"You are Icarus," Typhon said. He tore the wing from one arm and, as though he were tossing away a cockroach, threw the Guild Master over the side of the palace tower to the rocks below.

Everyone else stood there, stunned.

Typhon turned to them and shrugged. "He gave me the brain of a murderer. What did he expect?" He pointed at Mr. Socrates. "I demand safe passage off this island."

Mr. Socrates looked him in the eyes. "It would be immoral to allow you to roam free in the world."

"Then we are at an impasse. I've not discovered my own free will only to be forced to surrender it. I see only one avenue of escape." He heaved his bulk towards Mr. Socrates.

Tharpa let off two shots, but they only thudded into the creature's flesh.

Modo flew at the monster. He had always been amazingly strong; surely he could at least come between this thing and his master. But Typhon easily flicked Modo to the floor. Two more shots from Mr. Socrates' pistol and then the creature had his hand around the master's throat. He jerked him up and squeezed him against his chest, Mr. Socrates' face turning red from lack of air.

"Get too close and I will snap this old rooster's neck. I'll let him go once I've escaped this place. I promise."

He carried Mr. Socrates, now limp and speechless, into the lift and began his descent. Modo tore down the spiral stairs head them off. He shouted at the dragoons waiting below, "Back away! Don't fire!"

Modo trailed after Typhon as they left the palace, staying far enough back so as not to alarm him. Mr. Socrates' face had turned a frightening shade of purple. He saw Octavia running towards them and he motioned her to stay away.

The monster carried Mr. Socrates out into the water and dropped him unceremoniously into one of the *Triton* boats and climbed in after him. After experimenting for several seconds, he got the boat chugging out into the ocean.

"You are overly dedicated to your master!" he shouted.

"He is more than my master!" Modo yelled back. What could he do? He had no more weapons. No more words. His hand was broken. Modo pulled up his mask. "Typhon!" he shouted. "You're not the only monster here!"

He made his way slowly towards him through the water, the light falling fully upon his face, the waves creeping up his legs, his torso. Then he began to swim, tentatively, keeping his face above the surface.

"You see," he shouted, "we are both monsters of a kind." It was a last feeble gesture, Modo attempt to appeal to whatever tiny bit of humanity might still be floating about in Typhon's brain.

Typhon stared at him, bemused. He waved his little finger. "One day I would like to know more about you," he said, "but today is not that day."

As though he had done it all his life, he began piloting the boat out into the Pacific. With his enormous bulk it sat heavy in the water. He still had an arm around Mr. Socrates, who was now alert and struggling and beginning to holler.

"Let him go!" Modo pleaded. "You promised to let him go!"

"I did. You shouldn't have trusted a murderer." He paused. "But I shall keep my word."

And so he tossed Mr. Socrates into the ocean.

55

INTO BLUE WATER

Octavia kept her gun trained on Miss Hakkandottir from several paces away. The woman was pale as the marble statues surrounding her, but her blue eyes stabbed Octavia's.

"I will break every bone in your body," she said, spitting out each word though her voice was frail.

"Not today." Octavia smiled sweetly.

Dr. Hyde tightened the makeshift tourniquet on Miss Hakkandottir's arm. Then he stroked her red hair, which had fallen out of its braids. "You will live," he whispered. "My love. I will make you beautiful again."

Octavia felt like throwing up. Who would have thought these two could be lovebirds?

Modo's mother had curled up into a ball at the foot of a statue and seemed to be sleeping. Chloroform? Or exhaustion from the torturous things they'd done to her?

Ah, relief! A dragoon stooped to enter the door to take in the situation, followed by two Association soldiers, guns drawn.

"You must be extremely careful with her," Octavia said,

pointing at Miss Hakkandottir. "And tend to Madame Hébert. She'll need to see the ship's doctor immediately." Finally, Octavia scooped up Miss Hakkandottir's metal hand and said with great satisfaction, "I'll give this to Mr. Socrates myself."

Then she ran down the hallway and up a set of stairs into the Crystal Palace. It was good to see sunlight again, even if it was filtered by the quartz. No gunfire. The battles were over.

The Association soldiers stood at attention, uncertain what to do. Through the front gate she spotted Modo wading alone into the water, shouting something. And was that Typhon out in the boat? And who was he holding against him? Mr. Socrates! Typhon was throwing him overboard!

Seeing that Modo had already started swimming, Octavia dropped Miss Hakkandottir's hand, ran to the end of the half-shattered dock and dove in. The icy water took her breath away. She swam hard. She couldn't see Mr. Socrates, only Modo surfacing twenty yards ahead of her and the monster in the boat in the far distance.

She pushed harder, gasping for air. Tharpa had taught her better, but she was panicking. Then—Mr. Socrates's hand poked out from the water, waving, reaching for the air before sinking beneath the surface again. Modo dove after him, and Octavia kicked and kicked until she was closer to them, then dove herself, down, down, coral and brightly coloured fish all around her. Such a beautiful world.

In the coral lay Mr. Socrates—no longer struggling. His body gave only an occasional tremor. Modo attempted to pull him up, but with only one good hand it was impossible. The meathead would drown along with their master! She kicked harder, grabbed Mr. Socrates' shoulder, and together they pulled him up.

They broke the surface, the old man between them, pale and limp. A boat was already waiting for them. Tharpa pulled Mr. Socrates in, turned him onto his side and began pounding on his back. Modo clung to one side of the boat, Octavia the other, both gulping air.

After a minute or two, Tharpa let out a noise unlike anything Octavia had ever heard, but she knew its meaning. Overwhelming grief. The language of sorrow.

"Sahib!" he cried out.

There had been such devotion between them. Again he pounded his master on the back.

Mr. Socrates gave up the slightest sputter. Then a cough. He began to take in air, soon great gulps of it. Octavia and Modo climbed on board and worked on Mr. Socrates, helping him expel the water as Tharpa piloted the boat towards the *Shah*.

After a few minutes, Modo had to clutch his hand, grimacing with pain. Octavia stared at him, at his face. She didn't flinch. His eyes were so full of suffering. She studied the water dripping down his features, his patchy red hair plastered to his scalp. His breath came hard through his ragged mouth.

He turned towards her, caught her looking.

She smiled and said, "Next time you should let me do the swimming."

56

EVER SOUTH

Typhon kept one hand on the wheel of the boat, looking back as the *Shah* disappeared over the horizon. Soon the island of Atticus was gone and he was alone on the water. These little boats were fast. They wouldn't be able to catch up with him.

He thought of that last view of Modo. That was the young man's name, wasn't it? There had been something, dare he say, touching, about that. He'd shown him his face, and Typhon had been surprised: it was uglier than his own. They were indeed brothers, of a sort. At least they shared the same blood. He stroked the little finger on his right hand.

But that world was now behind him. What new worlds, what new places could there be for someone such as he? South was the best direction. South to Antarctica. Maybe there he would find peace—a place where no one would bother him.

He looked at the boat's compass, unsure about the direction. Still, he was pretty certain he'd find the way. After all, several brains were stuffed together in his skull. One of them would surely contain the map of the Pacific. And with that thought, he discovered a map in his long-dead memories. Life was full of little surprises.

He laughed, frightening the seagulls that flew above him.

57

ONE FOR THE ARMY, ONE FOR THE LORD

For the first two days of the journey to Esquimalt, Modo was so exhausted that he mostly slept in his cabin on the *Shah*. The ship's surgeon did what he could for his hand, resetting the bones but predicting he'd never have full use of it again. Modo didn't correct him, but knew it would be good as new in a few weeks. That's just how his body worked.

He wasn't allowed to see Mr. Socrates, who had not yet fully recovered. Tharpa assured him, though, that *Sahib* had already complained about the quality of the tea, a sign that he was on the mend. When he wasn't sleeping, Modo pulled on his mask and wandered along the deck and stared out at the ocean. Or he sat with Octavia, saying little. She, too, was exhausted. He ate sparingly, the grey sludge still being the only food on offer. Only two days out and already he couldn't stomach much more of it.

On one of his visits to the ship's surgeon he discovered that Miss Hakkandottir's life had been saved by cauterizing her stub. "She didn't let out a peep," the surgeon said, amazed. She was now manacled in a holding cell somewhere below deck. Dr. Hyde was in a cell on another floor. Both were guarded by several marines. Modo had no intention of visiting his enemy. He hoped the hangman's rope awaited her and Dr. Hyde.

All of the dragoons were on the *Shah,* too, though he rarely saw them. He was happy that Ester had survived and seemed to have no injuries. It wasn't until the third day that he ran across Oppie on the deck, sitting on a crate in the sun. The gash on his forehead had been nicely stitched.

"Mr. Modo," he said, with a broad smile. "It's a pleasure to see you, sir. We made it through to the other side."

"Indeed, we did," Modo answered. He sat beside him. It was still so strange that this man—who such a short time ago was a small boy—was now taller than Modo. A scruffy beard was attempting to grow on his face. "How are you?"

"All's well. I—I miss me mates. Three of 'em gave their lives, but I guess we all knew our chances going into this."

"Yes, you did. You are a very brave man, Oppie."

"Just did my job," he answered. "Some terrible things happened, sir. Truly terrible things." Then he laughed. "But we got the bastards, didn't we, sir."

Modo could only nod in response, then return his gaze to the horizon. They were silent for a few minutes. Modo remembered what Mr. Socrates had said about these dragoons. Every week they aged a month.

"What will you do now, Oppie?"

"Do, sir?"

"Yes, are you going back to England?"

"I'll be going wherever the army tells me to go, sir," he said.

"You don't get leave? Or perhaps you've done your part? I certainly think so. You could move on."

Oppie looked him in the eyes. "Do you really believe

there's a place for me in that other world, sir? My job at the inn again? Ha. No, this is my place now. My home is with my mates in the Lucky Sevens. No one else can wear my uniform, sir. There's still work for the Association to do."

"Yes," Modo said, though he felt for Oppie. "I suppose you're right. But listen, Oppie—you'll keep learning to read, I hope."

"I will, sir," he replied. "That's a promise."

Modo clapped him on the back and strode to the aft of the ship, his eyes set on the direction from which they'd come. How many times had he walked around this ship avoiding his most important conversation. He contemplated the view for several minutes before he found the courage to go down the stairs to the lower deck, past the surgeon's quarters to the recovery cabin. His mother had been here all this time, with reports on her health being delivered to his cabin a few times a day.

He lingered outside her door, having suddenly decided he should be bringing her a gift. She was his mother, after all. But it wasn't as though he could just dive off the ship and return with a bouquet of flowers. She would have to take him as he was. Perhaps she'd see his part in her rescue as a gift; perhaps she'd even be proud of him.

He adjusted his mask, then raised a hesitant hand and knocked.

A frail voice said, *"Entrez."*

He opened the door. Her room, lit only by the porthole, was relatively large for a cabin. It was littered with medical equipment and various supplies. His mother lay on her cot, propped up on pillows, a grey wool blanket covering her legs. He took two steps in and stopped.

Some colour had returned to her cheeks, though she

was still pale. He didn't know what to say. He stared at her face, looking for familiar features.

"Parlez-vous français?" she asked.

"Oui," he said. *"Je comprende."*

"I am told that you saved me," she said in French. "I remember you, though, as you know, I was not well. I thank you."

"It was my duty," he said. "I was only doing my duty."

"Still, I thank you. It was brave of you."

"Are you feeling better?" he asked. "Are you getting enough to eat?"

"Soldiers bring me horrible food. But the doctor speaks some French. He's not a religious man, but he's kind. He told me my husband is dead. I have not had any tears to weep yet. They will come. I've been praying for his soul. Had I died, it wouldn't have been so bad, to join him again in heaven."

Modo didn't know how to respond, except to say, "I'm sorry for your loss."

"What's your name?" she asked.

"Modo."

"What sort of name is that? British?"

"My name was . . ." He paused. What to say? He began again. "It's the name my father gave me." He hadn't meant to say *father,* but trying to explain his relationship with Mr. Socrates was too complicated otherwise. "My adoptive father," he added.

She nodded. "He has raised you well. But why do you wear a mask? Were you wounded?"

"I'm disfigured," he said. "At least some would believe that to be so."

She raised her eyebrows. "How did it happen?"

"At birth," he said. "I was born this way."

Her eyes narrowed. Was she thinking about his birth?

"I—" He had to spit it out. "I know you will find this diffi-cult to believe. But I have learned . . . that I was born in Nanterre. I am your son."

"You're lying," she said. Her eyes grew hard, her face like stone.

"It isn't a lie. The nursemaid's name was . . ." He searched his memory. What had Colette said? "Marie. And you left me at Notre Dame Cathedral. You left me there with Father Mauger. Don't you remember?" He hadn't intended to sound so whiny.

"I have no son," she replied. "My husband and I had no children."

Doubt crept in, but . . . her eyes were so similar to his. He thought about all the facts. No, she had to be his mother.

"Tell me the truth. You owe me that. Especially now. Did you not give up your son to the Notre Dame orphanage?"

Her face grew tired-looking and she sighed deeply, picking at her fingernails. "I prayed. I asked my God why he had given me an abomination. What had I done to deserve this? And my husband was a good, hardworking man. So it was me, my sinful thinking. Temptations I could not resist in my youth. So I gave the abomination up to the ones who would know what to do with it. You are not that child. You are only being cruel to me by pretending."

"What year was it?"

She paused to think. "1858."

"And this, this abomination, did you give him a name?"

"Why would I? It was a punishment visited on me for my sins. My family disowned me. We chose to change our names. To hide from them and from those who knew about God's punishment. I have been praying for his forgiveness ever since."

"Did you give your son anything?"

"I gave him his life. I gave him back to God."

"And if you could see him again, what would you say?"

"One does not speak to the devil."

He wanted to rip off his mask. Show her his tortured face. Really punish her. The room was blurring.

He breathed deeply, blinked back tears and summoned all of his courage. "I *am* your son," he said. "It's the truth. Whether or not you are willing to accept it is your own problem."

She covered her face. "Please, go, go . . . stop torturing me."

He thought of changing his shape, of showing her how magical he was, how powerful and strong—but no.

"I am Modo," he said. "I am your son who saved your life." He left the room, closing the cabin door firmly behind him.

58

A VAST DEPARTURE

The HMS *Shah* landed at Esquimalt in the late afternoon. Already there had been other ships alerted as to the position of the island. Modo wondered if, like the underwater realm of Icaria or the attack on the Parliament, this would never appear in the newspapers. The bodies of the Guild's half-men, half-monsters would perhaps be displayed one day in glass showcases. In the short term they would most certainly be shipped to cold storage in the basement of some well-secured building in London. Or maybe in the Arctic, for all he knew, to be dissected and studied.

He hoped they wouldn't discover the real secret, as it was in his blood. And his mother's blood, too. He wondered what she understood of what had happened to her. Or had she been so drugged that she would believe it to have been some horrible nightmare. Would the Association ever allow her to live a normal life again?

It wasn't until they docked that Mr. Socrates emerged from his cabin and Modo and Octavia saw him for the first time in four days. Tharpa pushed Mr. Socrates along in a wheelchair, a grey blanket across his legs. He appeared smaller, and more elderly, as though his time under the water had shrivelled him up. Mr. Socrates shooed Tharpa away and slowly wheeled himself across the deck.

"I owe you my life," he said matter-of-factly.

"Actually, Octavia and I pulled you out together," Modo said, giving her a nod.

"Yes, I owe my thanks to both of you, though I will take some of the credit for having trained you both so well." A twinkle returned to his eye.

"We chose how to apply it, though," Octavia reminded him.

"Yes, you have free will, too much of it at times." He chuckled hoarsely.

"It is all I have," Modo said.

"Come now, no time to be melancholy. We have accomplished great things. The Guild has been broken into pieces. There may be pockets elsewhere but they won't dare to rise up again for years. The good citizens of England have no inkling as to what threat we were under, will never know. Therefore, they will never thank you—but know that you did good work. We're now free to return to London to begin strengthening the Association."

"No," Modo said without hesitation.

"No?"

Modo had spent last night unable to sleep. His mother's rejection had rattled him, knocking some key part of himself loose. "I'm done with empires, Mr. Socrates. That was my last assignment. I mean to quit the Association and strike out on my own."

"Do you?" Mr. Socrates said.

"You said nothing of this to me," Octavia said, unable to hide her irritation.

"It's only become clear to my now, Tavia. I'm really best off alone."

"You can't just quit, Modo," Mr. Socrates said. "This is not a sporting club. You have oaths to fulfill, duties. There's much work yet to be done."

"Mr. Socrates. I care deeply for you. You're the closest thing I have to a father. But, through no choice of my own, I have given you fifteen years of my life. I want my next years to be my own. I may return one day, when I'm older. But right now I must act alone."

"What madness is this, Modo?" With the help of Tharpa, he rose from his chair and stood shakily on the deck. "I raised you. You would be nothing without me—just a cowering beast."

"Beast?"

"I didn't mean to use that word. I forbid you from leaving me—the Association. The care, the thought, the years I've put into grooming you and this is how you repay me? With betrayal."

"I'm not betraying you. I'm leaving you, that's all."

Mr. Socrates looked at Tharpa. "I have made him too much in my own image." Then he turned back to Modo. "I will not beg you to stay. But know this, Modo, if you walk away from me, you'll regret it. The world out there is cruel. You'll come crawling back."

"I must find my own place, sir." He locked eyes with Tharpa, who nodded subtly as though to say *I understand.*

Octavia said, "You're going alone?"

If she came with him, what kind of life would she have? Better for her to stay with the Association. To make a decent living. To find her prince.

"I am," he replied, then he walked down the gangplank and towards the gates of the naval base.

59

A WARM AND CALLUSED HAND

The cobblestone streets of Victoria were solid under Modo's feet. He felt solid, too, even though he wasn't certain about what he'd just done. The decision had come upon him so suddenly and so perfectly that he'd acted on it without the slightest hesitation.

He was deeply sad now when he pictured the disappointment in Mr. Socrates' eyes. He'd see him again, he was certain of that, but on his own terms. Living his own life.

Modo didn't have a plan for his future employment. He had the strength to work on the railways. Or in the mines. Or better yet, on a farm in the Wild West. He loved the idea of just bending his back to a task without worrying about the fate of the empire.

A swift step and a hissing noise alerted him, but before he could react a hard blow fell on the back of his head and he collapsed to the ground. He expected a knife between the ribs. Did Mr. Socrates mean to make sure he didn't leave the Association? He rolled over to face his attacker.

"Tavia!"

Octavia stood over him, hands on her hips. "You left without me, you . . . you nizzie, you nincompoop!"

"It's for the best."

"For the best? We're friends, Modo. You don't turn your back on a mate."

"But you have a good life with the Association." He was ashamed to hear his voice warble.

"You didn't even ask me if I wanted to go along!" His head hurt. What had she whacked him with? "You made assumptions you, you assumptious ass!"

"*Assumptious* isn't a word!"

"Don't lecture me, you traitor."

"Fine," he said with a huff. He stood, holding his head. "Will you come with me?"

"No. Not now, not ever!"

"Then what are you doing here?"

She took a deep breath, blew it out and stamped her foot. "Modo, you're so . . . so frustrating! A terribly frustrating, terribly . . . interesting man. And the silly thing is, I can't imagine not being around you. I do love your company."

He got to his feet, dumfounded. Had she said *love*?

"So?" she said after several seconds had paused. "What are your thoughts? Do you have any?"

"I—I— You know how I feel, Tavia."

"I do? How *do* you feel? Since you're so good with fancy words, tell me!"

But he had very few words this time. "I . . . can't . . . imagine not being around you, either."

"I would like to travel with you. Where, I don't know."

"And what of my face, my looks?"

"Modo," she said seriously, "that will take some getting used to. But I've learned to put up with your personality. I'm sure in time I'll learn to put up with that, too. Day by day."

"And I'll put up with yours," he retorted. "But there's a further problem: we have no money, no tickets."

She held up a familiar wallet. "I nicked this from Mr. Socrates. My final payment from the Association."

"You shouldn't have done that." Then he laughed.

"There's enough in here for two tickets. Anywhere we want to go, at least second class."

"Then where would you like to go?"

"San Francisco," she said. "I like the way it sounds. We'll see where it takes us next." She held up her hand. "But first, and this is my only condition, let us go hence to a bakery and eat cake."

"Cake? Why?"

"Because, Modo, I've lost track of the days, but we missed your birthday."

He counted in his head. It was the last day of October. "Actually, Tavia, my birthday is tomorrow." The thought of it, of celebrating his arrival on this earth, wasn't appealing.

Octavia grabbed him by the shoulder, squeezing so hard that it hurt. "Don't go all soft on me, Modo. Don't think about your foolish mother or all those other things. This is your first birthday, and we're going to do it up in style. You listen to me, I'm older than you, and therefore wiser. Are you game?"

She held out her hand. Modo laughed heartily and took it. It was callused and warm.

Hand in hand, they set off in search of a place to celebrate their new, and not so new, beginnings.

ALSO BY ARTHUR SLADE

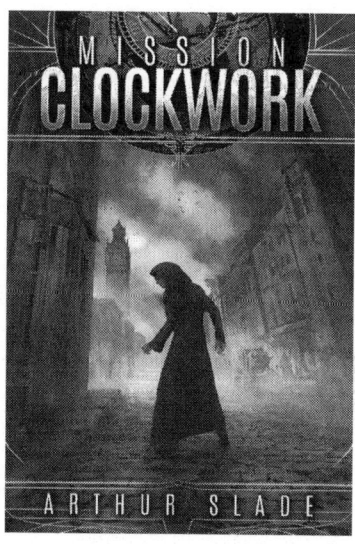

Book one in the series. Modo's grandest adventure of all! It will
take all of his skill to survive.

Mission Clockwork

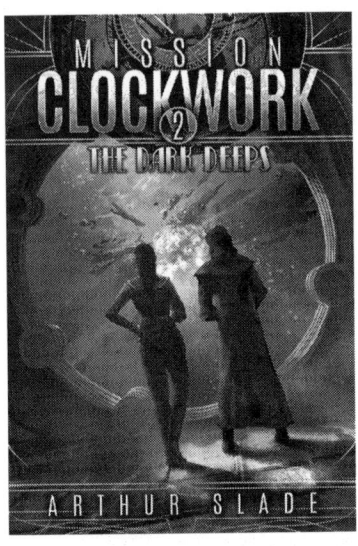

Book two in the series. A daring underwater adventure awaits
Modo.

Mission Clockwork 2: The Dark Deeps

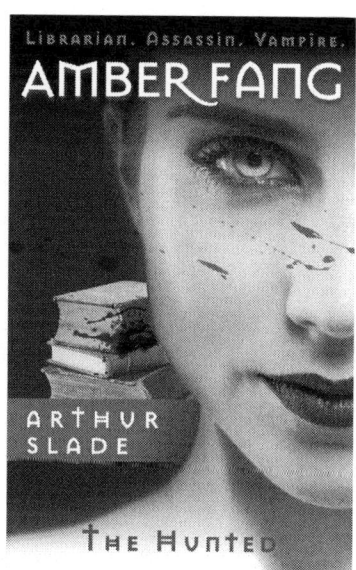

For older readers. The tale of a sweet librarian. Who also happens to be an assassin and a vampire...

Amber Fang

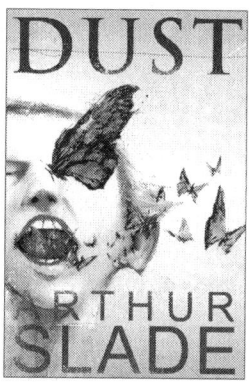

A rainmaker comes to town and brings much needed rain, but the children begin to disappear...

Dust

ABOUT THE AUTHOR

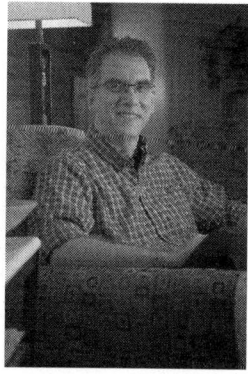

Arthur Slade was raised in the Cypress Hills of southwest Saskatchewan and began writing at an early age. He is the author of twenty books, including *Dust* (which won the Governor General's award), *Flickers*, and *Amber Fang*. He currently lives in the mythical city of Saskatoon, Canada where he writes on a treadmill desk while listening to heavy metal.

It's true.

Connect with Arthur Slade online:
www.arthurslade.com
art@arthurslade.com

Mission Clockwork #4

Island of Doom

Arthur Slade

Published by Arthur Slade

Copyright © 2012, 2018 Arthur Slade

Cover Artwork by Jeff Brown

❀ Created with Vellum